EMISSARY OF DEATH

Karne moved on along the rows of the wounded. Dashing back to Ontar would not find Charlotte any quicker, but the moment he spent with a soldier now might encourage the man to recover more quickly or to recover at all.

At the end of the next to last row, a man lay curled around himself in pain. Karne crouched beside him. The moment Karne was close, the man rolled onto his back, whipped a large knife out of hiding, and lunged upward. Karne threw himself sideways. The orderly brought the edge of his report board down on the man's neck. The man collapsed in a heap.

Safe. Karne felt a moment of blinding terror. Black blotches surged in and out before his eyes. *An assassin. An assassin!*

WINTER WORLD
BRANDER'S BOOK

C.J. MILLS

ACE BOOKS, NEW YORK

BRANDER'S BOOK

An Ace Book / published by arrangement with
the author

PRINTING HISTORY
Ace edition / January 1992

ISBN: 0-441-89447-X

To Art,
longtime First Critic and friend

PROLOGUE

The man in the gray habit of a deacon of The Way stared blindly out the window of his narrow cell. He did not move. Beyond the window, rain raced across the lake in sheets of water that trailed across the surface in waves and swirls. It slanted through the bluepines, making them bend and sway. It hissed against the Retreat House wall. The window glass, deeply set into the wall, received only an occasional spatter, bouncing off the ledge outside. After a long time, the man turned from the window and crossed the room to turn on the light. He unfolded the paper in his hand and read it again. He crumpled it and flung it at the wall.

"Damn that little bitch! Damn her sire, too! I'm Richard, Duke of Harlan, and I could have any woman I wanted, yet I've waited six years for her to come of age. Now she's not willing to wait for me."

He thought of Charlotte Rhiz as she had been when he had last seen her. She had been eleven and flirtatious and already beginning to show signs of the beauty that was now hers. She was a great beauty *and* had also been the genetic council's first choice for him as a wife. Harlan's mouth hardened.

The Guardians be praised the other Families don't know about our genetic council, he thought. We'd lose our advantage in bearing girls who survive the Sickness if they knew how we do it.

His mind touched quickly on Kathryn Halarek, who had lived

briefly, and unwillingly, in House Odonnel as his cousin's bride. There was a possibility she had carried information about the genetic council out when she had been so unexpectedly rescued by her brother and Nik von Schuss.

"Much good may it do them," he muttered.

Harlan turned his head to stare out at the rain whipping past the window. Hundreds of kilometers westward lay his holding and the power he used to wield. "I'm duke in Harlan," he said, needing to hear a human voice. "*Duke* in Harlan, head-of-House, and I wanted Kathryn. *I* wanted her, and the genetic council gave her to Ennis! When I took her from him, my vassals and cousins supported the World Council's attack on Breven to get her back. Now von Schuss has her."

The duke ripped the letter into shreds, muttering in a voice too low to be heard by the guards outside the door while he did it.

"Ennis shouldn't have been killed until I knew what he'd told her. Whether she knows about the genetic council, for example. Now he's dead and his child—who was to inherit House Halarek for us after the 'untimely' death of her uncle, the present Lharr— is dead, too, Kathryn's brother is still alive, and she's back in his protection. You'd think I was as incompetent as my father in getting rid of that self-righteous social reformer! That comes of having to use hirelings. I killed all the Halarek men except the one who was off-planet. *I* killed them! I killed the assassins who were after me in the Frozen Zone, and that was no easy thing. I should have killed that huge off-world friend of Halarek's, too, when I had the chance, but I never thought he'd catch me."

Harlan threw the paper shreds toward the wall, the ineffectuality of that enraging him even more. "Now the little bitch's father tells me he's pledging her to the Lharr Halarek. Of all the available men on Starker IV, the duke's pledged her to Karne Halarek!"

He picked up the nearest piece of furniture and hurled it at the wall, then the lamp, then the table it had been standing on. The crunch of impact eased his rage only a little. They would pay. Both of them would *pay*.

CHAPTER 1

Brander Harlan showed his identification to the Council guard outside the door to Richard's quarters. Ridiculous, showing them the same plasti card every time he came to visit, but that was the way bureaucracy worked. They searched him for contraband, then one of the guards opened the door. The door crunched over shards of glass from a broken lamp. Pieces of what had been a table lay in one corner of the room. Richard stood beside the window, a sheaf of papers in his hand. He rolled the papers, unrolled them, rolled them back up. He turned sharply when he heard the door shut. Brander noted the reaction and glanced again at the table fragments.

Upset, Richard? Jumpy? How unlike you.

Richard was almost always looking out the window when Brander came to visit. Visible signs of stress or anger were quite rare. Brander shrugged. There was little else for Richard to do but stare out the window and plan for the future, now the new abbot was enforcing Council's sentence exactly. The Retreat's library was small and limited and heavily religious and Richard was not much for reading, anyway. He could not use the tri-d to keep in touch with friends and allies, either. The new abbot had prohibited tri-d for Richard except on very important occasions. A gallop over the plains beyond the forest or a duel with rapiers or beamers against an opponent of equal skill—that would be more Richard's sort of activity, anyway.

3

Five more years of this strict isolation and inactivity and Richard will no longer be fit to rule. Maybe he's already unfit. That might be an angle to work with Isan of the Mark and others. Unfit to rule. No heirs. Soon no ability to make heirs, though I won't tell them that.

Richard began tapping the roll of papers against his thigh. Brander cleared his throat, as much to draw Richard's attention as anything else.

"Have things gone well for you this week, cousin? As well as can be expected, at least?" *Stupid beginning, but what can one say to a man who's permitted to do nothing?*

Richard made a harsh, unpleasant sound quite unlike his usual mellow laugh. "Well? Going well? I haven't had a woman since just before Kathryn Halarek was taken from me. I haven't had a good drink since emptying that bottle of Mirin wine Dr. Gebbits smuggled in almost a month ago. I'm no longer allowed even to walk in the garden if the other men are there." The roll of papers snapped against the stone of the window frame. "The other men. The innocents. The makers of retreats. But even on retreat men talk politics, do a little persuasion. And I'm shut out! I can't make contacts anymore or find new spies or even get aid bringing in some of the necessities of life. Like more Mirin. And the abbot is of House Rhiz, one of my own *vassals*!"

Mirin, Richard. I have more Mirin. Just like the doctor ordered. Brander made his face sober and thoughtful. "House Rhiz has turned on you twice, it seems. First the abbot, then Charlotte's marriage." *I'll save the news of Cherek's declaration of independence until later.*

Richard turned on Brander. "The new abbot. The beautiful Charlotte. The strict enforcement of Council's sentence." His voice was a savage imitation of Karne Halarek's. Karne Halarek, who had been involved in getting all three. Richard took a deep breath and continued. "None of these things would have happened under Gormsby's chairmanship. Our party considered the death of that uppity Halarek woman (though everyone knows I meant the knife for Lord Karne) a benefit to society." Richard's face was reddening and his breath coming faster. "She really believed the Council would accept her as regent in Halarek until Lord Karne's majority! She really believed Council would allow a *woman* to rule! Chairman

Gormsby wouldn't even let her *speak*!"

Richard laughed that unpleasant laugh again. Brander did not know how to interpret it and that made him uneasy. He knew mollification was necessary.

"The dead Lharr's Will, not Council, named her regent, cousin. Don't you think a ruler's word should be obeyed?" Brander steepled his fingers in front of his mouth and waited to see if Richard would fall into that trap. *With luck, I can use his own words against him when I take his place.*

Richard slapped the roll of papers against his palm. "No matter. The Larga's dead and Karne's still alive, when it should've been the other way around. What's the news?"

There'll be no protection for me in those words. His years in prison haven't entirely done away with his prudence. Brander glanced toward the roll in Richard's hand. "I suspect you already know it."

Richard looked out the window again. Brander could see some of the view over his shoulder. The sky, the lake, the frost-edged grasses—everything was fading to the bleak grays of coming winter. The bluepines had turned almost black. Brander could understand the anger that only barely covered Richard's despair. Five years and a thwarted escape gone, five years to go, in truly solitary confinement this time— that combination could drive anyone to despair. Only a month ago the entire lowest level of Breven had been Richard's, to hold parties and political gatherings (which the former abbot knew about); to have women (which the abbot did not know about). No amount of political advancement for his nephews or luxuries for his quarters could have made even that abbot wink at women in a male Retreat House. For that, his conscience was too tender.

Richard's hands clenched and the papers made a crinkling sound, drawing Brander's attention again. "I would have had Charlotte but for Halarek."

"He has a lot more to offer," Brander said, trying to keep impatience from his tone. *When will you get off your own troubles and start thinking about the House, Richard? Could you possibly believe a young and lusty woman would wait five years? Even for you?*

Richard might as well have not heard. "I should've forced Kathryn while I had her, but no, I had to wait to do it on

Council Day, to make my revenge on Karne Halarek even sweeter: He couldn't rescue his sister and attend Council both and he *had* to go to Council. So I waited and I lost her."

Timing is everything. Aloud, Brander said, "Your vassals wouldn't have tolerated rape. She was Ennis's wife."

A muscle jumped in Richard's cheek. "She went to Ennis's bed willingly enough, and he was as much a Harlan as I am. She would've been willing once I showed her how good it could be and her willingness would've added spice to humiliating Halarek. The humiliation would have lasted at least a generation, too. Kathryn would've carried it to her grave."

What would Ennis, her legal husband, have done afterward, Richard? You don't think about that, do you? Or you persuade yourself he would have accepted such an insult. "And Ennis?"

Richard turned away from the window with a snarl. "Ennis is dead, before he could be punished for his treachery!"

He would've told too much if he'd been left with his new allies. "Your vassals don't see the matter that way, Richard." *And many of them will be my allies against you.*

"I'd wanted Kathryn for years and the genetic council had passed over me to give her to Ennis, to *Ennis,* a son of a minor branch of the House!"

"So you decided to take her against her will and her husband's and your vassals'. The vassals rule Harlan now, remember? And you defied them!"

The papers tapped against Richard's leg more rapidly. "They found her too soon, Halarek and von Schuss did," Richard muttered. "I would have made in her a Harlan son for her to bear in disgrace."

Not if Dr. Gebbits has been doing his job, O cousin. A few more bottles of Mirin wine and you'll be unable to make any child at all and you'll never know why, because you'll never think to have your potency tested. The childlessness couldn't possibly be your *fault. No, never.*

Brander drew in his mouth disapprovingly. "Ennis alive would have treated the child as his, Richard. He would never have set Lady Kathryn aside. So where would the disgrace be?" *That's another reason why Ennis had to die, but I didn't imagine then that you'd delay taking the Lady Kathryn.*

Richard slapped his open palm against the stone wall. "House Halarek *needed* to be humiliated, disgraced, taken down."

Brander shaped his face into even more disapproving lines. "Well, it wasn't. Halarek gained by his gallant rescue. Harlan lost. Our vassals are talking about setting up a new branch of the Family as rulers in Harlan because of what you did, Richard." *And I'm putting my branch forward, cousin.*

Richard went white.

"It's too bad Ennis's baby died, out there on the caravan route," Brander went on conversationally. "Even a girl child of Harlan/Halarek blood would have been useful. It was sort of strange, her dying of the Sickness. Our House's girls seldom die of the Sickness. It must have been the Halarek blood that did it." *You haven't mentioned Ennis's child as heir, have you, Richard? You haven't been in any hurry to provide Harlan with a legitimate heir of your body, either, and now, with any luck, it's too late. That leaves the succession wide open, doesn't it, Richard, no matter what our vassals decide?*

"It would have been fitting, wouldn't it," Brander went on, "a half-Harlan female inheriting in Halarek? A female was the beginning of the feud, after all. It would be fitting if one were the end, also. From great-grandfather's Black Ship bride to Ennis and Kathryn's baby girl. A circle. A perfect ending."

Brander could tell his needling had gone home. Richard's face was whiter and his body had gone taut.

Too busy proving you're a great lover to take care of the line of inheritance, eh, Richard? And you didn't think anyone would notice? Why haven't you noticed your by-blows are occurring less and less often?

Richard's hand darted to his belt. Brander knew he would have died if Richard had had a weapon just then. But Richard had no weapon and he needed Brander for reliable word from outside Breven. He would remember that in a minute. Richard's visitors had dwindled. Now only Brander and two vassals (or former vassals), Dannel of Jura and the Lord of the Mark, came. Harlan vassals who had no interest in seeing the duke's position regain its strength.

No one used to dare talk to you so bluntly, right, Richard? But I don't expect you to leave here alive, cousin, so I'll talk to you as I please. "Can we leave the subject of women now? There are other matters, matters we can still do something about."

"Like?"

Brander could see the struggle it took for Richard to be even marginally civil, but Richard knew he needed Brander just now. He would not cut Brander off yet. "Paul III Druma is at the edge of death," Brander said. "Garren thinks now's a good time to demand a change in head-of-House. Paul IV is even more spineless than his sire. It should be easy."

"What's Garren doing about it?"

"He intends to put a proposal before the Frosttime Council as Druma's liege. If that fails, set siege as soon as possible after Thaw."

"I told him not to do that. Halarek won't stand for it."

"He expected you to say something like that. He said to tell you he's your friend and cousin, not your vassal, Richard."

Richard said something elaborately foul. "Does he think I'll save his hide when Halarek and friends come down on him?"

Brander looked away and did not answer.

"Well? Answer me!"

Brander shook his head. "I'm not privy to Garren's thoughts, milord."

Richard let that evasion pass. "A contest between Odonnel and Harlan now is out of the question, if it could ever be considered. We've been allies as long as anyone remembers. What else is going on?"

Brander's mouth twisted in distaste. *He wants more? Let him think about these for a few weeks.* "Cherek Rhiz has foresworn his allegiance to you. Gannet and Rooder have taken their holdings out of Harlan. They say they're independent now, but the fact is, they've gone to Justin for protection and it looks like they'll get it. Also, there's talk within the Family about replacing you as duke, even if the line of succession doesn't change. Many say your years here have turned you into a sybarite, unfit to rule. Your cousins question your fitness to lead—out of their own ambition, of course—but your vassals worry about the courtesan you had here. They've even talked to Halarek, the Heir in von Schuss, and the Council soldiers who raided this place about details. Everyone on Starker IV knew within days of the raid that you'd been drinking and whoring in a Retreat House." *Not a smart set of moves, Richard, but who was I to dissuade you?* "The scandal was amazing."

"Just what are you getting at?"

"The scandal and its effect on your reputation weaken our House. If Cherek Rhiz and Gannet and Rooder think they can escape your vassalage, so will others. Kath is already making noises about taking back that chunk of McNeece Holding his family has claimed for the last century or so, even though you told him not to. Druma's duke is dying, which tempts Odonnel almost irresistibly. Then there's Rhiz's new tie to Halarek—"

"How is that 'tie' to Halarek doing?"

"She is as she is. They'll be married on Council ground next week. I personally don't understand why either of you want her. *I* wouldn't want to wear the horns before all my friends. Though, from what I hear, only you and I and her sire even suspect her proclivities yet."

Richard looked speculative. "So. You've spied in House Rhiz?"

"You wanted the woman to wife, Richard. It was my duty to be sure she was fit." *And she certainly was willing to show me how "fit" she was if I'd wanted to take her up on it.*

"What she did in private wouldn't bother me as long as she behaved in public."

"She knows the value of the Halarek match. She's been very discreet. As I just said, I doubt anyone but her sire knows how far she goes in her 'flirting,' though members of her House probably suspect. There are many ways to give joy without breaking the maidenhead and I've heard she knows them all."

Richard chuckled. "Sly old fox, her sire. I wonder how he kept the lock on *that* secret."

"Told her what would happen to her if anyone found out, I imagine," Brander replied dryly. "Or beat her until she behaved. Halarek, now, isn't a man to beat his women, let alone torture them to keep them in line."

"His loss," said Richard. "Is she scarred?"

"Not visibly." *I remember when Lady Kathryn was brought to you how concerned you were that she had no scars from Odonnel's "persuasion." Interesting necessity for passion, Richard. Thinking of some way into Charlotte's bed still? Maybe I can arrange that. It would keep your mind occupied.*

Richard's face showed his mind had definitely turned to sensual thoughts. He came slowly, visibly, back to the stone room in Breven. "How bad are things at home really?"

It's about time you asked. "You must make some convincing show of power soon, or by this time next year only Harlan's skeleton will be left."

Richard clasped his hands behind his back and stared up at the ceiling, mouth pursed, for a long time. When he looked again at Brander, his face was set hard. "For starters, do these: Order siege set on Rhiz to bring him back into line; tell Kath again to step back from McNeece and send an assassin to pick off a few of the lower men in his line of succession if telling him doesn't work."

Brander threw his hands outward in a gesture of helplessness. *Now's the time for a show of sincerity and an excuse for matters going counter to his plans.* "That's a good start, but nothing's going to work well until you're out of here. 'A House runs best behind its rightful lord.' "

"Well, this House's lord isn't going to run anywhere for a long time. But I'll remember for a longer time anyone who fouls up my plans."

The harsh tone of Richard's voice alarmed Brander. "No offense meant, Richard!"

"None taken. As long as you remember who Harlan's rightful lord is. You may go."

Brander bowed slightly and went to the door. He turned. "Oh, I forgot to mention that Lady Kathryn expects a baby early in Kerensten."

Richard looked at his cousin through narrowed eyes. "Really?" He counted ostentatiously on his fingers, going backward through the months. "Kerensten to Nemb is one, Koort, Arhast, Uhl, Narn, Drak, Aden. Ennis's child." His face brightened. "That's good news, cousin. It will brighten my days for some time."

"Von Schuss, the Heir I mean, of course, marries Lady Kathryn this afternoon. The forty days of mourning for Lord Ennis are over."

Richard smiled. "Do you want to lay any wager that von Schuss will say it's his and early?"

Brander shook his head. "Once the marriage bond is made, not everyone waits for The Way to say the words. It could well be von Schuss's baby. They were trapped together several days before they were rescued." *And I have certain knowledge that Lady Kathryn and Lord Ennis slept apart after that baby was born. But make a fool of yourself with this claim if you want to, Richard.*

But Richard's mind was on his own thoughts. He smiled. "I could even add a little excitement to the battle for the babe and claim it's mine. It would be her word against mine and you know how Council looks at the word of women."

Do you always think of your reputation as a lover first, Richard? Brander smiled slightly. "Shall I save your claims until it's born or start now?"

Richard looked at him very seriously for a moment. "Save them awhile. We'll have to see how matters go at home."

Matters in Harlan deteriorated. Brander received from his contacts in Breven weekly reports about Richard. Richard made frequent attempts to escape. Each time he tried, he got no farther than the hall outside his door. Each time, the Council guards forced him back into his room again, cursing the guards and Council and Karne Halarek. No bribes could weaken their vigilance. Brander could understand Richard's frustration. He was allowed to leave his room, and then under heavy guard, only for brief walks in the garden and to nightmeal, which was his only contact with the other men in Breven. There had been no tri-d casts of planetary importance, unless one counted the von Schuss/Halarek wedding, which Brander and the abbot did not.

Maybe I should get him a caged bird for company. Brander enjoyed the thought for several hours, then dropped it. The parallel would come to Richard at once and he would kill the bird and toss the cage out the window. Perhaps he would even consider following the cage out the window onto the rocks below.

Maybe I should tempt him with Charlotte's lush body. Now that would be a challenge—the getting her in there and keeping her a secret—and it would make Richard very grateful.

CHAPTER 2

The flitter settled lightly onto the pad surface. Karne Halarek, Lharr in Halarek, sighed wearily, pushed himself out of the pilot's seat, and stepped out onto the flitter's wing. At least Kit and Nik were safely married. There had been some worry that House Harlan would object to her remarriage so soon after Ennis's death, though Kit and Nik had observed the minimum forty days' mourning, but there had been no objection. Neither House, von Schuss or Halarek, would be so lucky when the child-to-be became visible.

Karne circled his shoulders to work out the stiffness of the long flight, then tipped his head back and rolled it slowly around. Above him the pad shaft reached thirty meters to the surface, the dips and gouges of its hand-cutting never smoothed from the stone as they had been in other Houses, because the roughness symbolized for the first Lharr the founding, against heavy odds, of House Halarek, the youngest of the nine Great Houses. He rolled his head again, the bothersome bones cracked, and the tension in his neck and shoulders let go. It had been a long day. It would be a longer night.

Karne jumped from the flitter's wing to the pad surface. There was an Advent party tonight and, before that, the signing of his marriage contract with House Rhiz. Karne's mouth tightened. He did not wish to marry again, but his House needed heirs and money. If this marriage was not completed, the continued survival of House Halarek would be in question again. There were too many loans outstanding from the war with House Harlan. There were no heirs except Netta and Kerel's brainless boys, either. Karne strode across the landing pad toward the door into the manor house, his mind still struggling with the difficult problems ahead of him. Under Karne's leadership, House Halarek had won the war and four of Harlan's vassals besides, but it had cost more than Halarek could really afford.

"Guardians, how it cost!" Karne whispered. "But I couldn't let Mother's murder go unavenged, could I?"

Karne sighed. A marriage to Charlotte Rhiz would solve most of the money problems, but would probably bring others. Karne felt uneasy about the whole matter, but what else could he do? Beautiful, rich, greatly sought after as a wife, Charlotte was quite a coup for a man who had been thought a weakling and an incompetent only four years ago, but her House was a vassal of House Harlan, shaky as that House's control of any outside matters was at the moment. Whatever House Harlan's troubles in the wake of the Larga Halarek's murder were, Harlan was still the most powerful House on Starker IV and it held a generations-old hatred of House Halarek, a hatred that began with a stolen bride. Karne knew Richard Harlan would consider Charlotte stolen, though Lord Cherek Rhiz had sworn there had been no contract between them.

My great-grandsire *did* steal a Harlan bride, Karne reminded himself. He Sealed as his the woman the duke had already taken aboard their Black Ship. I'm only marrying a woman Richard wanted. Like he wanted Kit—

That thought led down a dark and dirty alley Karne did not want to travel. He found he had stopped at the edge of the pad in front of the locked door to the manor house. He roused himself from his gloomy thoughts and signaled the com center to let him in. One of the com-techs opened the door. Karne nodded to the man as he went through. He heard the door closed and locked behind him.

Necessary. Such precautions are necessary these days. Always precautions. No assassin can get into Halarek from the flitter pad. The conservatory skylight, on the other hand— if there were only some way to secure the skylight without closing it off.

Karne had not yet been persuaded that closing off the skylight was necessary. The conservatory was Karne's refuge of last resort. When troubles in Halarek pressed him too hard, he retreated to the conservatory and sat in sunlit quiet, surrounded by the smell of green plants, and imagined for a short time he had returned to green and peaceful Balder, where he had spent the happiest five years of his life.

Karne stopped in front of the lift. The lift would take him quickly to level 6 for a few reenergizing minutes in sunshine and clean, green smells. Orkonan and Freeman Weisman were waiting for him on level 4, though, probably with the completed marriage agreement. The Advent party would begin in less than two hours and he must host it. And he must approve the marriage contract first.

Debts. Marriage negotiations. The expectation that Harlan would demand Kit's baby. The impending death of Paul III Druma, Halarek's only vassal among the Nine. Troubles upon troubles. Karne wished again for Balder, the Altairian Naval Academy there, and the quiet life of a peace negotiator, the work he had been trained for. He had had to stave off wars, quiet interspecific prejudices, even persuade the cannibals of Ranha not to eat a Survey team, but all those problems had been much easier than the present ones, because they had not been his problems. Debts, Rhiz, Druma—

Karne suddenly realized this line of thinking was winding him up tightly inside. He glanced at his chrono. He did not have any time to spend in the conservatory and yet his body was winding up so tight, he felt as if he were about to explode.

He glanced at his chrono and at the lift again, then sprinted past the lift toward the stairs, which he took two at a time. He felt fierce satisfaction with the quick response of his muscles.

I'll survive, he told himself. I'll survive debts and another marriage. I'll survive Richard.

Karne stopped at the landing on level 4 to catch his breath and straighten his tunic. He ran a quick hand through his hair. This marriage contract was necessary, though he was not at all eager to marry again. Lizanne, with her cringing and crying and inability to carry a child to term, had been a trial. He had pitied her, but she had been a trial. When he had accepted her to wife, Halarek had desperately needed an heir and Lizanne had been the best Karne could get at the time. Well, Lizanne was dead and Halarek *still* needed an heir. No one considered Netta's boys seriously: They were almost as brainless as their mother. Kit's coming baby would be Heir in von Schuss, and in Halarek until Karne had an heir of his own. Harlan would also likely lay claim to Kit's child. Karne said a quick prayer that the baby would bear the forehead-to-nape birthmark hereditary in the males of von Schuss. He ran his hand through his hair one more time, then walked to the library.

Tane Orkonan and Frem Weisman were sitting at the long library table to the right of the door, Orkonan tipped back in his chair reading what looked like a letter, Weisman bent over the table, sifting through piles of papers with quick, nervous flicks of his hands. Orkonan saw Karne standing in the doorway and stood.

"My lord." He sketched a bow. He had been Karne's tutor before taking the job of Halarek administrator. Both titles and bows were only forms, not requirements, between the two men.

Karne nodded. "Tane." Then he looked at Weisman, the librarian, a small man with a sharp, eager nose. "Is the marriage contract complete and printed up, Frem Weisman?"

Weisman looked up. His hands stilled for a moment and his eyes darted from Karne to Orkonan and back. "It was here just a moment ago, milord. I can't imagine how it could have—oh, here it is!" He tugged out a half-dozen pieces of paper clipped neatly together.

Karne held out his hand for it, gave the top page a cursory glance, then walked to one of the wing chairs beside the room's fireplace. He waved a hand toward the logs. Flames shot up and a faint smell of smoke drifted into the room. Karne smiled.

"I see it works again."

"Aye, lord." Weisman started toward his seated lord. "The craftsman was in yesterday and—"

Orkonan made a sharp chopping motion. Weisman stopped speaking abruptly and returned to work at the table.

Karne looked up from the contract. "Summarize the details for me, Tane. I'll understand this fine print better if I hear the terms first."

Orkonan smiled. "You always did learn better by ear. Well, the main terms are these: Charlotte will receive from you the smallholding of Jura as her dower property; she is also to receive 1,000 Gildcredits for her personal use should you predecease her; children she bears must renounce all claims to Rhiz Holding. She agrees to use no preventatives for the first two years of this marriage. For his part, Lord Cherek settles 50,000 Gildcredits on you upon the signing of the contract plus 75,000 Gildcredits the day of the wedding; he presents a physician's certificate that the girl is intact, a virgin; he certifies that she has no prior contract with any man or House."

"That eliminates the worry of conflict with Harlan over her, milord," Weisman said from his place at the table.

"If Rhiz isn't lying," said Karne under his breath. He sighed. "Well, at least I know I was *her* first choice, though I'm under no illusions why. I'm free and healthy and coming up in the world, while Richard Harlan must spend five years more in Breven watching his House break up. Even considering our debts, which man would *you* pick if you were seventeen and your father gave you your choice?"

A small gasp came from the direction of the library table. Weisman looked up from his work, his long nose twitching in agitation. "*Her* choice? He really gave her *her* choice? Of marriage partner? What kind of fool is he?"

"Didn't you already know that?" Karne looked at the librarian with interest. "I'm surprised you object. I thought Freemen always chose their own marriage partners?"

"They do—I mean—I think—" Weisman cleared his throat and began again. "I've been in House Halarek fourteen years, milord, and I think as one of the Nine now."

"Hmmmm," was all Karne said. He looked toward Orkonan. "I heard from Duval just today that another Harlan cousin has declared his smallholding free of House Harlan's control and has taken protection with House Justin. Rooder, I think it was."

Orkonan looked back speculatively. "So. Justin's stepping into the Harlan mess again. I had thought once Lord Allet was free of acting as trustee for that House—"

Orkonan did not look as if he were going to say more, so Karne returned to reading through the contract. When he had finished, he carried the document to Orkonan.

"All I have to do now is sign this in front of witnesses and the matter's done?"

Orkonan nodded. "Lord Cherek insisted on your personal signature, given publicly, and on witnesses, too. He *is* a Harlan vassal, after all. He wants all arrangements to be public, so Richard can't claim that House Rhiz betrayed him. Two other Harlan vassals, the Lord of the Mark and Lord of Emmen, have agreed to be witnesses. And Abbot Godwin of Breven."

Karne whistled in amazement. "Harlan really is falling apart! Two Harlan vassals agree to witnessing the marriage of a third into House Harlan's worst political enemy . . ." He stood. "I realized getting Charlotte was a coup, but I hadn't realized what I was getting politically as well." He shook his head. "The abbot of Breven wants to witness this. I can't believe it!"

"He *is* her uncle," Orkonan reminded him.

"Then he isn't offering this as a leader in The Way, but as a member of House Rhiz, and that means this contract isn't just to the tastes of Lord Cherek. The Rhiz Family seems to agree on it. This *is* good news. After years of little but bad news, this is going to take some getting used to."

Karne looked over the final arrangements for the party and the contract signing, then went to the curving iron stair toward the rear of the room. The stair not only made getting books off the top shelves possible, but led from the library to a door on the next level. Karne gave the stair a shove to align it properly with the doorway.

"Lord Karne?"

Karne stopped with a foot on the bottom step. Orkonan crossed the room to him swiftly.

"Our eyes in Breven report Richard has received word of the marriage contract already."

"From the spy in this House that we can't find?"

"I believe Lord Cherek himself wrote."

Karne's fist slammed down on the stair railing. "By my Mother's Blood! Does he seek already to draw this House into another war?"

"I think not, Karne. I think he'll use this contract to break free of Harlan and I doubt there's much risk of war now, when Richard's vassals have made him essentially helpless. He should never have taken Lady Kathryn for his personal use while she was still his cousin's wife. Harlan vassals blame him for Ennis's assassination, too, for killing the husband so that what he planned to do to Lady Kathryn would not be adultery. Our eyes report that he's so isolated now by the abbot and Council that he isn't even permitted to watch tri-d casts unless the cast is of planetary importance."

"*Was* the assassin Richard's?"

"I think not. In Richard's mind, I'm sure he was doing nothing that would require Ennis's death. He knew Ennis loved Kit and would take her back, however long Richard chose to use her. Kit's feelings, of course, mattered not at all. She's a woman and an enemy to his House besides—"

"Who sent the assassin, then?"

"Someone in Harlan who wanted to pay Ennis back for helping Kathryn escape Odonnel and for telling McNeece she'd been taken to Breven and what was planned for her. Richard greatly underestimated his gentle cousin Ennis."

Karne thought about that for a moment, then clattered up the stair.

A little more than two hours later, Karne stood on the dais at the head of the Great Hall, watching the first of his guests come through the main door at the other end of the room. It was custom among the Nine that hostilities were laid aside for Advent, so friends and enemies met at the many Advent parties. On such occasions, members of the Nine Families wore their finest clothes and their best behavior. Members of the Nine and of the minor Houses mingled freely, something they did at other times of year only at Council meetings.

In the galleries above the main floor of the Great Hall, servants who had the evening off—also dressed in their best clothes—watched the nobles and entertainers below. The servants would be treated to a party of their own at midnight in the corridors and rooms around the kitchen on level 2. Even when money was as tight as it was now, Karne felt his serfs deserved at least that much appreciation once a year. He waved at the faces lined up along the gallery's stone balustrade and grinned at their answering cheer. The sound warmed him inside.

Orkonan, standing beside the huge box of gifts near the Great Hall's main door, motioned to Karne. Karne jumped off the front edge of the dais, instead of using either of the stairs on its ends, and strode toward the main door. His unlordlike manner of descent won a laugh and another cheer from the gallery. He waved again, then joined Orkonan.

A number of guests were waiting for Karne to arrive, though he was still a few minutes early for the party's official opening. Karne greeted each guest by name, shook hands with the men, kissed the air above the hands of the women, then gave each person a small Advent gift from the pile in the huge box. A gift symbolized the wealth of a House, and was thus obligatory at such parties.

A gift for every person, Karne told himself, even if a House must go into debt for it, or the word will start that House so-and-so can't afford the gift. Then that House's friends and allies will begin to fall away. That's not what Christmas is supposed to be for.

A slight commotion outside the Hall aroused Karne from his bitter thought. A knot of brightly dressed people was moving toward him faster than the general flow of the crowd. An aura of expectation surrounded them. In a moment Karne recognized the silvering hair of Cherek Rhiz and then the woman at his side. Charlotte Rhiz had spent the past year in the Retreat House for women near Erinn under the teaching of the deaconesses there. Now House Rhiz had dressed its favorite child richly in narsilk, fur, and chains and ribbons of gold, a far cry from the shapeless gray habit of the Retreat House. The dramatic blue of her narsilk dress played against Charlotte's dark beauty to stunning effect and the gold set off highlights in her dark brown hair. Being at the center of attention set Charlotte's dark eyes sparkling and put spring in her step. When she came even with Karne, Charlotte swept into a curtsy, which showed everyone nearby her grace and modesty and gave Karne a tempting look into the shadow between her breasts. She caught his look and stood hurriedly, blushing. Karne felt heat that was not in the room.

Charlotte offered her hand and Karne raised it to his lips, as was custom. A delicate, tempting scent rose from her soft skin. Charlotte glanced up at him briefly through thick, dark lashes and moved on. Karne felt stirred in spite of himself.

She may be only seventeen, he thought, but she definitely knows how to get what she wants. There'll be no need to force this one into bed as there was with Lizanne.

Her sire now stood before Karne. Karne swallowed and forced himself to focus on the man and not the woman. The man's eyes had a knowing look. Karne wondered suddenly if the Rhiz physician's report had been true, or if he had been bribed to say Charlotte was still intact. He wondered if Charlotte's innocent seductiveness had been a ploy, or had Lord Cherek had some reason other than religious instruction for confining Charlotte to the Retreat House for the past year?

At long last, the stream of guests ended and Karne was free to dance and drink and watch the jugglers, troubadours, acrobats, and dancing dogs with everyone else. He was at last free to begin to know the young woman who was to be his wife.

CHAPTER 3

It was his wedding day. Karne stood in the hallway that surrounded the circular Council chamber, leaning against the cold blue tiles of the wall for emotional support. Only minutes more and he would again be a married man. After the witnesses showed up. After the bride's party showed up.

His heart was pounding faster than he liked. His palms were sweating as if this were the first time.

What's the matter with me? he asked himself. I've been married before.

Van McNeece and his plump little wife came around the curve of the hall and stood in front of Karne.

"Good morning, Karne. You don't look so good," said Van in his booming voice.

"Good morning, Van, Ahnah. I don't know what's the matter."

McNeece laughed. "Pre-wedding jitters, Karne. You'll get over them when Pastor Jarvis starts talking."

Ahnah patted his arm. "It will be all right."

Somehow the trite words, said in Ahnah's comfortable voice, became true. It *would* be all right.

Childreth Konnor joined them. He and McNeece and Nik von Schuss were to stand as witnesses for Karne. Abbot Godwin of Rhiz, Dannel of Jura, and Isan Grent, the Lord of the Mark, were standing witness for Charlotte. When all six men had arrived, they entered the Council chamber through its double center

21

doors and walked down the main aisle to the chairman's desk in the center of the room. Hareem Gashen, Council chairman, stood there alone, waiting for them. He had decided there would be no observers of this wedding, because the risk of assassination or kidnapping by the allies of one House or the other was too great. People died on Council ground frequently, of course, but these were the losers in judicial combat *à outrance,* and died either on the dueling grounds outside or in the dueling arena set behind the Council building. Only once had anyone ever been killed in the Council building itself, the Larga Halarek, and Cherek Rhiz was vassal of the man who had killed her.

House Halarek's Pastor Jarvis slipped in a side door, still adjusting his stole to lie flat around his neck, and took his post beside the chairman. The big double doors opened soon afterward and were held open by men in the brown, green, and blue livery of House Rhiz. Charlotte came to the entrance and stood there dramatically for a moment. Her long wavy hair hung free over a bridal dress in Rhiz colors. Her father waited a step behind her, the wedding shawl, which Charlotte would wear after the ceremony, hanging over his arm; it was the deep blue with dark green edging of House Halarek.

"Tactful," McNeece murmured in Karne's ear.

Karne nodded, his blood stirring at the sight of his beautiful bride. Charlotte came toward him, moving in a manner subtly sensuous, yet entirely within even conservative bounds of propriety. Karne wondered how she did it. He wondered who had taught her. No matter that she had spent the last year in a Retreat House. No matter what the Rhiz physician said, this was not an innocent maiden. Karne was quite sure Charlotte knew the effect her movements would have and had planned them for that effect. That thought led to other reactions that made Karne grateful he was wearing his long ceremonial tunic, so Charlotte could not see how successful her plan was. This woman was to be the mother of his children. The making of them was clearly not going to be the chore it had been with Lizanne.

Charlotte stood beside him and rested her hand on his arm. Her delicate and beguiling scent—

Karne turned with her to face Pastor Jarvis. The pastor read the service, pausing in the appropriate places to wait for one or the other of the bridal pair to reply. At the end, he joined their hands, wrapped the hands with the end of his stole, and anointed each forehead with fragrant oil. Because Karne had no overlord to give him the kiss of peace, Pastor Jarvis passed him the kisses. He placed one on each cheek and Karne gave the kisses to Charlotte. Pastor Jarvis then unwrapped the stole from around their hands. They were officially wed. Karne looked down at Charlotte's glowing face, glad there was no overlord to claim his right to take her maidenhead. If she still had one.

The witnesses signed the contract Reed held out to them and then the wedding party went outside into the crisp, late-autumn weather. A crowd of various personal families, invited from among the Nine Families and the minor Houses, cheered when they saw the bridal couple and threw flower petals and small grain at them. Flowers for joy, grain for fertility. Karne and Charlotte made their way slowly toward a long table set under some trees to the near side of the landing pad. They sat in flower-bedecked chairs and received the congratulations, and gifts, of their guests.

The receiving seemed to last for hours. When the line of guests finally ended, the eating began. Guests could choose from several meats, platters of domestic and exotic vegetables, bowls of jellied meats or fruits, plates of salads, baskets of fruit. Barrels of wine, beer, and ale lay iced and waiting. The guests sat in the sun or under the trees on the grass to eat. Karne sat back in his fragrant and uncomfortable chair and listened to the buzz of conversation, underlaid with the laughter and shouting of children. It had been good, this idea of receiving guests outside. It had been Charlotte's idea and Karne noticed he was not the only one enjoying it: Guests came up to Charlotte frequently to tell her how much they liked this original way of serving a wedding feast.

After receiving their guests, a wedding couple must circulate among them, seeing that everyone got enough to eat and drink and was having a good time. Karne stayed by Charlotte's side at first, but there were so many people and she performed so well that he soon left her to her work and went about the host's, which was too often soothing hot tempers, dragging drunks out of traffic patterns, and separating fighters. Whenever he had the chance, he watched Charlotte to see how she was doing without him. She was introducing herself to the guests she did not know, introducing strangers to each other, making sure empty barrels and baskets were replaced with full ones, checking frequently with the Freeman who supplied the food to be sure that enough was always available to satisfy everyone's hunger. She would do Halarek proud as its hostess.

After separating the twentieth or thirtieth pair of fighters, Karne wondered if it had been a good idea to forgo the customary feast-time entertainers. Clearly, for some men, there wasn't enough to do, but going without jugglers, dancers, acrobats, magicians, and trained animals had been Kit's suggestion from her experience at her own wedding. He told himself she had probably been right, that the fighting and drunkenness would have been the same whether there were entertainers or not.

After the feasting and the fighting came the dancing, for all those still able. Seven bands provided music in widely separated locations around the Council buildings. Karne delegated his mediating work to McNeece and led Charlotte for their first dance together. She melted into his arms in a decidedly delicious manner and he held her as close as propriety allowed. It had been so long, so very long since he had felt such stirrings of desire and he intended to enjoy every possible moment of it.

The band started another tune and Charlotte's father requested his turn to dance with her. Karne began the host's round of duty-dances, the first round with unattached females, though with the shortage of females among the Houses, there were only a few of those. Next came unoccupied married women. He had just begun a *trakka* with Lady Elizabeth Roul when he noticed a sudden halt to the dancing about fifty meters away. Karne let his hands fall away from his partner.

"You must excuse me, lady. Something is wrong over there." And he indicated where with his head.

Karne sprinted across the grass and pushed through the crowd. Benjmin II Roul lay motionless on the ground. A thin, middle-aged woman, probably his dancing partner, leaned white-faced against a younger man. Karne glanced quickly around. No one was leaving the area. No one was slipping a weapon out of sight. This was not likely an assassin's work, then. He gave only a second's thought to the possibility that this was a hoax to get him to leave his own back unprotected— Roul had been at odds with him since Karne had punished him for rebellion—before he knelt at the man's side. There was not a mark on him. Karne felt for a heartbeat. There was none.

Karne looked up at the faces around him. "Get a physician." He looked pointedly at the white-faced woman. "What happened?"

"We—we were dancing the *trakka*, Lord Karne, and he just—he just—collapsed."

Karne pitched his voice louder. "Is there a physician here?" The Freemen who catered such events were customarily required to hire a physician in case of emergencies, but Karne did not know what this contract required: The reception had been Rhiz's expense.

A man in Gild uniform shoved through the crowd. "Here, sir."

Earning a little extra money on the side, Karne thought. Didn't know the Gild permitted that.

"He's dead," Karne said to the Gildsman. "Why?"

The physician examined Roul quickly. "Heart attack, sir. That's an educated guess, but I can't do more without an autopsy and . . ."

Karne knew why the Gildsman let the sentence hang. Members of the Houses rarely permitted autopsies. Tiny needles, or stab wounds, or blows to the head or some other vital organ were too often found. Then an "accidental" death or a death "from natural causes" became murder. Assassination. Life was precarious enough, frightening enough, without acknowledging that there were secret ways to kill. Most Houses did not want to know.

Someone led Lady Elizabeth through the crowd. She dropped to her knees beside her husband. After a moment, she bent over her lap and burst into a thin keening that tore at the heart. Benjmin had always intimidated her, but he had been all she had. Now he was gone, and her sons were not required to provide for her if they did not wish to. Karne put a tentative arm around her. Someone behind him roughly jerked it away. Karne turned and looked up into the furious face of Benjmin III Roul.

"What have you done to him?" the young man demanded. He drew back his foot as if to kick his overlord, then thought better of it. "He's dead. You've finally killed him."

Karne stood and straightened to his full height. It gave him a few centimeters' advantage over young Roul. He took a deep breath, shoved both his wedding night and the death from his mind, and thought of his role as Lharr in Halarek. The Academy's careful training paid off again. He shed the image of happy bridegroom and became one of the Nine. He could see his change mirrored in young Roul's face: It stiffened and turned an unhealthy gray.

"I'll forget what you said just now," Karne said, his voice cold and hard. "You're overcome with grief. I'll ask Abbot Godwin to instruct you again in the proper ways to address your lord."

Young Roul's Adam's apple bobbed. He squared his shoulders. "I will no longer be under the abbot's control, my lord. My sire is dead. I'm now lord in Roul."

Karne looked at him questioningly.

"I administer my sire's Will, my lord, and his Will frees me from being his penance in Breven. My brother Danver will take my place."

The young man's eyes were hot and angry. He hates me for his sire's sin, Karne thought. Roul rebelled and it cost him most of his children and a great deal of his fortune. *Roul* rebelled. I get the blame.

Yet, in a way, Karne understood how the young man felt. It had been Karne who had ordered Roul to bring himself and his children as hostages to Ontar, though it was late in Uhl. The lateness in Uhl, however, had been Roul's choice. He could have yielded much sooner. For Karne to have shown mercy to a rebel would have been fatal to his authority over his vassals: The Gharr did not understand mercy. But in Benjmin III's eyes, Karne was to blame because the flier had crashed in a storm, killing everyone but Roul and his little daughter Mikette. "Roul chose rebellion and he chose to delay yielding until far into Uhl. I'm not to blame."

Karne did not realize he had spoken aloud until he saw the young man's eyes flame. There would be no convincing him. Deep inside, Karne had often wondered if there might have been some other way to bring Roul into line, though his mind knew any other course would have been fatal to all of Halarek. He still felt guilty about the children.

Karne turned from the new lord in Roul. He would have to be dealt with later. Right now, the old lord must be taken care of. He ordered some of Ontar manor's Blues to take the body to Gildport for an autopsy and arranged for Childreth and Durlene Konnor to take care of Lady Elizabeth for several days, until the worst of her grief and fear abated. By that time, it would be clear whether or not her sons would accept her into a House they now ruled. Karne wished he knew more about internal matters in Roul, but he did not. He would not allow the Lady Elizabeth to be set adrift, though, even if he had to take her in at Ontar manor. The idea was not comfortable, because he had never liked timid and weepy women, but it might be necessary to keep her from starving, or freezing during the coming winter in some distant and ill-kept smallholding of Roul's.

As for the autopsy, if it showed a heart attack, no one could accuse Karne of eliminating a troublesome vassal by hidden means. In a matter of such importance, his need as overlord for facts overruled any hope the personal family, or the Family Roul for that matter, might have had of prohibiting such investigation. And the autopsy had to be done by a Gild physician, because no one would question a Gild physician's conclusions: To do so would be to accuse the Gild of partiality and the Gild never favored one House over another.

Roul's death put a damper on the celebration. Guests began leaving for home not long after. Before sunset, the fields around the Council building were empty of people and fliers.

CHAPTER 4

Brander stood to one side of House Justin's Great Hall. It did not have magnificent clerestory windows like House Halarek or House Odonnel, but then Justin was too old for such things. This was the last party before Christmas. Brander looked around. Almost everyone who was anyone was present. As a neutral House, Justin had a much broader choice of possible guests than House Harlan did. There would be good hunting at such a party. Already Brander had spotted the new lord in Roul and Paul IV Druma, who was representing his terminally ill sire this night. Perhaps Paul III was on the edge of death. Perhaps he was already dead and buried, all unannounced, to keep Odonnel off Druma's back until winter made any kind of siege impossible. Brander shook his head.

Paul IV's not that devious and not that smart.

Because Justin was a neutral, its parties were considered safe for introducing young women just coming of marriageable age. There would be many, many more females than usual here, to look over marriage prospects and to be looked over. Females had always been Brander's best source of information about the Houses and their business. They were so easy to flatter into talking about almost anything. Males, better trained and more aware of danger, seldom could be led to say anything of use to Harlan or its allies. Brander again thanked the Guardians for the hormone deficiency that made women as vital to him as furniture or carpets, objects of beauty or usefulness and no

28

more. It gave him a great advantage in dealing with them.

He began the tedious but necessary process of finding a male relative of each of the young women he wanted to meet to introduce him. After introductions, he set about charming the young women, one by one. His charm was a skill of which he was justly proud. Even after women discovered they had no sexual power over him, many remained his friends.

Brander had met six or seven of the up-and-comings when Charlotte Halarek came through the Hall door. The noise near the door diminished noticeably for a moment in tribute to her beauty, which was truly spectacular. Brander did not wonder that Richard had wanted her, still wanted her. Brander admired a rare work of art as much as the next man, and there was as much artifice in the face Charlotte Halarek presented to the public as there was nature. Brander watched her progress across the floor. He would have to get to know her a little. She was the daughter of a vassal. Former vassal. Richard had not done anything about that defection yet, more fool he. The vassal relationship was enough to start an entirely proper conversation, though.

Dance music began. Brander worked his way into the circle around Charlotte by dancing with the women in it one by one. Patience, he often told himself, was one of his strong points. He would dance with Charlotte eventually. In the meantime, he was a very good dancer and valued as a partner. He could have fun and, perhaps, pick up useful bits of information.

Eventually, luck smiled on him and he was returning his latest partner to Charlotte's circle of friends at the same time a minor cousin in House Gormsby was returning Charlotte. Brander extended his hand to her, then bowed with practiced grace.

"May I have the next dance, milady?"

Charlotte smiled and blushed prettily and put her hand in his. "Certainly, Lord—?"

"Call me 'Brander,' milady. I haven't been called 'Lord' for years. Too stiff." *And too threatening to Richard. He doesn't like that title for anyone else in Harlan.*

"And what House?"

"A friend of Rhiz for many years." *Which is true, in a way, but it's not an introduction and she should not dance with me.*

Charlotte looked at him with sparkling eyes. "A riddle, milord. How droll. I've never danced and riddled at the same time before." She moved ahead of him toward the circle forming for the next dance.

Hmmm. Bold. Interesting. "Start guessing."

The quick, bouncing steps of the dance required concentration, so Charlotte's guesses came on jerking breaths of air. Brander expected her to show some concern, feigned or otherwise, and perhaps refuse to dance with him any more when she learned her partner belonged to her new Family's strongest enemy, but when she finally hit the right name, her face lit up.

"Harlan? Really, my lord? My sire has spoken often with admiration of Lord Richard's cleverness and sharp timing."

So highly that he pulled out of alliance with him as soon as it seemed possible? Who's lying, you or your sire? "Lord Richard will be glad to know he's admired by someone. Life in Breven is very lonely for him now. The abbot keeps him very strictly confined."

Charlotte's eyes narrowed. "He did commit murder."

"The Harlan/Halarek feud has been long and hot. He didn't *intend* to kill the Larga."

Charlotte turned out of the dance circle. "No, he meant the knife for my husband. I think you had best take me back to my friends. *I* don't like dancing with someone who would prefer to see my husband killed and Karne wouldn't like seeing me dance with you, anyway. You had such an interesting face and he wasn't here—" Her mouth shut like a trap. "Take me back to my friends, milord." And Charlotte stepped out of the circle completely.

So you will do out of Karne Halarek's sight what you won't do in it. Interesting.

When Brander turned to lead Charlotte back to her group, he saw Karne Halarek standing just inside the main doors, looking over the crowd. *So. You saw him come in. Perhaps the sentiments so loyal to your husband were for the ears of the dancers around us. There's more to you than I thought, Larga Charlotte.*

Brander left the group before Karne reached it, but not too soon to hear Charlotte explain to her friends that she had not known who her partner was until moments before, at which time of course she had stopped dancing with him at once. Brander resolved to keep an eye out for her after Christmas at Twelve Nights parties, though there were not likely to be many at which both Harlan and Halarek were guests.

CHAPTER 5

Karne sat at the library table, staring into the flames across the room and thinking of the business he must take care of before the season's last Council. Christmas was over for another year. It had been a hollow celebration. There was always too much going on for him to devote time to gifts and decorations, and Charlotte had not wanted to take charge. The lack of sufficient gifts had put her into quite a pout. She had apparently expected a mountain of gifts for herself, at least.

There was the matter of Roul, too, but that would hang quietly in the background for the winter. It would take young Benjmin that long to feel even tentatively sure he could control his House and Family. Roul's first test would be in his personal family, a question of whether his sole surviving brother, Danver, would agree to take Benjmin's place in Breven, meaning whether he would agree to be House Roul's penance for rebellion. Benjmin III's speech to Karne at the wedding did not bode well for relations with Roul, however, nor had Benjmin made any move toward conciliation, even after the Gild autopsy reported the senior Roul had died of a very ordinary heart attack.

Karne stirred restlessly, then got up as Charlotte came in, dressed in the frilly coat she wore over her nightclothes. He felt the now-familiar stirring in his loins. She *was* very desirable. She floated into one of the wing chairs and looked at Karne expectantly. He glanced quickly at his chrono. She was not early. He was late.

He looked reluctantly at the papers spread on the table. Druma. The Mark. Alderman Duval's reports. Spy reports. Letters to write or to leave as notes for Weisman to do tomorrow. And Charlotte, waiting expectantly for her story. Karne rubbed a hand across his eyes. He wished he had thought to ask if Charlotte were literate. He was so used to the women of his family that he had not considered the likelihood that Charlotte could not read or write much or calculate at all, even though most noblewomen could not. The Houses seemed to think they had no need to. So he read to her each night before bed. It was one of the few bonds they had found, so he kept on with it, though he disliked it more every night. It put her as child to his adult. That was her place in law, but—

Karne got up and walked to a low stand beside the fireplace and took up their current book. The stories Charlotte like were *very* adult, sometimes too "adult" for Karne's taste.

Karne read for half an hour, then the two of them went up the iron stair and across his room to hers. They never made love in his bed, because Charlotte considered his room stark and unfriendly. Karne felt a strong and unexplainable reluctance to let her change it. He had disliked the room intensely himself when he first moved in, but the mural Egil painted for him had helped soften that dislike a lot. Karne let his eyes glide across the painted wall as they crossed the room: Heimdal at the Rainbow Bridge, with sunset flaring its last and the Jotuns looming at the bridge's far end. Lizanne had never come here, either.

Two hours later Karne sat on the edge of his own bed. He was a skillful lover. He knew that. Charlotte could not shake his confidence in his skill, but his endurance . . .

Allfather, have mercy! The woman goes on forever and then whines and weeps and storms when I have no more to give! No man could satisfy her. I should have let her wait five years for Richard! She'd shake even that bragging bastard's confidence.

He lifted the coverlet and sheet and slid into bed. Even after many nights of ego-destroying effort on his part, Charlotte showed no signs of being with child. It was as if she had access to preventatives, though their contract made plain that no preventatives were to be used in the first two years of marriage. Karne pulled the covers up over his shoulders and turned wearily onto his side. Then there were the parties. He had agreed to accompany Charlotte to several parties between Christmas and Council. He was not looking forward to it. Charlotte loved parties and sulked when Karne refused to go to one because of pressing business. Since Charlotte had quickly developed a circle of friends among the young people of the Houses allied with Halarek, Karne had sometimes allowed her to go to parties by herself. Until spies and then reluctant friends began reporting suspicions of improprieties.

Weisman had reported seeing Charlotte flirting with a merchant from Neeran. Weisman suspected she thought to wheedle a fur from the man in return for her attention. Karne wondered how far she had planned to go. Weisman had been appalled, but then Weisman was very conservative, especially for a Freeman.

Karne turned onto his other side and pulled the pillow over his head, but the thoughts buzzing in his head would not let him sleep.

Van McNeece had reluctantly mentioned seeing Charlotte talking to Brander Harlan and behaving seductively toward Cyril of Melevan. Karne had paid more notice after that. The sting of Cyril of Melevan's rebellion against Karne's overlordship had not yet gone away. Maybe Charlotte's flirting covered spying for Harlan. Rhiz had been a Harlan vassal for generations. Perhaps Richard, through Charlotte, was stirring up Melevan to rebel again. Or perhaps Charlotte thought to get the satisfaction from other lovers she was not getting from him. Karne told himself even a seventeen-year-old woman would not be so stupid as to search for lovers publicly.

Karne flopped onto his back and stared up at the dark ceiling. He had repeated and repeated that to himself. Until more, similar, reports came in from Halarek spies in various Houses. Charlotte was too friendly with male guests at parties, especially when dancing. Charlotte allowed men not related to her to touch her during conversations. Charlotte sometimes touched them back. Charlotte had been seen talking to Brander Harlan twice. These were too much to ignore. If Charlotte's behavior had alerted his spies, it alerted other, enemy spies also. So Karne had decided Charlotte would go to no more parties without him and that meant either cutting deeply into the time he had left to prepare for Council or keeping Charlotte home. He had reluctantly decided that, if his marriage was to be even tolerable, he would have to go to the Twelve Nights parties. At that time, he had not known that decision would add worries about the political preparations he was not making to his worries about Charlotte's, and therefore his, reputation. It seemed like hours before Karne finally fell asleep.

The most important of the Twelve Nights parties was the Freemen's Ball. It was always the next to the last party before the Frosttime Council, though this year House Konnor would have a party following a pre-Council meeting on 19 Narn. The Ball was always silly and it was always held in a freecity, one of the few times outside Council when Freemen and lords met other than on matters of trade. Only Free*men* attended. Free*women* stayed at home, because the Sickness had made noble women scarce and the freecities feared intermarriage with the Houses more than wars between them. It was a masked costume ball this time. Karne knew Charlotte would enjoy it, so he arranged his schedule to allow time to go. Preparing for it, Charlotte had been as excited as a little girl.

After sunset on 16 Narn, the Lharr and Larga Halarek stepped across the threshold of the Alderhouse of Neeran and into the noisy, smoky room beyond. Bodies dressed as aliens, animals, folk-tale characters, circus people, and Gypsies milled around, drinking, eating, talking. Sometimes it was hard to tell what sex the person inside the costume was, let alone *who* it was. Karne instantly felt apprehensive. This was dangerous. He had not thought about the risk attached to a hundred or so anonymous bodies in one room, at a party where allies and enemies mixed, and he knew he should have. Masked balls were rare among the Houses, but Karne had been off-world too long, and too preoccupied lately with his emotional battles with Charlotte, to think carefully about why: Masked parties offered too many easy opportunities for assassinations or assignations. Before he could open his mouth to tell Charlotte they were returning home, she had slipped away into the crowd.

He looked after what he thought was her curly head for a moment, considering going after her. He reassessed the risks and shook his head. It would probably be safe enough. He knew what her costume was. The swan-lady would have to behave like a real lady tonight.

Karne himself wore no costume, because almost any costume hindered free movement and a mask narrowed vision. He *had* thought that far. The Lharr Halarek could risk neither in a room full of enemies. Karne saw Emil von Schuss's balding head across the room, waved, and headed in his direction.

Emil wore no costume, either. The short, plump chicken beside him put an arm around Karne and squeezed.

"You're chicken, too," Kit's muffled voice said.

Karne laughed and squeezed Kit back. "Not chicken. Smart. If I'm anyone's target, I don't want any mistakes made."

"Want to dance?"

Karne looked at the round, feathered shape. "That's going to be hard to manage, isn't it?"

"Not as hard for you as it will be for me."

Karne laughed and led Kit toward the open space where a pair of goblins, a Gypsy, a Rigellian pirate, and several soldiers in uniforms from Starker IV's past were dancing. Two swan-ladies stood watching and Karne knew Charlotte had not yet had time to put on her costume.

He stopped and stared. Charlotte had known. She had probably arranged this with her friends. A joke on a husband she looked at with contempt? Distractions? Though the first guess was a likely one, Karne's instincts told him the elaborate deception had been arranged as a distraction. Charlotte had created distractions so she could carry out whatever business she wanted to at this party and Karne would not find out about it, or he would find out about it too late. Rage blinded him for a moment.

The little bitch! Bitch, bitch, bitch, bitch!

"Karne, what is it?"

Karne turned to Kit. He had to force his voice out through thickness that threatened to strangle it. "Charlotte's made a fool of me, Kit. She's had some of her friends wear the same costume, so I won't know which of them is which. And that means she's up to something here. I'm sure Nik's told you what our spies are reporting." His fist smacked into his other palm. "By our Mother's Blood! Why can't I find a docile, obedient wife, like you are to Nik?"

The chicken's rotund body jiggled, as if laughing. "You're joking, of course."

Karne looked at Kit for a long moment, then smiled a little himself. "You've never been docile in your life, have you?"

"Except with Father."

"Yes, except with Father. He would've killed any of us who weren't, even Jerem, and without a qualm, too." He ran a hand quickly through his hair. "What do I do now?" His voice was low and uneven. "What do I *do*? I've bound myself to that vixen for life."

"Find her. Label her with a ribbon or pin or something else she won't notice. Follow her or have someone else follow her. She's not doing this just as a joke on you. There has to be more to it than that. A joke on you, she'd flaunt herself. When you get home, try talking to her about the danger this kind of trick creates. Lock her up if she won't listen."

Kit's feathers rattled as she turned abruptly. Karne looked where she was looking. Cherek Rhiz stood against the wall near a side door. "Her sire's responsible, in the end," Kit continued in a low, hard voice quite unlike her, "but it's too late for him to do anything now. Can you imagine our sire letting either of us refuse the spouse he had selected for us? Richard of Harlan is as high a match as a girl can even dream of—though the match *would* require a five-year wait—and this chit turns him down." She turned back to her brother and lowered her voice still more. "Get her pregnant, Karne. That will slow her down for at least a few months." Kit touched her own belly, well disguised by feathers and bulk, with tenderness. "Go. Emil will dance with me. Find out what Charlotte's doing."

Karne turned to go. Kit grabbed his sleeve, then pulled his ear close to her face. "Watch her sire, Karne. She's his favorite child. She'll visit him sometime tonight and that will identify her."

Cherek's favorite child. Godwin's favorite niece. It sounded like partial explanation for Charlotte's willfulness. Karne circled the dancers and stood near enough the pair of swan-ladies to hear their voices, which were undisguised because they did not know he was behind them. Neither was Charlotte, but one was Richard's sister Galliana. Help from Harlan. They had probably been friends since childhood. Karne wished he knew which theory to believe, adultery or treachery.

Karne felt in his pockets. There must be something he could use as a tag. All he found was lint and, finally, a pen. That would have to do, though how he could make a mark big enough to see from a distance he did not at the moment know.

Over the next couple of hours, Karne danced or talked with all five of the swan-ladies. All of them spoke to him in deep, seductive, unrecognizable voices. None of them visited Lord Cherek. It was the dancing that revealed Charlotte. Karne knew her body too well to mistake it for any other woman's. She whirled from him to the next man in the circle. Karne made no sign he had recognized her. She would come back as part of the pattern of the dance. He palmed the open pen, letting the thin, blue fluid run slowly into his hand. He touched his next partners only with the fist of that hand.

Charlotte whirled back the same way she had whirled away. He let the pen fall and spun Charlotte around in the next move of the dance, his blue hand flat and low on her back. When she moved on again, he saw with satisfaction that she now wore a blue blur behind. The dance ended. Karne thanked his final partner and dropped out of the circle.

Nik von Schuss was easy to find: He was standing with an arm protectively around a plump chicken. Cinkaid of Justin was only a little harder. Karne drew all three aside and asked them to keep watch on the side doors and, if a swan-lady with blue on her back left, to follow her. Karne went to the main door, wrapped himself in a cloak from the pile he found there, and waited just outside, in the shadow of a pillar. He was sure Charlotte would make some betraying move as soon as she decided he was not coming back to the Hall immediately.

More than an hour later, a swan-lady smudged with blue passed along the intersecting corridor with a rattle of feathers, followed discreetly by Cinkaid. Karne dropped in beside his friend.

"Thanks. I'll tell you later what's going on." He pulled the cloak's hood over his head, let Charlotte get well ahead of him, and walked close to the side wall.

She turned into a poorly lighted corridor and stopped for a moment just inside it. She pulled a tiny locket out of the neckline of her costume and squinted at the paper she took from it. It must have been hard to read in the poor light. She nodded, put the piece of paper back, then the locket, and walked on. Karne waited until she turned a corner ahead before he followed. He reached the place where she had turned just in time to hear a door close. Too late. He was too late. Then he saw a thin line of light beneath a door down the hall.

If I were going to an assignation, or to meet a spy, I'd do it in the dark, he told himself.

He walked very quietly down the corridor and stood where the door would conceal him for a moment when it opened again. The door opened surprisingly soon, too soon for any kind of an assignation. A high, light voice told Larga Charlotte goodbye until the next time, then Charlotte came out, her mask in one hand, a green box in the other. She shut the door carefully. Karne sprang. One arm fastened her arms tight against her sides, the other clamped over her mouth so she could not scream. She squirmed and kicked with surprising strength.

"It's me, Charlotte." Karne heard the cold hardness of his voice and did not care. "Drop what's in your hand and I'll let you go."

She struggled harder. The door opened again. The man's head snapped toward the sounds of struggle, then he whirled and ran away, but not before Karne had seen jutting from beneath an eye mask the high, thin nose that marked strong Harlan blood.

"Do you bargain with Harlan, Larga?" He wanted to strangle her and his voice showed it. "For my life, perhaps? Is your sire in this, too?"

Charlotte stopped struggling immediately. She shook her head as best she could against Karne's hold.

"Are you going to scream, Charlotte? It could be very embarrassing—for *both* our Houses—if you did."

Charlotte shook her head. The box she had held in her hand hit the floor with a metallic clang. Karne released Charlotte and swooped up the box in one smooth motion. He dragged her into the better-lighted corridor, then opened the box. Several hundred round pink pills lay jumbled inside. Preventatives. Had she believed his desire for her was so great he would forgo children just to have her?

"Preventatives, Charlotte?"

She swallowed audibly. Her face paled. She nodded slowly.

"You signed a contract with me, Charlotte. No preventatives for the first two years. You're an adult woman now, Charlotte, and adult women are required to keep the contracts they sign." Karne shook the open box in front of her eyes. Pills spattered out onto the floor. "Halarek *must* have heirs. You knew that. You know that. NO PREVENTATIVES!"

Karne hurled the box down the corridor. Pills clittered across the stone and bounced from the walls. The box hit the floor with an empty clang. Charlotte dropped to her knees, sobbing, scrabbling for pills.

"I won't be pretty anymore," she wailed. "I'll get fat and waddle and—"

Karne jerked her to her feet. "That's what happens, for a short time, when a woman's pregnant, and pregnant is what you agreed to be. Come on." He wrapped an arm around her and forced her to walk toward the Alderhouse's entrance. "We're going home."

CHAPTER 6

Brander Harlan settled his flitter carefully onto Konnor's snowy landing pad and took a last look around the craft's interior. There was no sign of the bag of gem-quality orak stone the new lord of Roul had given him at the Freemen's Ball, not even dust. It was custom in Konnor that guests' fliers were cleaned while they attended parties or political events on the holding. It would not do for even a cleaning serf to find orak in a Harlan flitter. He had not asked where Benjmin III had gotten the stone, some underground deal with Cyril of Melevan, probably. Or—

It doesn't matter. It's a symbol of the pact between us. Hidden Harlan support for a young rebel. Come spring, both Richard and the Halarek will be surprised. Unfortunately, the Halarek won't be as surprised as I'd hoped. I told Charlotte to be sure no one followed her. Now he knows she has Harlan aid, at least for the preventatives. He probably has the note, too. Had to print in words so simple my six-year-old nephew could read it. Stupid bitch!

Brander stepped out onto the flitter's wing and looked down at the grass poking up yellow-brown through the snow. There would not be much flying weather left. They would all settle into a nice, quiet winter, Harlan, Halarek, and von Schuss. Brander laughed inside at the thought.

He counted the fliers already on the ground and made mental notes of who had arrived and who was yet to come. This was an important meeting, called to attempt to work out details of some very sticky political problems a day before Council. There was to be a party afterward, too, Durlene's way of smoothing all ruffled feathers. It would be most surprising if any lords of the Nine stayed away from this meeting, or very many of the minor lords, for that matter. The hospitality of House Konnor was world-famous.

Halarek was here already, and deVree, and Justin, plus many of the minor Houses and a few fliers from freecities. The presence of Freemen was unusual. Freemen did not concern themselves with anything they considered "the business of the Houses." It had been a "privilege" for him to be invited, because Isan Grent, Lord of the Mark, was, of course, still the official spokesman for the trustees of Harlan. Brander had his own guess as to how the invitation had come about.

Wouldn't do to have no one with the Harlan name at this meeting, would it, Isan? And you know I have Richard's confidence.

Brander jumped from the wing into the snow. *Doesn't have a flitter shaft, does Konnor, or he's not letting most of us use it.*

He crunched across the pad to Konnor's entrance shelter. The prox sensor opened the lift doors the moment he reached the protection of the windwalls. The meeting was not the only reason for coming. At the party afterward, Brander could meet Charlotte Halarek again and reassess her role in her new House and her uses now the preventatives had been discovered. Clearly, she was not going to be hindering the conception of a Halarek heir anymore. Harlan spies reported she behaved in overly familiar ways with men at parties. That interested him. Such women were excellent candidates for blackmail or enlistment as spies or even for kidnapping, although another kidnapping by his House of another Halarek woman would perhaps be more than the current political climate would bear.

The political meeting in Konnor's Great Hall was already in session when Brander arrived and it was going badly, as Brander had expected. He seated himself toward the rear of the gathering and kept his mouth shut. None of his cousins wished to give up the chunks or crumbs of Harlan they now held and, without an overlord to compel obedience with his army, Council had no way to force them to. That problem, by its very nature, was unsolvable. Brander was sure that had been clear to everyone before the session was called. Nonetheless, the debate went on for hours, with Odonnel, Brassik, and even some representatives of the Freemen urging Council to send its army to pry loose the smallholdings and manors wrongfully taken out of House Harlan's control. Halarek and von Schuss sat silent, even though Halarek, at least, had a strong stake in what happened in Harlan.

Fools. Halarek, von Schuss, deVree, and Justin, at least, won't lift a hand to put Harlan back together. It's not in their interest. But the Freemen are worried. That's very interesting. They've probably had meetings of their own to discuss what to do. Have to check on that. That even a few Freemen would urge Council to use its army against one of the Nine . . .

In the end, the members of the Houses refused to consider using Council's army, with Halarek and its allies leading the attack on any action to restore order in Harlan, just as Brander had thought they would. Though the destabilizing of Harlan endangered many of them, they could not come up with any alternative plans. The time for nightmeal came and the meeting adjourned without taking any action at all.

Serfs quickly set up benches and trestle tables. The moment the setting-up was finished, Durlene Konnor entered the Hall, accompanied by many wives of attendees.

You'd think Durlene could have fed all the wives earlier or elsewhere. What reasonable person wants his meal spoiled by a female's constant chatter? At a party is one thing, over food quite another.

Brander considered saying he was not hungry and eating later at the party, but Durlene Konnor was justly famous for her meals and a chance to sample one was too good an opportunity to pass up, just because he did not want to have to share a platter with a woman.

There were far fewer women than men and there were no unattached ones, so Brander, to his delight, was allowed to eat alone. Sampling some of this and some of that, he came to the conclusion that this meal would do nothing to damage Durlene's reputation. The meats swam in inventive and delicious sauces. The vegetables came piled in bowls, each vegetable cooked to doneness, yet retaining its color. Often several vegetables had been mixed, so the colors pleased the eye. The bread was the best Brander had ever tasted. The wine was top quality and freely poured. By the time dessert arrived, Brander was feeling very relaxed and comfortable.

After dessert, Durlene invited the wives to come with her to freshen up, leaving the men to relax still more over more wine and to talk about matters other than politics. This evening, though, it seemed no one wanted to talk about anything *but* politics. Brander noticed that some of the most important political players—Halarek, von Schuss (both baron and Heir), Justin, Konnor, McNeece, and the aldermen from Lews, Loch, and Neeran—seemed to have disappeared somehow before the women did. Brander listened carefully anyway, glad that his rank out of immediate succession in Harlan gave him an excuse to say nothing.

Everyone knew Kath was going to try to take a chunk of McNeece come spring, and some men were laying wagers that Van McNeece would send Kath packing within days.

The matter of Odonnel and the overlordship of Druma came up, too. Few doubted that Halarek would go to war to prevent his vassal from being overthrown in favor of another branch of Family Druma, weak-willed and cowardly though Paul III and IV were known to be. It would be a matter of principle for Halarek, and few of the men present would consider any alternative other than war were they in Halarek's position. On the other hand, if Odonnel could take more land into his hands without heavy losses . . .

Allet of Justin, claiming poor health, had sent his Heir, Cinkaid, to the meeting. Behind the young man's back, men talked about the likelihood that Allet had stayed home to settle on some means of protecting Gannet and Rooder Holdings, now he had taken those Houses under his protection. The mention of those rebellious vassals brought up House Rhiz's renunciation of all ties with Harlan on the basis of the marriage into Halarek, and that subject led to discussion of Benjmin II Roul's sudden death.

"What think you, Harlan? Was it an accident, or was it assassination?"

Brander looked at the lord of Emmber curiously. "Why do you ask me? His death's of no interest to me. I have no power in Harlan." *Though that will change before autumn.* "I'm just

Lord Richard's messenger and sometimes his adviser."

"Wouldn't it be interesting if Halarek were responsible, him with his alien ideas and alien friend?" Lord Hyndrik of Emmber went on, looking around the room at the other lords of the Houses.

You'd better hope both his alien friend and his alien ideas stay home. They have more power than you understand, you ninny. Brander cleared his throat, the polite signal that an inferior wished to speak. "Murder is beneath the Halarek. Besides, Roul was his vassal." *And the young Roul will soon be mine.*

"But Roul rebelled. I wouldn't trust such a man again as head-of-House," one of the other minor lords put in.

Brander looked at the two young men in disgust. "Roul lost all his children but three. Most men would learn something of their overlord's power from that." *And I gain nothing by talking more with you.* Brander stood to leave their company.

Konnor's seneschal ceremoniously opened the main doors of the Hall just then and the women reentered, bright in party gowns and headdresses. Brander watched Childreth Konnor walk to his wife, bend gravely to kiss her hand, and look down at her a moment, his face alight with more than pride in her abilities as a hostess. The look lasted only a moment, but that was long enough for Brander to see that here was a powerful pressure point in this House, should he ever need one. It occurred to him that there might be other such connections that could be useful. If Richard had known about the powerful emotional tie between the Heir in von Schuss and Kathryn Halarek, for example, he would probably have planned his seduction of her differently. His ignorance had been an important factor in losing her and the leverage a child got on her would have brought. If Richard could have. If Dr. Gebbits had been doing as he promised, if the little pills he claimed he had been giving Richard in the Mirin wine did as he had promised, twenty years would not provide enough time for Richard to get a child.

Whatever the odds of success might have been for a child by Richard out of Lady Kathryn, Ennis had spoiled everything. Ennis had taken Kathryn out of Odonnel before Richard's escort to Breven could reach her. Garren Odonnel had perhaps been a factor in that, at least in turning his back to possible escape routes, because Richard's plans for his cousin's wife were too much even for Garren to swallow. Though he *had* done a convincing job of torturing her to find out where Ennis and the baby had gone.

Brander watched Garren and his beautiful wife pair off and join a cluster of couples. No, Garren was not an absolutely reliable ally. Ennis had escaped the caravan ahead of Garren's soldiers. This should not have been possible. Ennis had hidden or killed the baby that could have been so useful. Brander did not believe the child had died of the Sickness, as Kathryn and the Gypsies said. It was too neat, and against recognized genetic likelihoods.

Charlotte Halarek made her entrance. She looked around. No Lharr Halarek to be seen. She made a small nod and a crowd of admirers absorbed her and hid her from view. *And her husband not here. How interesting.*

Brander strolled over to the edge of the group and hovered, waiting, listening. There was still much he did not understand about Charlotte Rhiz-Halarek. She had not been out much socially before her marriage. In fact, she had spent the past year in the Retreat House near Erinn. That detail had bothered Brander since he learned of it. He had never considered House Rhiz as especially religious.

Charlotte spent the first hours of the party wandering from one part of the Hall to another, watching the jugglers and then the acrobats, petting a performing dog, tossing the bait for a friend's hawk, behaving as a proper young wife should. Except she always had a young man near her, often improperly near, like a brother rather than a friend.

Soon, apparently bored with entertainers, Charlotte joined the dancers. Her husband was still nowhere to be seen. Brander watched and noticed she seemed to cling to her partners. When he looked closer he saw she was touching and touched as was not right for a married woman. Or an unmarried one for that matter. She interested him more and more. Perhaps the religious retreat had been enforced on her, and not for religious reasons.

Toward the end of the evening and after checking again to be sure Karne Halarek was still out of the room, Brander asked Charlotte to dance. They danced a *trakka,* keeping up a here-and-there conversation, as allowed by the pattern of the dance, then he persuaded her to stay with him for the waltz that followed. As the music began, Brander pulled Charlotte into his arms and held her indecently tight. She moved close to him and smiled at him, her eyes lazy slits. They continued a light bantering conversation. Brander let his lower hand wander a little. Charlotte hummed the dance tune and did not object.

As he danced, Brander kept an eye out for Karne Halarek. Recently, he had been sticking quite close to his new wife. Brander toyed for a moment with the idea of finding out where Halarek and his allies had gone and what was keeping them away so long, but decided it would be too risky. Besides, Charlotte was a very skillful dancer and her skill gave him pleasure. In addition, he was becoming more and more convinced that a relationship with her other than as the purveyor of preventatives might be most profitable. Looking for Halarek and friends might betray to someone how interested he was in what Harlan's enemies were planning. Their plans were not the business of a first cousin, especially not an unsenior first cousin, but of the lord of the House and his brothers. There were no brothers anymore, of course. Richard had killed them, Natan in self-defense and Olan for reasons no one could understand, because Olan had been too damaged mentally to be a real threat, though he was the oldest brother.

The waltz ended and Brander relinquished Charlotte to another partner, but he watched her unobtrusively for the rest of the evening. She danced most of the dances and seemed to move closer to some of her partners than propriety allowed. Some of her partners responded by pulling her closer and putting hands where none but a husband's should go. Some responded by turning red and sweating. A few hurriedly broke off their dance and returned her to her cluster of friends. Brander assumed few if any of these transactions were noticeable except to someone watching as closely and continuously as he.

Was she bored already? Was Halarek lacking in skill? Was she a woman who needed constant excitement, and teasing men provided it? Did she go beyond teasing, even without the protection she had paid for with small Halarek secrets? He would have to listen more carefully to what was being said about her. Charlotte could be setting herself up for a charge of adultery, though she was being moderately discreet. The possibility of setting up such a charge would interest Richard.

Anything to keep Halarek aware that Richard was alive and that the feud was nowhere near over would interest Richard.

Brander had never regretted, not after adolescence at least, his hormone deficiency. He considered it a blessing, since, as a cousin out of the line of succession, he had little chance of finding a wife from among the small supply of women among the Houses, let alone among the Nine. This night, he could see he would have understood Charlotte better if his body had reacted to the subtle questions hers had asked it.

No matter. I know plenty of men who "function" normally. I'll find out what's going on with Charlotte of Rhiz and what, if anything, it has to do with what's going on in Halarek.

CHAPTER 7

Karne stood in the mouth of an entrance shelter, dressed in a survival suit and mask and clinging to the handholds. Wind whipped snow past in a blinding fog. Uhl had come roaring in with vicious storms like this one, the sort of storms that usually did not occur until toward the end of the month. Karne felt drawn by storms and had come up to watch the wind pile the snow high against the entrance shelters and make drifts two meters high across their ends. The murderous wind could suck the breath out of a man who wore no mask. Karne wondered if it was the contrast to Balder's sunshine and soft rain that drew him, or the violence.

This year's early storms had been so severe that Gild deliveries from the orbital, which often lasted until the end of Uhl, had already stopped. This would be Karne's last trip outside, even in a survival suit, until spring. Already his finger joints ached from resisting the tug of the wind. Tomorrow or the next day, Uhl's winds would be strong enough to rip him away from the handholds no matter how tightly he held on.

Karne regretted the ending of these small adventures. His minutes outside often cleaned away the pressures of being the leader of a Great House. They also often refreshed memories of games he had played in the snow on Balder, where people could play outside all winter, and those led to other play ideas that would help keep the Halarek Family amused for another week or two. Keeping amused was important. Generations of experience with Starker IV's winters had taught the Gharr the importance of keeping hands and minds occupied. When several hundred people lived in close contact in one house for 160 days, boredom became dangerous, even deadly.

The wind rose, tugging at Karne irresistibly. Reluctantly, Karne pulled his way from handhold to handhold back to the lift and safety. He paused inside the lift door to look back one more time. Snow swirled in around his feet. He stepped back from the opening and pushed the door control. The lift started down.

In House Halarek, winter was a succession of Family game nights, parties, and riddle contests, plus individual activities such as horseback riding, weapons practice in the arena, fine stitchery, and tri-d contact with friends, just as it had always been. This winter, before even Uhl was over, it was clear to everyone that the usual activities were not enough for Charlotte. Unable to do more than *see* her friends, real as they looked on tri-d, Charlotte grew moodier and moodier. Games, contests, riding—nothing amused her. She regained her smiling good humor only for parties.

Karne knew that even when she was smiling, she was still planning to get back at him for taking her preventatives away. He had learned early in their marriage that Charlotte let no slight or crossing of her will pass without retaliation, and taking the preventatives away had been no mere slight. She had already denied him her bed. Karne had not forced her, at least not yet, though it was his legal right. He remembered how it had been with Lizanne and had resolved to wait until Arhast before considering force.

Force turned out to be unnecessary and Arhast and Koort passed without the expected retaliation. Charlotte behaved like one of the most gracious ladies of the Nine while Karne waited, feeling a tension in the air like that that comes before lightning, knowing something was coming and yet not knowing what, nor when it would hit. The tension impaired his concentration. Added to that were the rumors, whispered in Karne's ears by cousins and Blues, that Charlotte was flirting with her Blues guards and lying with other men, men of the Family. To lie with a cousin who lived in the manor was incest. That, then, was the form Charlotte's retaliation would take, a scandal that would alienate Freemen and many of the more conservative Houses. Charlotte's reputation was Karne's reputation. If she destroyed her own, she also destroyed his.

Karne kept a close eye on Charlotte after those rumors began and assigned his household officers to watch her when he was not around. The rumors stopped, but Karne knew that was only temporary. Watching her constantly could not be a long-term solution. A few minutes would be all Charlotte would need to start a disastrous scandal. He had to stop Charlotte and to do that, he had to *see* impropriety, see something even Charlotte could not laugh off or explain away.

On the first day of Nemb, Family Halarek gathered in the Great Hall for another winter-party. Karne stood with Kit on one of the narrow galleries above the Hall, both of them against the wall out of sight from below. Daymeal was over and the musicians were tuning their instruments. Soon the dancing would begin and Charlotte would come to the open space in front of the dais. Charlotte loved dancing and Karne had mentioned to her as she was dressing for this party that business with Tane would keep him in the library for most of the afternoon. Karne would see for himself how much of the reports about her were true.

"Spying. On my own wife," he muttered. It still seemed a violation of the trust a married man and woman should share.

Kit set a comforting hand on his arm. "You must. You can't confront her with rumors, Karne."

They stood for some time in silence. Karne stared at the crowd below. He put an arm around his sister without looking away from the Hall and she leaned against his shoulder. She stroked her bulging belly occasionally with awe and pleasure.

Above the galleries, artificial "noon" light flowed through the clerestory windows, illuminating the center of the Hall floor. Bright flags and streamers fluttered over the people sitting, standing, talking, or eating below. In one corner, a minstrel sang. In another, a cluster of men threw dice, shouting encouragement to the cubes of polished ulek horn. At the head of the Hall, the platform that had held the dining table for the Lharr Halarek, his personal family, and his House officials now held a troupe of jugglers and tumblers. The dance space lay open below it.

Karne watched, alert for Charlotte's emerald-green dress, hating the necessity for watching. "A man who cannot control his wife cannot control his house." It was one of the Gharr's oldest and most strongly held beliefs. It was a standard to which all Gharr men, noble and free, were held. Karne dared not let himself be seen as being lax with Charlotte. If men of the Houses saw him as cuckold, or even as just a besotted fool unable to control his wife, the gains he had made in the last year would vanish and Starker IV would again be on the road to its own destruction. Little as Karne had wanted to leave Balder to return to this icy world, even less did he want his world to die in serf uprisings, feuds, and wars among the Houses.

Karne felt deep anger and bitter disappointment. He had tried to give Charlotte the benefit of the doubt. He had tried to keep her in line with admonitions and chaperones. A man should be able to trust his wife, at least not to damage his reputation. Thank the Guardians the rumors had not yet become party conversation. But they would, if Charlotte were not stopped. Karne looked out over the crowd and longed for just a few months of peace.

Kit looked up at him and her hand slid onto his arm. "You're clenching your jaw, Karne. I can hear your teeth. I'm your *sister* and you're trying to hide from me how hard this business with Charlotte is on you—"

Her sympathy was too much for Karne's already strained control. "I'm supposed to," he snapped. "I'm the Lharr." Then he added in a more moderate tone, "I'm sorry, Kit. I suspect many of our cousins expect something exciting to happen. That's why so many of them stayed here instead of going home to their own smallholdings for the winter. They're hovering over us like carrion-eaters. Well, I don't intend to provide them with any food for gossip at my expense and I won't allow Charlotte to."

Karne looked out over the Hall. There was more, so much more, but it was his load to carry. After what Kit had been through, he would not disturb the joy she had now for the world.

Kit took Karne's head between her hands and forced him to face her. "There's something else bothering you, though, isn't there? More than Charlotte. More than Roul."

Karne sighed. Kit had somehow always been able to read him, ever since she learned to talk. He might as well try to hide his thoughts from a Gypsy fortune-teller. But he did not want to talk about Richard's probable claim on her baby, the baby she and Nik looked forward to with such anticipation.

Kit's fingers clamped down on Karne's arm and he could not in all courtesy keep looking away, not unless he wanted her to think he was angry with her.

"Tell me!" Kit insisted. "It's not just the baby will be 'early' and Harlan can yell 'adultery,' is it? You expect Richard to pressure you and Uncle Emil to give up the baby. Because of Ennis."

Karne nodded.

Kit threw her arms around him. "I was afraid of that." Her voice came out muffled. "I'm so sorry, Karne. You know how many years Nik and I didn't even *touch* each other because we were supposed to make other alliances. We couldn't help it in the trap, though . . ." Kit pulled away a little to touch her stomach tenderly. She did not look at Karne. "It could be a bad fight, couldn't it? And coming on top of everything else—" She sighed. "We wouldn't willingly put more trouble on you for anything!"

Karne held Kit tightly and stared blindly across the Hall. He did not answer for a long time. Charlotte. Roul. This baby. When Kit and Nik had made this baby, they had believed they would be dead within hours and so were hurting no one. But they had been rescued and the pregnancy had come too quickly after Ennis's death to avoid scandal.

Music floated up from the dance floor. Pairs formed and re-formed, moving onto the floor and off again as the music called them or ceased to appeal. Charlotte had come, somehow, when Karne was not looking, and was accepting invitation after invitation. She stayed a proper distance from each partner, lingering after the dance with each one no longer than propriety dictated.

Karne looked down at his sister. "Charlotte's arrived. She's being very circumspect. Maybe my story about business with Tane didn't fool her and she knows I'm watching."

Kit said nothing, just turned her head to look out over the crowded Hall. A *trakka* came and went. A waltz began. Karne enjoyed the waltz himself, but many people, especially among the Old Party, said the dance had been revived only because it permitted a man and woman who were not married to each other to get indecently close to each other's bodies. Many laid the blame for its return on Karne Halarek and his off-world ideas, though he had had nothing to do with it. Dancers floated and swirled over the floor, though there were far fewer than there had been for the *trakka*. For a moment he lost himself in the swirling colors and the music.

Kit pinched Karne hard. He followed her pointing finger. In the center of the dance area, Charlotte whirled in the arms of a stocky young man. There was no proper open space between the emerald-green gown and the gold brocade tabard. Karne thought bitterly that Charlotte would not of her own choice dance that close to *him* this night.

"With what you've told me lately and what she's doing down there, I think I see why she spent that year in the Retreat House," Kit murmured. "It wasn't for religious reasons."

Karne thought of Charlotte's intense and insatiable appetite for bed-play and understood Kit's point only too well. "It was entirely away from males," Karne growled. "I wonder how Lord Cherek concealed her nature, even from my spies, until the contract was signed. Surely others, outside her Family, noticed."

"Apparently not. You'd have to believe all the witnesses could be persuaded to keep quiet before you could believe that." Kit went on more hesitantly. "After you met her, though . . ." She swallowed. "She made you blind with desire, Karne. I saw that. She must have, too. You wanted her for more than her beauty or her dowry or the fact that Richard intended to have her. Your desire gave her power. Two years with Lizanne probably made you much more susceptible."

Karne looked at Charlotte, still whirling around the floor with the stocky young man, and nodded. "Charlotte's behavior isn't my fault."

Kit squeezed his hand harder until he met her eyes. "That's not what I meant, but you're right. You *must* stop her. Now. Tonight. Nothing would suit Richard better than to file a charge of adultery against her." She looked away. Her voice fell almost to inaudibility. "Adultery means death."

Kit was staring at the dance floor. Karne guessed she was remembering she had escaped a similar charge only because an assassin had killed Ennis and because Nik had married her. Karne felt a little guilty. His thoughts had been about the consequences of Charlotte's behavior for him. He had not considered the consequences for Charlotte.

"Could you charge her, Karne?" Kit asked finally, her voice almost a whisper. "She's only seventeen and she doesn't believe she'll get caught, let alone die!"

Karne looked long at his sister. When he was "only seventeen," he had not had the privilege of doubting that death was right around the corner. He had been called home to rule after his sire and four brothers were killed. Untrained and adrift in forgotten customs, he had *known* any slip would be fatal. Kit knew that. Now here she was making being seventeen an excuse for the spoiled daughter of a Harlan vassal!

Karne spun on Kit and snarled, " 'Only' seventeen? At seventeen, I was ruling this House. At seventeen, she's been a woman almost two years. By the Four Guardians! You knew better than to behave like that before you were twelve!"

Kit's face went white and Karne felt instantly sorry for his harshness. She was only twenty herself. He reached out and laid his hand against her cheek in apology.

Kit lifted eyes bright with unshed tears, but when she spoke, it was not about her own hurt. "What would such a charge do to you politically, Karne?"

Pride in her replaced his sympathy. She was hurt, but she was still thinking like a Halarek. "The damage, even from conviction, would be less than if I play the blind fool. I'd lose allies, freecity alliances." Karne closed his eyes for a moment, the pain of being unwanted as strong in him again as it had been as a boy. Slowly he banished it to the black pit deep inside him where all his ancient pain lurked.

Kit was watching him intently. She was not quite as pale. "Could she be a spy for Rhiz and Harlan?"

Karne looked at her, surprised at how close their thoughts ran. "I doubt it. I was free and Richard wasn't. That was enough. Charlotte isn't given to complex thoughts or postponing satisfaction."

He spun around to hide from Kit the pain his face would show. He had not expected love from a wife, but he had expected loyalty. Loyalty was necessary. Love was dangerous. Childreth and Durlene loved each other. So did Nik and Kit.

Karne lived in constant fear of what loving could cost them. They probably did, too. Karne was learning desire was almost as dangerous. He clenched his hands. In spite of the Academy training of which he had been so proud, he was not in control of himself anymore. His body responded to merely thinking about Charlotte, to watching her move. After four years without pleasure in a woman, who could blame—

Other things. He must think about other things! The danger from the Harlan cousins, for example. They were destabilizing Starker IV's entire political structure and their treacheries and betrayals within Harlan led Houses like Kath, Brassik, Rhiz, and Odonnel to reach for advantage and greater power, too.

Then there was Paul III Druma, very old, very sick, and with mixed allegiances—he was vassal to Harlan's sister-House, Odonnel, as well as to Halarek—and he had never been known for courage. Garren Odonnel and the Lord of the Mark had both suggested strongly that Paul IV would not be a satisfactory replacement for his sire. Wolves, circling a potential kill.

Finally, there was his own childlessness and the coming quarrel over the bloodlines of Kit's baby. Those were sobering enough thoughts. As good as a cold bath.

Karne straightened and turned toward the Hall again. He had his face under control and his physical reactions to thoughts of Charlotte had gone, but the pain had not. "I've been married most of the last four years," he murmured. "Other men would have three children by now."

Kit sighed and gave Karne a hug. "That's the way things are. Don't blame yourself. You don't have any children and I have a child I can't claim. Van hides her even from me to protect her from Harlan."

Karne kissed her cheek and held her close. "Ennis loved you both and he kept Narra safe at the cost of his own life."

Karne felt a shudder run through Kit and knew she was struggling against tears. He hugged her tighter, Charlotte for the moment forgotten. "Van's always been good about inviting us at New Year's and on his little 'cousin's' birthday. His own children's birthdays, too, of course." He kissed Kit's ear.

Only the Gypsy caravaneers and six people among the Nine knew Narra was still alive. Thanks to Ennis, Van McNeece kept her safe and hidden, more, perhaps, out of hatred for Richard

Harlan than friendship with Karne Halarek. Still, Narra was as safe as was possible on this world.

Kit stiffened suddenly. "Charlotte's leaving the floor with Shjell, Karne."

Karne looked. Charlotte was heading for the door under the far balcony. To leave the room with a man and without Karne's permission was as good as saying she was going to bed him, and to bed a Halarek cousin was incest.

As Karne watched, Charlotte leaned against her partner, who wrapped an arm familiarly around her waist and began nibbling her ear. Karne's face went cold as the blood drained from it. He put his hands flat against the wall for a moment to steady himself against the sudden light-headedness. There was no possibility Charlotte thought that kind of behavior would go unnoticed.

Karne's fist slammed into the wall behind him. "Enough! I've seen enough!"

In one stride he reached the balustrade, dropped his left hand over the edge, and swung it back and forth once. Below, ten Blues separated themselves quickly, but without an appearance of hurry, from their games and conversations and moved toward the Hall's doors. Karne flew down the stairs two at a time, his hand only lightly touching the railing. At the foot of the stair he paused to check his hair and clothing to be sure both were smooth and unwrinkled. He wanted no one to deduce from rumpled hair or twisted tunic that he was angry and in a hurry. He intended to show only a cool, stern refusal to permit his wife to behave this way. He wrapped the role of husband around himself and strode onto the Hall floor and into Charlotte's wake.

The familiar noises of a festival in the Great Hall closed around him. People talked, laughed, and cheered the entertainers. Men shouted their bets on dice or hawks. Musicians played their instruments. The dogs of guests howled at the music or fought with each other over tidbits of food left on the floor. With half an ear, Karne heard Kit close behind him, unobtrusively sidetracking guests and Family members who appeared about to stop him for questions or conversation.

They're probably eager to tell me my new wife is already throwing herself at another man. It wouldn't be as bad if we'd been married for years. Or if she'd already provided me with children. Lots of women have lovers, discreetly, after they've provided children.

This was nothing like his marriage to Lizanne. Lizanne had never been bold. Lizanne had never been passionate. The year he contracted for Lizanne, he had just begun disproving his sire's valuation of him as weak and "womanish," and his prospects of survival against Richard's power had been dim. Lizanne had been the best he could get. Charlotte was a result of being in too much of a hurry to replace Lizanne after she died. Karne still felt ashamed of that hurry, but in Halarek only he and Kit and Kerel's boys were left and, with Sindt of Durlin's nonchalance about protecting the boys, they were not likely to be left long. Now, trying to catch up with her in a crowd, Karne was stingingly aware he should have checked Charlotte out personally. He should have talked to people who knew her, most especially the abbess at the Retreat House.

Karne lost sight of Charlotte for a moment. He stopped and looked intently around. She could not leave the Hall now, but he would prefer to catch her himself. There. Nearer the dais. She had changed direction. Perhaps she had seen one of the Blues. Karne's blood pounded in his head. She would have to live under lock from now on. There was no other way to protect Halarek from her recklessness. If that was all it was.

He stopped Charlotte with a hand that dug into the fine bones of her shoulder. She spun around, furious at the presumption, then had the sense to cover her anger with a quick-drawn breath and lowered eyes.

"My lord," she said, in her husky, seductive voice.

Even now, here, and after what she had been about to do, Karne responded to that voice and to the lovely body that contained it. Lizanne had had to be forced. Every time. Charlotte—

Karne took sharp rein of his thoughts and looked down at the head bent so humbly before him. He looked over her shoulder at the stocky young man behind her. "Your company is no longer wanted here, Shjell." Karne spoke in a cold, quiet voice, too quiet for others to hear. "You're lucky that I don't challenge you to a duel over this gross impropriety with my wife."

The coldness, the effort of speaking very quietly, the formality of mentioning challenge—all helped Karne regain emotional control. He had been the Academy's top cadet negotiator, in part because he had had such powerful control over his feelings. This woman had shaken that control to pieces.

Shjell bowed and opened his mouth to say something, then shut it, spun away, and left the Hall. Karne paid no further attention to his cousin. The man had succeeded in luring Charlotte away from her duties and loyalties. Or she had lured him. The fear on her face acknowledged her guilt more clearly than words. She knew she had stepped too far out of bounds. He would take care of her behavior in private, later. Right now, he must minimize the damage. He would not make more dramatic the stories that would come from this night by hauling her away to her room, a move he knew she would protest loudly and vigorously.

Karne led Charlotte back to the dance floor and drew her into his arms. Perhaps observers would think he had gone after her just for the dance. It didn't hurt to act as if that was what they would think. Charlotte stiffened as he pulled her toward him and her full lips pouted charmingly.

"Woo me. Win me back," her actions said.

She's recovering, Karne thought.

The pouting lasted for only a minute or two, then Charlotte snuggled against Karne in a way that heated his blood and made his heart beat faster, in spite of his intention to stay aloof. She had "forgiven" him.

The piece ended. Karne came back too slowly to the Hall and its crowd of guests. He realized he had been lost in his body's feelings. Again. His desire made him unwary and that was dangerous. He would have to learn to control this feeling as he had learned to control the others. Charlotte, on the other hand, was not likely to learn control, or even to want to, and that made her very dangerous for Halarek. It did not matter if it was her hungers that drove her or a desire for revenge. It did not matter if she were part of some Harlan plot. The end result for House Halarek would be the same—ridicule, humiliation, then lost political and economic power, then death.

CHAPTER 8

Karne escorted Charlotte to her quarters and ordered Blues to guard the exits, including the one into his quarters. He did not want to have to cope with Charlotte's so-desirable body in the night. Karne himself did not sleep. He paced his room and thought and worried. He had just, this year, reached a position where the men on Council listened to him without the condescension or contempt they had had at first. He had finally conquered the image of him as a weak incompetent that his sire had created in the minds of others. He had finally shown he could rule in his House, that he could control even the vassals he had captured from Harlan in the war that followed his mother's murder.

She had been a good wife, Alysha Halarek. She had had charm, beauty, a sharp intelligence, and an iron will. She had ruled Halarek well in the months between the deaths of Trev and his sons and Karne's return from Balder. How had his brute of a father found himself such a prize? How had he, Karne, managed to go wrong twice?

Karne felt like tearing his hair. He ran a hand through it instead. Men of the Houses left the selection of brides to their mothers and advisers, because personal involvement in such an important political decision was unwise *and* unmanly. Karne had violated too many other customs already to violate this one. Lizanne, then Charlotte were the results.

Karne paced. He sat down. He stood up. He sat down again.

He ran his hands through his hair so many times that it stood on end. There was no graceful way out of the position Charlotte had put him in.

Live and learn, he told himself bitterly. I wish I knew what Charlotte's sire did to keep her demure and sedate until after the wedding. Maybe it would work for me, too. She was a virgin when I took her, though it could only have been by some miracle or some very effective threat by her sire.

Karne stopped and stared down at the brass bands and rivets on his leather Rigellian chest. He could keep his Family and its servants quiet about Charlotte and Shjell. It was winter. The first impulse to gossip would be long dead before the more careless members of the Family had contact with people outside Halarek in person, and Charlotte's behavior was not something one talked about on tri-d. But come spring . . .

Come spring, she must have a baby in her.

In the small hours of the morning, when the lights in the manor courtyard were graying to "dawn," Karne found a solution to his problem. He could not trust Blues as guards for long. Charlotte was too skilled and too tempting. Deaconesses of The Way would guard and chaperone her. They could be with Charlotte day and night, as soldiers could not be. They would be immune to her sexual come-ons. Spies and close friends could spread some tale about her religious interests, along with a quiet reminder that she had spent her entire sixteenth year in a Retreat House. Few would believe the tale, but even fewer would argue with it. The Houses knew a lot about the need for polite fictions.

It would not do to bring in deaconesses from Erinn, though. The possibilities for corruption through friendship or pity were too great. How to avoid that? Find a Retreat House abbess who would not sympathize with "the poor child."

Karne thought immediately of his Aunt Alba, who was an abbess. Her Retreat House lay just over the equator in the open plains beyond the Great Swamp. Alba had never liked him, but she had no tolerance for breaches of ethics, no matter what the reason. She despised self-indulgence and self-concern, and she was devoted to House Halarek. He wished he could send Charlotte to *live* in Alba's Retreat House, but Halarek had to have heirs, therefore Charlotte must continue living in Ontar manor.

Until a son is born, Karne thought savagely. Then I can lock her away or confine her with Alba the way Richard is confined at Breven.

The thought, farfetched though it was, gave him comfort. He went down to the tri-d room and made arrangements with the abbess. By the time their conference was over, Karne felt considerably better. As soon as the thaws came and travel was possible, the abbess would send a number of strong, determined women who were capable of physically restraining Charlotte if necessary. In return, Karne would send a sizable contribution for the repair of the west end of the Retreat House's outer wall. Karne walked down the hall to the library whisper-whistling an old folk song.

Karne skipped nightmeal that night, claiming manor and Halarek Holding business. In truth, he did not want to face Charlotte. Loyalty, at least in public, seemed a minimum sort of expectation of marriage and Charlotte had failed to provide even that.

It was late when he at last climbed the iron stair to his quarters. He said good night to the Blues prefet outside his door and went in. A servant had left clean nightclothes from the rok-hide chest for him. Karne put them on and began getting ready for sleep. He still felt too angry at the Larga's behavior to visit her room at all. Getting a child could wait one night.

Charlotte must have been listening for him, because she burst into his room only seconds after he sat down on the bed. "I'm not your child, to be punished this way. I won't be confined!" she fumed. "I won't be watched! Take those soldiers away from my door at once!"

Karne looked at Charlotte in silence. What had she offered the soldier who should have been between his room and hers? Or had he himself just forgotten to post a guard this night? She had seduction in mind, too, he noticed. Filmy gown. Hair floating in a black cloud around her lovely face. A sweet, intoxicating scent following her into the room.

Does she think she's going to change my mind that way? Karne wondered. She knows I'm entirely within my rights and within the law. If she disobeys me, and she has, I can do just about anything I want to short of killing her. To be watched day and night is mild. "The soldiers will be there until Thaw, Charlotte. Aunt Alba is sending deaconesses to take their place."

Charlotte's face went white. Karne felt a surge of satisfaction.

At least that got through to her. She couldn't bring herself to seduce a woman, not Charlotte, even if the holy women were interested in sex.

"Please don't do that, Karne," she whispered. "I'll do anything you say if you'll just take the soldiers away."

Charlotte slid her arms around Karne's neck, pressed her very desirable body up against him, and ran her fingers up into his hair. The tip of her tongue wet her lower lip. Karne focused his mind on her behavior toward other men and ignored his body's reactions. He made his voice stern.

"You brought this on yourself. I warned you to behave as a wife of the Nine is expected to behave."

"I greeted all your guests. I danced with most of the men. I'd done my duties for the night."

Karne felt anger rising, burning. "Your duties include being discreet. Your duties include protecting this House—its secrets, its heirs, its reputation. They do *not* include bringing a bastard baby into the line of succession. You were very obvious last night, Charlotte. You danced indecently close, you let Shjell nuzzle you. Worst, you were leaving the room with a man who was neither your brother nor your husband. Everyone who saw drew the same conclusion I did. And you had no preventatives."

Charlotte stepped back from Karne and ran her hands over the rich curves of her body. "So what? A girl needs some fun. You're gone a lot and you're busy a lot and when you come to me all you're interested in is babies."

She knew the last was not true. Karne was quite sure she knew how fiercely he desired her. He could not tell whether she believed for the moment everything else she was saying or if she was only stirring up the old fight. Fighting excited her. What she actually believed did not matter.

"After you give me two heirs, you can have as many lovers as you wish, as long as you're *very* discreet. Which you haven't been up to now."

Karne watched her hands make a second trip over her curves and his hands itched to do the same. Sweat broke out on his forehead. He must not give in. Not this time. Fawning over a man in public like that was—

"Shjell knew I was only playing." Charlotte's low, husky voice played along Karne's nerves like fire. "*You* want me to spoil my figure. Babies make a woman sag. And get thick in the waist."

"Shjell's baby wouldn't?"

Charlotte's lower lip began to droop. "I wasn't going to go that far with him. Like I said, I was only playing."

"Other observers didn't know you were playing. Shjell didn't know you were only playing."

"Who cares?" She turned to go with a flounce.

Karne lunged for her and spun her around, all the anger at her recklessness, all the frustration, all the pain showing themselves in the white and red outline of his fingers appearing on her upper arms, in the roaring in his head that urged him to shake her until she got some sense of responsibility. But Charlotte was unlikely to learn responsibility.

"I care." His voice vibrated with anger. "Anyone who lives in this House and wants to survive cares. You'll live under guard from now until my heirs are born, longer if you learn no discretion."

"I'll tell my sire."

Karne gave her one hard shake. "Think, woman! Your father turned all authority over you to me with our marriage vows."

"I'll tell my sire. He won't like it that you're keeping me prisoner."

"Prisoner?" Karne snorted. "You think you're a prisoner? What you're getting is a personal guard, and a female one at that. Talk to Kit. She'll tell you what it's really like being a prisoner." Karne shoved her away. "Get out of my sight."

When the first thaws came, Nik and Kit went back to Von Schuss Holding. Kit was very near her time and the baby needed to be born on the holding it would inherit. Charlotte still showed no sign of blooming into motherhood and Karne had begun to be concerned about that.

Kit and Nik's baby was born on 13 Kerensten. It was a healthy little boy and they named him Jerem, after Kit and Karne's oldest brother. Karne got his first look at the baby by tri-d. Small and wrinkled and bluish-red, with his head bonneted against drafts, this was the second-in-line heir in von Schuss and the heir in Halarek after Netta's boys. Karne could see, just visible under a fringe of wispy brown hair, the fat red fingers of the von Schuss mark. Karne breathed a prayer of thanks for that. Looking at the sleeping face, Karne saw for a moment the face of his own baby daughter, who had lived only a month before dying of the Sickness. There was a resemblance to their personal family, then, even among newborns.

On 14 Kerensten, Kit and Nik made a tri-d announcement of the birth to all the Houses and to Council, as was customary with a new heir-in-House. Watching and listening to the announcement, Karne imagined the pain Kit was probably feeling at the same time: Her firstborn must remain hidden and unknown, separated from the family that was now beginning. Though rule in either House would pass first to the male, Jemmy, of course.

Congratulations came to both Houses, floods of them. Even House Harlan, in the person of Brander Harlan, made formal congratulations on the arrival of a new heir. Only a day later, however, very early in the morning and just hours before Karne had to leave for Council, a page called Karne to the tri-d room to receive a message from Richard Harlan. Surprised and curious, Karne put down his shaving equipment and followed. The news had to be urgent for Richard to be allowed out of his room to use Breven's tri-d.

Karne paused a moment in the tri-d room doorway, able to see Richard but unable to be seen. Richard stood stiffly in the center of Breven's carpeted, paneled, luxurious tri-d room. The recently deposed abbot—who had let Richard live his own life in the Retreat and had been partly responsible for his escape— had loved luxury. Halarek's tri-d room was stark by contrast, though Karne had had the walls painted since his father's rule and a magnificent York carpet laid. Karne walked into camera range.

Richard stood so straight he might as well have had a steel rod up his tunic. "I receive word that Ennis's son has been born and declared heir in Halarek." Richard's voice was as stiff as his posture. "And in von Schuss, which is obviously absurd. I demand that the baby be returned to its father-House."

Karne needed a moment to absorb that. That word of the birth would get to Richard quickly, he had expected. That Richard would try to claim the baby had even been a possibility, but Karne had not expected this speedy a demand.

There would likely be a demand made to Council, too.

Karne watched his opponent. He had not seen Richard face-to-face since the afternoon three years before when he and Egil had cornered Richard after a long chase and forcibly returned him to Breven and his sentence. What was he playing for? House Harlan had plenty of heirs. Too many heirs. In fact, the shredding by the heirs of what the Family Harlan had spent generations building was the chief reason Richard had escaped Breven, to put everything back together. What did he want one heir more for? And why had he not been told that little Jemmy bore the distinctive birthmark of von Schuss males? Did someone wish to embarrass Richard in front of Council?

"On what grounds, milord?" Karne made himself speak and act as though the idea of a fight over Jemmy were a minor matter.

"This child is my cousin's son and so belongs in Harlan."

"On what grounds do you say he is your cousin's?"

"By counting the months!" Richard snapped. "The Lady Kathryn and Lord Nicholas have only been married a little more than six months."

Karne studied Richard's face a moment with eyes the Academy had trained to read subtle emotions. Perhaps he was sincere. Kit and Nik had married quickly, immediately after the minimum forty days of ritual mourning for Ennis. In that forty days was the missing month between Jemmy's conception and birth.

"I deny your claim, milord. Lord Jerem bears the von Schuss mark from forehead to nape. Your spies are failing if you don't already know this."

Richard's eyes shifted quickly away, then back. "A lie," he said. "I've seen pix of the child, taken from the tri-d."

"Someone's making a fool of you, Richard. Place the matter before Council if you will, and discover how much a fool you are."

Karne hoped he was right. Nik and Kit had known this claim was coming. They had to have planned some response. Kit would probably have to admit she lay with Nik before Ennis was dead. That would be embarrassing at best and dangerous at worst. She and Nik could be charged with adultery. But surely Council would understand the extremely unusual circumstances—

The adultery charge would be the worse of the two, since Jemmy's birthmark was so obvious. The charge would have been much worse if Nik had not married Kit. It would have been much, much worse if Ennis had still been alive. As things stood, there was no power in either charge. Richard, in his isolation and helplessness, was grabbing at straws. Had he already made a similar call to von Schuss, or was he threatening Halarek because of the feud?

"You think you have the power in Council to win this, Halarek?"

"No, milord, this is not a matter of power. Von Schuss has right on its side and Baron Emil and Lord Nicholas shall prove it." Karne cut the transmission link, but he stood in the center of the broadcast area a long time afterward, lost in thought.

CHAPTER 9

The Council chamber was almost full by the time Brander reached it. So far everything was going well. He had persuaded the abbot that the matter of the von Schuss baby required Richard's presence on tri-d, to defend his House against the false claims of von Schuss and Halarek. And it had gone well. The abbot had not checked with von Schuss. Richard was suitably angry, Halarek suitably cool and righteous.

Self-righteous prig, Halarek.

Brander took his assigned seat, on the bench behind the Harlan prep table's bench and right on the aisle, where he could easily leave the chamber on some errand of the duke's.

Errand boy. That's what Richard sees in me. Not a possible Heir. Not a man even, because I don't have his lusts.

Isan, Lord of the Mark, sat in the chair that belonged to the dukes of Harlan, with his advisers among the other vassal-trustees on either side of him. Resentment burned through Brander, thinking of the man's presumption.

He could have left the chair empty and set one beside it. He's not Duke of Harlan. He won't ever be. Nor will Richard return to claim his place, if I handle matters right.

Brander imagined for a moment he was sitting in that chair, dressed in the rich clothes and jewels of the Duke of Harlan, his many sons arrayed on the benches behind him. A moment's indulgence was all he allowed himself. He was only a cousin, though a first cousin, and daydreaming would get him no nearer the succession. He did not have enough power even to win himself a woman for a wife. Yet.

Brander let his eyes drift across the semicircle of prep tables of the Nine. Kingsland's prep table, directly across the semicircle, was empty still.

Ingold's likely off on some business of his own and none of the others dare sit until he does. Very suspicious man, Ingold.

Halarek and his advisers came next, then Odonnel. Cousins and nephews in Odonnel hovered around the table, shifting like a field of grain in a breeze.

There's where Richard's complaints against von Schuss will come from. Isan Grent apparently has more sense. Garren has more loyalty than sense, thank all the gods.

Brander wondered briefly how Karne Halarek felt, sitting there with enemies on both sides, then his eyes moved on to Gormsby.

Most useful in the past, old man. You held Old Party principles too tightly and that lost us the Council chairmanship forever.

Gormsby shifted in his chair, almost as if he felt Brander's thought.

Wonder how much longer the old bastard has? His Heir is at least as bad. Ingold Kingsland, now, he's much easier to work with than Nellis was. Thought of the "accident" to clear his sire out of the way all by himself, too.

Baron von Schuss and his Heir were standing in the aisle beside their table with the Duke deVree and Paul IV Druma. Brander saw some younger Justin men in the group, too.

DeVree, Druma, Justin. All Harlan's enemies, or potential enemies, are on our side of the circle. Though deVree would've held neutral if Richard hadn't allowed Arl deVree and the entire wedding procession to be massacred, just to get Kathryn Halarek. It's a mistake to kill an Heir so blatantly. DeVree put great store in Arl. Stupid, stupid, stupid!

Hareem Gashen, Freeman and Council chairman, walked down the aisle that separated the Nine's section from the Freemen's, passed Brander, and stood beside the chairman's desk. A brief blare of trumpets announced his arrival to the inattentive. Standing Council members took their places, making a noisy muddle of low voices, shuffling feet, scraping bench legs. Then there was quiet.

"Welcome to the Thawtime Council," Gashen began. "There will be the customary outdoor meal and social time afterward. For those of you who haven't noticed, we set up large tents for your women and children, and several play areas for the children around behind the building."

Gashen looked sideways at the notes on his desk. "The most pressing matters of business here today seem to be the official acceptance of Benjmin III Roul as lord in Roul and a charge from the duke-designate in Harlan that House von Schuss has possession of a Harlan heir, newly born. Lord Richard is demanding the child's return."

From the corner of his eye, Brander saw Nik von Schuss start to rise and Baron Emil yank him back into his chair before the younger man had fully gained his feet.

"There are other matters here vital to order. Kath claims four hundred square kilometers of the southwest corner of McNeece Holding. House Rhiz declares formal independence of all its oaths to Harlan. The lords of Gannet and Rooder swear allegiance to Allet of Justin. Last, and probably most important, some of the remaining vassals of Harlan demand changes in the line of succession."

The men in the room gasped almost as one in astonishment. *They didn't know. Good. Surprise is almost always an effective tactic.*

Garren Odonnel stood. "Garren Odonnel, Lharr in House Odonnel," he said, identifying himself as was required, though there was no one in the room who did not know well who he was. "Lord Richard Harlan has asked me to present his demand for the child recently born to Lady Kathryn Halarek."

Gashen nodded recognition. "I hear you, Lord Garren. However, Lord Richard contacted me very early this morning, wishing to present this matter himself."

Odonnel stood a moment more, looking befuddled, then sat down. Gashen waved his hand toward the tri-d techs' window into the chamber. The giant tri-d screen behind the chairman's desk lit up, then the tri-d room at Breven appeared. Richard stood at ease, awaiting the Council's attention.

Brander smothered a smile, not knowing where the Council chamber's tri-d cameras were trained at the moment. *This* is

*a two-way exchange, after all. Wouldn't do for Richard to
see that. There he stands, on tri-d, in spite of being sentenced to solitary confinement. He's a champion manipulator,
is Richard. Even the current, most upright abbot isn't immune
to appeals to reason: Richard should present his own claim
because it will be so much more effective that way.* Brander
suppressed the pleasure that would have shown on his face if
he had allowed himself to feel it. *The embarrassment or refusal
will be so much greater, delivered to him in front of the world
on tri-d, and I've protected myself from suspicion with an orak
stone alibi: I was in a flier on the spring search for Harlan's
ulek herds. I couldn't've seen the tri-d cast from von Schuss,
so I couldn't have warned him. Though I did warn him.*

Brander waited for Richard's speech to end, a speech the two
of them had prepared as soon as they had heard Kathryn was
pregnant. It was much the same speech, actually, as Richard
had given to von Schuss and Halarek when he tri-ded them.
There were added details, of course, for those among the
minor Houses who might be a little misty on the details of the
Harlan/Halarek feud. When the speech was done, only Garren
Odonnel stood to add his agreement to Richard's demand, and
his voice lacked the authority to make him sound truly sincere.

*Garren's seen the baby, but Garren owes too much to
Richard, not the least of which is a very desirable wife, to
do anything other than support him. That wife brought gold
and Gildcredits and export contracts to Odonnel.*

Chairman Gashen looked at Richard for a long moment after
he quit speaking. He looked at the rank upon rank of minor
Houses in the benches to the left of the screen and the ranks
of Freemen to the right. He did not need to turn to know the
opinions of the Nine. The opinions of the Nine on this issue
were as predictable as the rising of the sun.

"Have you considered this demand carefully, Lord Richard?"
Gashen said at last.

Richard gave a curt nod. He was not used to being questioned.

Gashen cleared his throat. "The heritage of the child is clear,
milord. There can be no question of who his father is."

Richard snorted. "Von Schuss has only had her six months.
A baby requires seven. Lord Nicholas came forty days too
late."

Gashen straightened the papers on his desk, his head bent, making his face unreadable. He made a sharp outward motion with his hand. One of the doors at the back of the room opened with a creak and then closed.

Brander let his head nod thoughtfully, not a movement that would give Richard a clue to his thoughts, should the chamber camera be pointing in his direction. *This is uncomfortable for Gashen, too, is it? The obvious conclusion from Richard's claim is adultery. Freemen are very sensitive on the subject of adultery. Prudes even. Nicholas and Kathryn would've gotten away with it, too, if the dice hadn't fallen against them and the evidence of their crime appeared too early.*

Gashen lifted his head and looked Richard in the eye. "The child could not be Ennis Harlan's get, milord. His head bears the mark of all the males in von Schuss." Gashen turned toward the back of the room.

Richard's face froze. Whatever he was feeling at the news was hidden behind that mask, but Brander knew Richard's quick mind was searching for a way out.

You should've cross-checked my story, Richard. Careless of you.

Nik von Schuss came down the aisle toward his Family's prep table, carrying his infant son. He crossed the empty carpet between the prep table and the chairman's desk and carefully folded back the blanket wrapping the child's head. He held the tiny boy up for inspection first by the Nine, then the minor Houses, then Richard, then the Freemen. The dark red von Schuss mark began just ahead of the fuzz on the baby's forehead and ran over the top of his skull to the nape of his neck. Von Schuss handed the child to Gashen and lifted the hair away from his own forehead. The same fingers of dark red marked him, though age had faded them. He turned and folded over the collar at the back of his neck. The mark was the same.

He took the baby back and looked up at Richard. "We thought we were to die in that trap, Kit and I," he said simply. "We took comfort from each other, believing it was the last thing we would ever do." He looked down tenderly at the baby in his arms. "It wasn't."

Brander snorted. Obviously, von Schuss did not feel guilty. *I should have held off the assassin until later in the week, then*

Ennis would have been there to greet his wife and her lover when they emerged from the tunnel and this entire matter could have turned into a very interesting distraction. Brander watched Nik cross the carpet and start up the aisle again. *Yes, very interesting. But Ennis had to die. Richard agreed with me there, afterward. But I didn't tell him I think their child is still alive.*

Richard had done a lot of agreeing, but had taken very little action on his agreements. He had not ordered out enough men to do anything serious about besieging Rhiz, and his assassins had not been able to get into Kath. Not that Richard's orders mattered a lot anymore, unless they also suited the wishes of the vassals who now ruled Harlan. Richard had not yet realized how strong a hold the vassals now had and there was no one but Brander to tell him. Isan Grent and Dannel of Jura certainly were not going to. *Poor Richard.*

Richard, disconcertingly suspended in lifelike realism behind the chairman's desk, was studying his carefully manicured hands. He looked as if he could touch Gashen if he leaned down. "It seems I missed some vital information," Richard said, not looking up. "The child is clearly Lord Nicholas's. Proof of an adulterous relationship."

The Council chamber began to hum. Men shifted in their places. A voice from among the minor Houses said, just loud enough to be caught by the tri-d equipment, "What business is it of yours, lady's man? You've just been luckier than von Schuss when spreading your seed."

Brander turned to hide the smile he could not stop. Richard had precious little seed left.

Nik von Schuss stopped where he was and turned toward the ranks of minor Houses. He opened his mouth, closed it, turned again, and left the room.

Good. Good. Restraint on the part of the hot-tempered Heir. Don't dignify the charge with a response. Et cetera.

Other voices protested.

"You talk? After taking whores into Breven?" The angry voice came from the Freemen's section.

"Aye, what business is it of yours, lady-killer?"

That's a good one. "Lady-killer." Double meaning.

Gashen rapped his gavel on the desk twice. "Order, lords and Freemen. None of you identified yourselves." He turned again to Richard. "I'm sorry for the interruptions, milord. Did you have more to say?"

"I charge Lady Kathryn Halarek and Lord Nicholas von Schuss with adultery on behalf of my cousin Ennis and our House—"

"My lord"—Gashen was being painfully polite—"you're clutching at wishes. I'll let you go no further. Adultery needs an injured party. The lady's last husband is dead. There is no crime against the planet, so there is no charge. Lastly, my lord, you do not now speak for Harlan in any case and therefore may lay no charge on behalf of your House." Gashen gave Richard a hard look and pointedly turned his back. He waved to the tri-d techs and Richard's image disappeared.

Brander imagined with some glee Richard's rage, both at Gashen's dismissal of him and at his own helplessness to prevent it. There was some satisfaction, too, in the murmuring in the chamber. The fragments Brander caught from across the aisle had to do with Richard losing control, those from behind him with envy that Lord Nicholas had seized him a wife, even though he did so a few hours before she was actually free of her first husband. Brander understood the frustration of the young men and was again grateful that he had no physical need of a wife. He himself would take a wife only for the power she brought as dowry. Children would be only for custom.

"If there's no disagreement, I suggest the Council proceed with the installation of Benjmin III Roul as lord in his House and witness the oaths of Houses Gannet and Rooder to House Justin. Are there objections?" Gashen looked pointedly at the Lord of the Mark, who shook his head.

Letting them go, Isan? Every defection weakens our House, but that's to your benefit, isn't it? Ambitions to add the House of Grent to the Nine in our place, perhaps?

Bile swam into Brander's throat and he choked it down. He could do nothing just now to prevent these dangerous concessions. Isan Grent held power over Harlan direct from Council, and the weaker vassals supported him.

Time. If I only had more time. Brassik and Jura are with me, except Jura technically belongs to that bitch Halarek married. Lynn will come along soon.

At the chairman's desk, Benjmin III Roul was accepting the charters of his House from the hands of the chairman.

Absurd custom, returning the charters to Council when a head-of-House dies. That should be a matter for the Houses. What do Freemen have to do with who controls what? Brander stared at the chairman and chewed a hangnail off his forefinger.

Gannet and Rooder came to the chairman's desk and Allet Justin gave each of them the kiss of peace and the symbolic gifts of vassalage.

Brander felt anger rise. *What's the hurry, gentlemen? You want your alliance firmed up in case of attack and don't want to wait for a proper ceremony in the Great Hall at Justin? What are you afraid of? Harlan's in fragments or you'd already both be dead.*

Gannet and Rooder resumed their seats among the minor Houses, looking pale and relieved at the same time.

"Now to the matter of Kath—" Gashen broke off as Obert, lord of Kath, rose to be recognized.

"I ask that Council postpone this matter until the next Council, Frem Gashen. There is the possibility it might be solved by negotiation."

A disapproving murmur ran through the benches of the Nine and the minor Houses.

I see the hand of that Halarek upstart in this. Negotiation! Women negotiate. Men fight!

Obert's already ruddy face got redder, but he did not withdraw his request.

"Then we've come to the Harlan line of succession." Gashen sat down at his desk and picked up several plasti sheets. "A majority of Harlan's vassals request a change in the line of succession for the following reasons:

"One. Richard Harlan stands in solitary confinement, has been out of touch with affairs in Harlan for four years and will be for five years more. Harlan needs one strong man in control, not many.

"Two. Richard Harlan, in his time at Breven under the previous abbot, has shown himself to be a libertine and that he holds the laws of The Way in contempt."

That's a self-serving argument if I ever heard one. Half of you have mistresses or make regular visits to the whores in your manor towns.

"Three. Richard Harlan has refused to provide House Harlan with a duchess and heirs."

They don't know he can't. That's why he's never gotten caught like Lord Nicholas.

"Four. Lord Richard has brought disgrace on his House by killing a woman.

"Five. Lord Richard further disgraced his House and brought dishonor to himself by committing murder in the Council chamber, where no man brings weapons."

There's the rub. If he gets away with bringing weapons in, no man here is safe from his enemies.

Gashen looked up from the charges. "Is there discussion?"

Of course there's discussion, you freecity fool! Why stick to the formulas for something so obvious?

In the discussion that followed, Garren Odonnel and some of the Harlan cousins urged maintaining the line of succession as it was. Other Harlan cousins and most of Harlan's vassals wanted the line changed. Not for the benefit of the House, Brander felt quite sure. His line, thanks to a lot of gifts and promises, was the one most proposed as the replacement, though the lines of other first cousins had their supporters, too. Slowly the debate among Harlan's circle swung toward Brander's Jennen line.

Good. Good. I've done good work here! Shows what the right words, said often enough and unobtrusively enough in the right places, can do. And my name hasn't even come up. There are two cousins senior to me, but cousins should be no problem. Look how Richard eliminated his brothers.

Agreement among House Harlan's members and dependents was not enough to make the change, however. The Nine and the minor Houses had to agree to any change, also, and here the agreement ran into the Old Party, usually a Harlan ally. The Heir in Gormsby spoke, at great length, about the sacredness of leadership and the devotion of a rightful lord and his descendents to his House. The Duke deVree reminded the lords that no House had changed its line of succession, except after the death of all direct heirs, for three hundred years. Lord Meryd Vesco spoke of Richard's powerful mind and strong grasp of politics, which a new lord might not have.

Not the subject under discussion, Meryd. Wake up, Meryd.

The lord of Kerex spoke of the tradition, now fallen mostly into disuse, of settling a succession question by single combat à outrance.

*Oh, very good, Kerex. I'm not a duelist and even if I were,
it would be extremely stupid to get into a battle to the death.
I prefer subtler methods. Apparently I was too subtle when
explaining the advantages, to you as well as me, of ousting
Richard.*

Finally, when the debate was making a third trip around the
same old arguments pro and con, Gashen called for a vote.
Because this was a matter among the Houses, the Freemen did
not take part. The vote went narrowly in favor of keeping to
tradition and the original line of descent.

Brander was so angry he trembled with it, yet he could not
leave the room without drawing attention to himself. *I'm not
to blame that my sire was a younger son, lords and Freemen,
and I will yet prove I am more than Richard's messenger boy
and spy. This is just the first round!*

CHAPTER 10

The Council members flooded out of the chamber to the food and music waiting outside. Karne waited near the chairman's desk with Tane Orkonan, Obert of Kath, and Van McNeece, each with his holding administrator. Emil von Schuss sat behind his prep table, staring thoughtfully at the ceiling. Garren Odonnel had refused to participate in such a "cowardly" solution as negotiation. In a few minutes Chairman Gashen would be able to join them, as soon as all the other Councilmen left the chamber. Karne felt nervous and edgy. He had to succeed here or no one would try negotiating such a dispute again in his lifetime. It had been a miracle that Kath and McNeece had been willing even to consider a negotiated solution to their quarrel. That Obert would speak of it in front of the other Houses was beyond believing.

Perhaps my dream of helping Starker IV catch up to the Inner Worlds and the Federation isn't entirely a dream, he told himself. Maybe their willingness at least to talk about negotiation is a result of my four years' work, talking myself blue in the face about progress and necessary changes. He felt himself relax a little.

The bustle and the low roar of voices in the outer corridor disappeared when Chairman Gashen himself closed the chamber's central doors. Gashen then walked down the aisle to the center of the room and the men waiting for him. He motioned to the administrators to bring chairs from the prep tables to his desk, then looked with bright-eyed interest at Kath.

"Lord Obert, I'm both surprised and pleased to hear you say you'll consider negotiation in this matter. No Houses have been willing to give up their—excuse my saying this—their twisted ideas of honor long enough to attempt to avoid bloodshed before. Nor have any ever accepted a Freeman as official mediator. I commend you." Gashen looked at McNeece with equal directness. "And you, also, my lord."

McNeece looked if anything a little angry at the praise. Karne watched with amusement. Van had never been one to take a compliment easily. It had taken courage, of a different sort than the courage to face an armed enemy, for Van to participate in such a meeting, especially after that meeting and its "dishonorable" purpose had been made public: The Houses of McNeece and Kath had argued over that piece of land for at least a century *and* the two men belonged to opposite sides in the battle for the soul of Starker IV.

The chairman motioned the men into the chairs. Karne watched them settle themselves, Kath and McNeece avoiding each other's eyes.

Gashen spoke. "You've come, as I understand it, to attempt negotiation of a very old property quarrel between your Houses. Is that correct?"

McNeece and Kath both nodded.

Gashen went on. "We asked your closest allies to come, primarily to conceal the fact that Karne Halarek, and not I, is to negotiate this session. The Lharr Halarek has exceptional skills in this area. I'm not taking his word for his accomplishments, either, my lords." Gashen looked at Obert Kath when he said that. "I checked his credentials with the Altairian Naval Academy myself when this meeting was first suggested back in Koort." He paused to glance toward the chamber's main doors. "We relied on the Lharr Odonnel refusing this invitation. Had he come, negotiation would not have been possible within the political rules as the Houses now understand them. Am I correct so far? A Freeman does not always understand the ways of the Houses."

"You are correct, Frem Chairman." An undertone of amusement lightened McNeece's voice.

He knows what a sly fox Gashen is, Karne told himself.

The chairman is trying to be polite about customs he considers criminally stupid.

"Then I turn the matter over to the Lharr Halarek. When this meeting concludes, to everyone's satisfaction, I hope, the Lharr Halarek, Baron von Schuss, and their men will leave. We'll sit here one half-hour longer, to leave the impression that they were here only as interested observers. Is that plan acceptable to you both?"

Kath and McNeece nodded and Karne began, first asking each man in turn his family's interpretation of the land quarrel, then prodding carefully for any areas of agreement, then expanding those areas of agreement. Both men were very prickly at first. They had risked much just agreeing to negotiation. They had reputations to lose if they were seen as giving up too much. This was a very important point, reputation. Houses had risen and fallen on the strength or weakness of their reputations for honor and power or dishonor and weakness.

Hours of negotiation passed. Karne called a break for eating. In a short time, two Council soldiers brought in a nightmeal from the remains of the food being served outside. When the negotiation resumed, moods were mellower. Within another hour, the men had worked out an agreement that would protect their reputations and settle the dispute, they hoped for all time.

Kath was to issue a formal grievance announcement and then attack McNeece, leading everyone to believe negotiation had failed, thereby saving both lords' reputations for settling serious disagreements with honorable combat. Kath and McNeece would forbid the use of beamers in battle for whatever convincing reasons they could come up with and would also secretly rewire the stunners their soldiers carried so they could not kill, though the "kill" level indicator would work as expected. McNeece was to respond on tri-d to Kath's attack with outrage, at which he was very good, then the two Houses would fight for ten to twelve days, depending on weather, before settling. Kath would get the corner of land separated from the rest of McNeece Holding by the Zimar River, a natural boundary both men agreed would have been a likely property marker in the first days of the feud.

Kath could claim victory, because he received some of the land. McNeece could claim victory because he drove Kath off his holding, except for the worthless piece of land on the other side of the river. He could also point out that he had given up far less than Kath had demanded and could argue convincingly that the cost in casualties of crossing the river to win that piece back from Kath would be higher than that wet and infertile strip was worth. No blood would be shed, unless Odonnel decided to intervene on behalf of his vassal and that seemed unlikely, because Druma was a much bigger prize and Paul III Druma was reported finally to be on his deathbed.

The negotiation completed, Karne and Baron von Schuss left the chamber, both shaking their heads and walking as if discouraged. They joined the partiers outside, but without visible enthusiasm. Inside, Karne was dancing with elation. The fakery of the battle would eventually come out. No one could keep a story like that secret for long, but the fighting would look real long enough to make at least some lords wonder if killing were truly the only way to settle such disputes, and the settlement would last: Kath and McNeece were both honorable men who had inherited a quarrel they did not want to continue.

Almost an hour later, Van McNeece appeared, red-faced and sweating. He roared for beer and began complaining about the obtuseness and stubbornness of Obert Kath. Kath followed Gashen out, looking rather white and shaking. Only Karne knew he had spent enough time in the Council kitchen's refrigeration unit to get that way. Kath snarled at the first three or four men who tried to stop him to talk and went pointedly to the food table farthest from McNeece and his beer before he took anything to eat or drink.

Karne went looking for Charlotte, whose chaperones for the day were Durlene Konnor and Kit. It was his turn to watch her. He had not had the heart to forbid her the first social gathering of the season, but he had arranged to have someone watching her every moment, as he had had to do at Family parties over the winter. Kit and Durlene had agreed to stay with Charlotte today, in shifts, so their watchfulness would not become a subject of gossip, for as long as Karne was in the Council building. This was not the first time Kit had given Karne this kind of help; it was just the first time the arrangements had been formal. It had been obvious, from the moment the issue of allowing Charlotte to attend the Thawtime party came up, that the dour gray presence of husky deaconesses would not do for chaperones. Lifelong deaconesses did not go out among males often, anyway.

Karne found Charlotte's chaperones first. Durlene was sitting with her family under a tree, telling her older children a story while she nursed her youngest. She glanced up when Karne's shadow fell on her and nodded her head in the direction of the Sanitaries without missing a word in the story.

Karne walked in the indicated direction and found Kit sitting on a grassy mound near the Sanitaries, watching one of the small temporary structures and looking worn. She gave Karne a weak smile of greeting.

"I've got an uneasy feeling about this, Karne. She's been in there a long time, but I can't really go over there and ask her what's going on, can I?"

Karne bent to kiss her cheek. She'd had too much to bear this past year, he thought. He said, "You've helped me beyond the call of duty, Kit. Go find your husband and baby boy and enjoy the rest of the party. I'll take over from here." He extended a hand to help her up.

He watched her go with half an eye. She drooped. He would find someone else to chaperone Charlotte when necessary and let Kit relax. He felt a moment of fierce anger that a woman of seventeen had to be watched as closely as a child of four or five.

Karne thought he saw something move behind the Sanitary supposedly occupied by Charlotte. Karne sensed trouble. Was there a rear door? He had never seen a temporary with a rear door. He crossed the grass to the little structure as quickly and quietly as he could, but he was not quick enough. A man peeked around the side of the Sanitary and ducked back behind it again. Karne broke into a run, but the man had already reached the trees edging Council ground before Karne reached the back of the Sanitary. The glimpse Karne had of the man's nose convinced him the man was Harlan.

"One of the flaws of the close breeding Harlan does, that nose," he murmured to himself. *And I'm one of very few people outside Harlan who know about their genetic council and its breeding program.*

Karne turned to examine the back of the Sanitary carefully. He heard the door in front open and snap closed. The back was smooth. The thin wood had no visible holes, but the man and Charlotte could probably have talked through it without much difficulty.

And what may Charlotte be doing, talking with a man from Harlan through the back of a Sanitary? Plotting treason? Plotting escape? Arranging an assignation?

Karne hurried around the structure to catch up to Charlotte before she discovered Kit was gone and hid herself in the crowd. He saw her looking for Kit. Her step quickened. He sprinted to her side and took her arm. She jumped in surprise at the touch. She looked to see who had her arm, and her face turned white.

"What did you discuss with the Harlan man, Charlotte, in that place where everyone else wants to be very private?" His voice was as hard as he felt.

Charlotte threw her head back and her eyes blazed. "I wasn't talking to anyone, you jealous fool!"

Karne stopped and jerked her around so he could grip her other arm, too. He longed to beat her with the narrow rod, a recommended punishment under the law, but in his head he knew he could not: He had seen his sire use it on Kit far too often; he had felt it too frequently himself.

"You're hurting me," she gasped.

"You're hurting my *House*. I'd be entirely within my rights to beat you until you bleed for seeing another man secretly."

"I didn't see h—"

Karne tightened his hands until she winced, and gave her a hard shake. "Don't lie to me, Charlotte! I *saw* him!"

"Like I said, you're a jealous fool and that makes you see things that don't exist. I talked to no one."

Karne slapped her hard, then wrapped his arm around her tightly and hurried her to his flitter. He tossed her up onto the wing and ordered her into the cabin. When he saw her rebellious pout beginning, Karne ordered the soldiers guarding the flitter to use their stunners on her if necessary to make her stay, then he returned to the party long enough to make his farewells.

When he climbed into the pilot's seat a few minutes later, Charlotte glowered at him from the passenger seat, into which one of the soldiers had fastened her, not only with the safety webbing, but with wrist cuffs, so she could not free herself.

"Looks like you gave the guard some trouble," Karne remarked.

Charlotte glared, but refused to answer. In his present mood, that suited Karne just fine. He did not know how he could have talked with her at the moment and still kept his temper. Four years of work pressing for changes in Starker IV's political and social systems, and, just when he began to see hopeful signs of change, his wife set out to destroy his reputation and therefore his credibility.

Karne wished he could believe her actions were a plot by Harlan and Rhiz to bring Halarek down. Plots he had learned to handle. Plotters could be bought, frightened, persuaded to change. He could not believe this was a plot. Charlotte was acting on her own, for herself. She would have to be as strictly confined to Ontar manor as Richard was to Breven, and there she would have to have a chaperone who could give her full attention, someone who did not have children and husband to attend to, too.

Lady Agnes. Whenever the word "chaperone" was spoken in House Halarek, the image that came instantly to mind was tall, gaunt Lady Agnes, distant cousin, nurse to all the Halarek children, tutor in lady-like behavior, and the strictest chaperone among the Nine. Lady Agnes would make the perfect chaperone and she would come if he asked because she loved him. She could watch Charlotte inside her quarters, while the deaconesses guarded the door.

Karne remembered how Kit had fretted under Lady Agnes's strict rules. Kit the tomboy. Kit the rowdy. Kit the outspoken. Kit had only gotten out from under the estimable lady's thumb by marrying Arl deVree. Yet Lady Agnes had attended Kit at her lying-in, by Kit's invitation, even though Kit was in House Odonnel. She had taken care of the baby up to the time Ennis and Kit escaped. Karne's mouth twitched upward, imagining Kit's reaction to the reappearance of Lady Agnes in House Halarek.

At least I haven't entirely lost my sense of humor, he told himself. I wish I could be around when Kit hears. Kit knows what life will be like for Charlotte after Lady A arrives and she'll rejoice that she now lives in von Schuss. Charlotte won't have any idea, any idea at all.

Karne felt a surprising rush of satisfaction, thinking of Charlotte's reactions to her new supervisor. There were few women he could say this of, but Charlotte *deserved* Lady Agnes.

Back at Ontar and after Lady Agnes had been politely summoned by tri-d, Karne called together his military advisers in the library. There were Generals Wynter and Roth, Captains Jenkins, Phillipson, Obren, Yan Willem, and Dennen Willem. Together they planned Halarek's strategy for a "rescue" attempt of its ally, McNeece. The action must appear genuine, from the air as well as the ground, yet do damage only to the landscape. No one doubted that lords who might profit from exposing the battles as frauds would buy satellite pix from the Gild to check in detail what was going on. Many uninvolved Houses would buy pix, too, just to see what the others were interested in.

Dennen Willem fiddled with the knobs on his sheathed beamer. "I suppose there's no chance we could quietly persuade the Gild to let something go wrong with the cameras that week, could we?"

Yan Willem glared at his brother. "You can't really think the Gild would violate their neutrality by even as little as that. Or can you?"

Dennen glared. "Why not? No one would know—"

General Wynter cut off further argument with a slice of one lean hand. "How long until Kath attacks, milord?"

Karne shrugged. "No telling. When he feels the time is right."

Lady Agnes arrived three days after she had been summoned, bringing with her one moderately small wardrobe case and a library large enough for a long stay. Tane Orkonan escorted her to Karne, who was at daymeal.

"Karne." The gaunt old woman made a little, stiff bow, the stiffness accounted for only in part by aging joints.

Karne rose from the table and made a bow. One did not embrace Lady Agnes. One did not touch Lady Agnes. "My lady."

"Where is my charge?"

"In the Larga's quarters, Lady Agnes."

"Then if you will excuse me." She made an even smaller bow and turned to go.

Orkonan moved forward to assist her down the steps from the dais. The lady gave him an icy stare that made him drop his hand and step back.

"I'm not so old and decrepit as that," she snapped. "And you don't need to escort me to the Larga, either. I was finding my way around this manor house before you were born, young man." Lady Agnes looked over her shoulder at Karne. "However, it *is* customary for the Lharr to introduce members of his Family to his wife."

Karne rose from his meal and followed Lady Agnes to the lift, feeling like a little boy again. It was not that he *had* to obey her, but following her orders again after so many years gave Karne an odd sort of comfort. His old nurse loved him, and for the greater part of his life, she had been the only adult who had.

Kath invaded McNeece a week later. A week after that, in the gray hours before dawn, Karne was at the controls of a flitter, leading two centuries of soldiers to the aid of McNeece. Two centuries was not a lot of support. On the other hand, this was not going to be a big battle. Laying siege to a manor and fighting off the besieged demanded large numbers of men. Defending empty land at the edge of the plains did not.

As Karne flew over the southwest corner of Druma Holding, he wondered about the health of Duke Paul III. At last hearing, he was still hanging on to life, though not aware he was. If Paul IV had been a man like Richard or Ingold Kingsland or even Tam Brassik, the old man would already have died "in his sleep." He was too far gone for anyone to believe in an "accident," though. Well, that trouble would come when it came and he would have to face Garren Odonnel in battle over who would succeed in the House that was vassal to both.

Karne and his soldiers landed about five kilometers downriver from the battle. Van had been "surprised" by a Kath invasion force that had come halfway across the holding before he "discovered" it. His men had forced Kath's army back almost to the river but had been unable to push it farther. That was what Karne was supposed to do: add enough men to push Kath into the water.

Because McNeece lay on the very edge of the northern Frozen Zone in the shadows of the mountains of Zimara, spring came later there than on Halarek. Though it was near the end of Verdain, the grass was still only greening. When Karne stepped out onto his flitter's wing, he noticed that the edges of the Zimar River were thinly fringed with ice. The uleks had come down from their wintering places, though, and grazed on the crisp remains of last year's tallgrass. Karne looked at the animals speculatively. Their stolid presence might make fighting more difficult, since stunners did not make enough noise to disturb them and no one would be using fliers and their beamers in this battle.

Karne shook his head. They would have to be herded away. A stunner on "kill" would take even a ulek down and their presence would reveal to observers that the battle was a farce. Lying in their droppings to fire would not be pleasant, either.

Karne sent a messenger to Van and, within hours, riders from the manor had come to move the herds out of the way. The centens, meanwhile, double-checked all stunners for range and power, then some of each century began setting up barracks-domes. The rest marched toward the fighting, if taking careful advantage of what shelter the open land offered could be called marching.

The "battle" was mostly boring. Karne rotated his men to the battlefield and then back to base every third day—those who did not come in as "casualties," that is. Casualties came in according to their "wounds." Men who felt only numb from a stunner beam reported themselves wounded and returned to base in ambulances. Men who were knocked over or out reported themselves killed and spent the rest of the day of their death in the burial cart. These returned to Ontar in body bags, only to get into another transport a few days later and return. It would look like casualties and reinforcements to outsiders.

Each side kept careful count of how many men were hit, because the battles were, in fact, exercises in marksmanship and the course of the battle varied according to who had the most casualties each day. If Kath had more, it retreated. If less, it advanced. The arrangements relied on absolute security within each House. Charlotte, therefore, was told nothing of the fighting beyond that her lord was still all right. Reports from Ontar to Karne said Charlotte did not even offer to do a Larga's duty and visit the wounded.

After nine days, both sides were ready for the important and showy battle for the northeastern riverbank. Van McNeece had choreographed a dramatic, watery escape by overwhelmed Kath forces, who—hopelessly outnumbered due to casualties, of course—would cross the river however the men could. Downstream, in the willows hanging over the shallows on both sides, men would wait, out of sight of the Gild orbiter's cameras, to catch any men who happened to be washed away.

The night before the battle, Frem Weisman brought Karne the message that Paul III Druma had died and that Garren Odonnel had immediately attacked Druma's border farms and smallholdings. To everyone's surprise, he had not declared siege. The law required forty days' notice before setting siege. Forty days allowed non-combatants and women to leave a holding. Forty days gave the defenders a chance to prepare. Attacking the farms and smallholdings was almost never done. Karne would have to leave the Kath/McNeece drama immediately and go to the aid of his vassal.

Karne did not return to Ontar, but sent a message back to Wynter, ordering him to send four centuries to Druma at once under Roth's command and Karne would join them there. Roth's soldiers had been waiting at Ontar for weeks. Moving them to Druma should take only eight to ten hours, but Karne needed at least that much time to tie off his responsibilities to McNeece and select someone to leave in charge for the final hours of fighting. While he was doing that, McNeece received word that Odonnel had given the forty days' notice of siege on Drumanton. Forty days to ravage the smallholdings and serf farms. Forty days for Paul IV to sweat and wring his hands and cry to his other overlord for help.

Odonnel's timing and tactics clearly intended to take advantage of Karne's being occupied at McNeece Holding. By suddenly attacking outlying properties, farms that belonged to serfs, Odonnel threatened Paul IV without doing him or his Family any serious harm. The serfs had no real value, nor did the temporary structures they raised each spring. The smallholdings were about as impregnable as the manor house itself. The damage to crops and surface buildings would only make Druma's survival through the next winter less comfortable, not less likely. Karne saw a large flaw in Odonnel's plans almost at once: Odonnel could not imagine anyone putting a serious effort into protecting serf property, so his forces on Druma Holding were thinly spread, killing time with harassing serfs until time to set siege. Karne intended to show Odonnel this was a serious miscalculation.

CHAPTER 11

Karne circled over Druma before landing. Halarek forces had been scattered by half-centuries among the trees of the many deep valleys on the west of Druma Holding. Karne found them only because he had been forewarned they were there. Karne knew Roth had brought them in as unobtrusively as possible over the past thirty hours. Now he could see the general had hidden them carefully. Surprise might help defeat Odonnel and his allies, scattered as they were while they systematically destroyed every pitiful surface structure they found. Karne did not want *his* men surprised, however, and was therefore pleased to see that Roth had not only set double lines of sentries, but that he was drilling the men hard, ridding them of the sense of invulnerability the battle on McNeece had given many of them. The stunners and beamers in the Druma battles would be on full power and there were no secret rules forbidding air attacks with heat beams.

It was midmorning when Karne set his flitter down on the flats beyond the camouflaged lean-to that was the temporary command center. The foothills around him lay dotted with flowers of yellow, pink, red, blue, purple, and white. The air hummed with bees. A light breeze carried the scents of flowers. It was hard, in such beauty, for Karne to think of men fighting, killing, dying.

Karne jumped from the flitter's wing onto the grass and looked south at the mountains of Zinn. Snow still clung to their upper slopes. Beyond those mountains lay Halarek Holding. And Charlotte. He longed for Charlotte, in spite of her treachery. He had not bedded any other woman since their marriage. He doubted Charlotte would have been as abstaining of men if she were not guarded night and day. Still, his body longed for hers, though he knew how dangerous that attachment was. He shook off such thoughts and walked to the cluster of men under the lean-to's shelter.

General Roth, Karne, and the lower officers had decided, before anyone left Ontar, that they would not attempt to meet any large Odonnel force until after House Halarek's vassals arrived. Now Roth explained what he had ordered to fill the waiting time. To avoid the effects of hours of tedium on the men, and considering that no one could drill indefinitely, Roth had extended to everyone the equipment checks and manual labor that were usually left to reserve forces, and had offered sorties against small groups of Odonnel soldiers as an incentive to do top-quality work. Squads that met Roth's criteria for top-quality work were given sufficient stunner or beamer charges and supplies for two or three days and turned loose against Odonnel. From what Karne had seen on his way into the lean-to, the soldiers were working cheerfully and talking about the damage their squad would do to Odonnel.

After the meeting, Karne walked around several of the scattered camps. Each half-century's transports and fliers were being gone over carefully so they could take off safely on a moment's notice. Some soldiers were carrying the gear in them into barracks-domes or cook tents. Others set up beds of installed portable Sanitaries at the edge of camp. Centens sent out scouts, their weapons cleaned and restored, if necessary, to fully functioning condition. Karne was glad to see the weapons check. It would catch any altered stunners that might have gotten into Roth's munitions from returning McNeece "casualties" and alter them back. The one-legged weapons master who had altered them at Ontar had been brought along just for that, but he had not arrived yet.

By the time Karne returned to his landing area, a command dome had been erected. Karne pushed through the air-lock door. The weapons maker's worktable had been set in good light on the opposite side of the dome from the tables of papers and maps to be used by Karne and his advisers. A pile of McNeece stunners lay on the table.

The air lock opened and the weapons maker swung into the dome on his crutch and headed straight for his place. A prefet followed closely with a litter full of weapons-making-and-repairing tools. The man settled into place and pulled the first stunner toward him. Karne turned to the maps and papers on the table behind him.

"And to think, in my place, my sire would have cashiered him as useless, even though he lost his leg protecting Halarek at Farm 3," Karne muttered. "Best weapons maker since Wayland Smith, or close." He sat down to go over relief maps of Druma thoroughly.

The transports from Labar, Nomer, and Durlin arrived only hours after Karne did, though Sindt of Durlin sent only one century. Melevan's and Nerut's came by evening, with Jura's and Brassik's close behind. Jura and Brassik each sent two centuries, which surprised Karne. He had expected only the most token support from these two captured from Harlan only a little more than two years ago. Roul sent no one. Lest his overlord miss the point, Benjmin III did send a message. The com-tech brought Karne a transcription of the message, not daring to bring such words verbally. Karne read the message aloud to the vassal lords present.

"I will contribute no help to my sire's murderer."

Karne scanned the words a second time, then crumpled the transcription in his hand. "There's no fool like a young fool," he snarled. "He's only been official oath-holder a month and already he thinks to violate his oath of fealty! If he thinks I'll ignore this because of pressures here, he's very wrong."

Phillipson, commander of the pilots and Karne's friend for years, looked up from the contour map he had been studying. "I'd wager he thinks you're going to be occupied here for weeks. That's plenty of time for him to dig in, perhaps find allies. Lynn and Skabish, for example. Those Houses sent no one to help you."

Karne nodded thoughtfully. They had not. But there might be good reasons for that. Skabish, for example, was too poor to send men except on horseback, and that would take weeks. He wondered if he could use the absent Houses against Roul. They were closer to Roul Holding than Halarek's forces were at the moment. Karne reminded himself to ask Wynter about that possibility. Druma was more important to Halarek than Roul, though Halarek's export balance needed Roul's blown-glass art goods. Because of Druma's importance, Karne and his army had to stay at Druma until Druma was rescued or lost. Halarek and its allies heavily outnumbered Odonnel's forces now and Odonnel could not count on any help from badly splintered House Harlan.

Weisman ran the spy network. It would be easy to order Halarek spies to sabotage any efforts Benjmin made to get allies. Benjmin was too new and too rash to have the trust of his sire's spies yet, and if he had behaved in customary fashion, he had already executed most of his sire's highest advisers, putting him at further disadvantage.

But operating underground took far more time than military attacks. Karne took a deep breath and then another. Roul had picked his time carefully. Karne could not leave Druma. But he could make it appear that he *would* not leave Druma, that House Roul was too insignificant to attract his personal attention. That would make a big difference in the political impact of his rebellion, both in Roul and elsewhere. Karne turned to the com-tech, who was still hovering at the edge of the map table.

"Take a message," Karne snapped, angry at Roul for provoking him at such a time, at any time.

"Yes, milord." The tech grabbed a stylus and pad from the table and stood poised to write.

"To Benjmin III Roul, greetings.

"Eight hours after receiving this message, the fuel lines to Roul will be turned off, as they were when your sire rebelled. You may sit in the heat with your machines silent and sweat until I decide what to do with a young pup who begins biting his lord's hand the moment he slips his leash.

"Or, unlike your sire, you could give up rebellion now, pay a 2,000-decacredit fine, and send two centuries at once to Druma Holding."

The com-tech read the message back to Karne and then left to send it. Karne looked around him. None of the vassal heads-of-House who had been in the dome minutes before were there now. Karne looked at Phillipson.

"Where is everybody?"

"They just left, Karne. Like they had some sort of agreement."

The seven lords filed back into the dome minutes later, with Generals Wynter and Roth bringing up the rear. Karne looked at Wynter in surprise and disapproval.

"Lord," Wynter said, "I'll go back to my duties at Ontar as soon as you hear what these men have to say. It's very important. They asked me to come because they know you listen to me."

Nerut spoke then, with some hesitation. "We have voted, Lord Karne, the seven of us and Lynn and Skabish. The com-tech will verify that we talked to them. We're telling you to stay out of the fighting, Lord Karne. You have no direct heirs. Your new nephew is far too young to be acceptable in times like these and any battle over ascent to the title will tear Halarek apart, leaving us easy meat for the wolves among the Nine. Our vote doesn't have the force of law. We know that. We're respectfully requesting that you heed it, anyway."

Karne just stared at them for a moment. A vote? By his vassals, new and old, to keep him at the rear? The Gharr instincts in him reared up in outrage. The Balder-trained parts whispered his vassals were right. Their vote was an important step toward change for Starker IV. To Karne's knowledge, no such vote had ever been taken before: Vassals did not stand up to their liege lord. These men were also providing him an honorable excuse to keep safe. He stood a moment, caught between tradition and a beneficial change that went against his immediate desires. He wanted to fight Odonnel. He owed him for trying to prevent necessary Gild medical help from getting to Egil. On the other hand, he had no heir who could take over if he were killed.

"I value your concern for my line," he said at last. "I'll do as you ask, though it will be a hard, hard thing to do."

Wynter smiled slightly. It was approval. The seven lords bowed in acknowledgment and scattered to their duties inside or outside the dome.

The armies of Halarek, commanded by General Roth, spread out and moved against Odonnel's camped forces hours before dawn, using a plan General Roth had worked out while waiting. House Halarek took the center, the vassals' armies the wings, and they moved against the single bivouac Odonnel had set up.

General Roth had done his planning well. A day and a half later, the battle was over. Roul's two centuries arrived just as Odonnel's forces were pulling back. Odonnel withdrew over the boundary of the Frozen Zone, apparently deciding a change of dukes in Druma was not worth the casualties he was taking. He loaded his army aboard transports and took it home. He left so suddenly he did not even take all his wounded. If they were behind enemy lines, he left them.

Karne, looking out across the battlefield, could not understand abandoning men to an enemy unless his own army's condition was desperate. Odonnel's army had not been desperate. He walked along rows of wounded and dying—both allies and Odonnel—being assembled as quickly as possible for transport. A soldier orderly, who identified each man to Karne if asked, followed him closely. Karne spoke to each of the conscious men and made sure their immediate needs were being taken care of. Perhaps one in ten was Odonnel. He wondered what he was going to do with them. He did not want so many enemies inside Ontar, yet he could not leave them and he must decide before the transports began loading.

One of the com-techs appeared at Karne's elbow. "Excuse me, my lord. A very important message has come for you." He swallowed. "The Larga Halarek has disappeared, my lord."

Karne's head whipped around to face the tech.

The tech started, then recovered himself. "She was going to Lews shopping, milord, to buy upholstery fabric and a new rug for her quarters. You had not forbidden shopping, lord, as long as she was thoroughly escorted. Two deaconesses and a squad of soldiers rode with her, just as you required."

Karne felt light-headed. He had authorized no shopping trip. How could this have happened again? And the trade road to Lews was as safe as any road on the planet. This could not be true. It was a mistake. "Gone?"

"Yes, my lord. Someone stunned them from ambush. When her escort woke up, the Larga and her mount were gone."

Karne felt a wave of relief. At least the entire party had not been murdered this time, as Kit's had been. At that moment, if he could have done so in honor, he would not even have ordered a search. She was more trouble than any woman was worth. But honor demanded he find and punish the thief who had lured or stolen away his wife. The needs of his House demanded he find and punish whoever had stolen the intended bearer of Halarek's heirs. And he still desired her.

He noticed his fixed look was making the tech fidgety. He looked away from the man's face and asked, "What's been done to find her, or to find out who did this?"

The tech shrugged. "I delivered the message that was sent, milord. I know no more." He handed Karne a transcription.

"Fine. Thanks. Dismissed."

Karne examined the details without emotion. No one killed. The Larga and her mount gone. Perhaps that meant the kidnappers had only a little way to ride. Into Lews, perhaps, or to a flier? Where could one hide a flier on the open plain around Lews? The hills west of the Great Swamp were the closest concealment, and the kidnappers would have been visible on the way there for hours. Karne turned to the orderly beside him.

"Call Wynter. Have him check with the Gild for pix. Tell him I'll be home as soon as I can manage it."

Karne moved on along the rows of wounded. Dashing back to Ontar would not find Charlotte any quicker, but the moment he spent with a soldier now might encourage the man to recover more quickly or to recover at all.

At the end of the next to last row, a man lay curled around himself in pain. Karne crouched beside him. The moment Karne was close, the man rolled onto his back, whipped a large knife out of hiding, and lunged upward. Karne threw himself sideways. The orderly brought the edge of his report board down on the man's neck. The man collapsed in a heap.

Safe. Karne felt a moment of blinding terror. Black blotches surged in and out before his eyes. *An assassin. An assassin!*

"My lord!" The orderly's voice was urgent. "You're bleeding. Sentry!"

Karne focused his thoughts. That would help keep fear away.

The knife must have been very sharp, Karne told himself, because I don't feel hurt. I could've been dead if my reflexes had been slower.

The pain came then, liquid fire running along his left arm. Karne gasped. A sentry appeared, assessed the situation, drew his stunner, dialed it to "kill," and pointed it at the assassin. Freed of guarding, the orderly crouched beside Karne and began pulling away Karne's slashed sleeve.

"Don't kill him," Karne ordered the sentry through clenched teeth. "Evidence. Assassin."

The sentry nodded, stunned the assassin into unconsciousness, bound the man's hands and feet, hoisted him over his shoulder, and headed toward the command dome. Karne demanded a litter and notice given his pilot to get his flitter ready to leave immediately. The orderly protested. A transport of wounded was loading now. It would leave for Ontar in a few hours. Karne struggled to his feet.

"Can't wait. Larga stolen. Got to get home *now.*"

Karne's flitter arrived at Ontar eight hours later. Karne felt so woozy he could barely stand. Of necessity, he accepted his pilot's help getting down from the flitter's wing. He paused a moment on the pad surface, right where his feet landed, and waited for his head to stop spinning. Odonnel had been defeated. The Larga had disappeared. Someone had sent an assassin. Odonnel? Harlan? Roul? Charlotte?

Trouble always comes in threes, they say. Karne bit back a bitter laugh. *Or fours or fives or sixes.*

His dizziness intensified and he clutched at the pilot's arm.

"My lord?" The pilot's voice was soft and worried.

"I'll—I'll be all right in just a moment. Lost a lot of blood." Karne heard his own breathing coming faster and faster. *Going into shock. Got to see Othneil.*

"Wouldn't wait for the transport of wounded, eh?" The acerbic voice cut through Karne's spinning head like a saw. "Transport has several medics, you know."

Karne would have recognized that voice anywhere. *Othneil. Wouldn't wait to be called to my quarters. Of course.*

The black-robed, fiftyish man in front of him swam gradually into focus. He was frowning.

"My lord, I credited you with more sense."

"Transport's shtill on ground," Karne muttered, swaying.

"And you'd still have some of your missing blood if you'd stayed with it. Late is better than dead, milord. Late is better than so bled-out you can't take care of matters that need taking care of. Like the Larga's disappearance." Othneil beckoned imperiously to med-techs behind him, who came forward at once with a litter and had Karne flat on his back on it before he could assemble his wits to say he could walk to the lift.

Karne lay still, watching the lights along the ceiling edges pass by. *It would have been a mistake, arguing. Never won an argument with that man yet without pulling rank. Stupid to pull rank on a physician. Knows what to do. Always has. Even when my back got burned so bad, Othneil figured a way to keep me off it* and *lying down.*

The litter floated smoothly but slowly, which told Karne he was not in such serious condition that the techs needed to carry the litter themselves to go faster. *So smooth. Could go to sleep. Sleep.*

Karne awoke what had to be several hours later, because the light beside his bed was on. It was "night" in the manor and he was in his own bed in his own room. His left arm was so stiff he could not bend it at all. Surely, the knife had not gone so deeply that it damaged his elbow? His throbbing head turned to look only grudgingly. Relief made him shut his eyes for a moment. It was splinted. That was all. The gash had been so long Othneil had splinted it.

Karne lay half awake for a long time, trying to remember why he had come home in such a hurry and seeing only the men dying around him on the grass. Odonnel had given up. Van and Obert had negotiated *and* saved face (and men). Karne's own vassals had voted and expected him to abide by their vote. There *was* hope of change. He turned his eyes to Egil's mural, where also there was hope. On the wall, Heimdal was holding off the Frost Giants. On the wall, the giants never reached the Rainbow Bridge. In the myth, they did, eventually, and the war that followed destroyed the world. Things were changing on Starker IV. Perhaps the giants would not win. Perhaps his efforts to turn Starker IV into a new course were finally having some effect. Perhaps this world would not die. Karne slept again.

The right side of the bed sank under him, waking him instantly. His right hand flashed for the stunner under his pillow before he had half opened his eyes. Kit grabbed his hand before it had moved more than a few centimeters.

"Karne, it's just me. Tane commed us. He said an assassin made an attempt at you and you'd lost a lot of blood. Nik came to see if there's anything he can do to help search for Charlotte (Tane told us about that, too) until you're strong enough to do it yourself. I came to see for myself that you were no worse than Dr. Othneil said."

Karne's mouth twitched in a smile he felt too weak to finish. "Have you ever known Othneil to soften a diagnosis? Or to lie about one?"

Kit shook her head.

"You could have trusted him."

Tears glistened in Kit's eyes. "You're my brother and I love you and I was worried about you." She leaned over him and hugged him with great gentleness. She kissed his cheek and sat up again. "I can't stay long. Jemmy will be hungry soon and he hates ulek milk and acts like water is poison. Uncle Emil will be at his wit's end in a few hours."

"You didn't bring him to show to Lady Agnes?" Karne tried to make his voice light and teasing. What came out was rough and croaking.

Kit smiled with love. "You idiot," she said, and kissed him again. "If I showed him to Lady Agnes, I wouldn't get him back for a week." She stood to go. "Uncle Emil's sending a flier for me so Nik can stay as long as you want him." She left the room and shut the door quietly behind her.

She did not leave Karne with a peaceful mind. Her very presence reminded him of the horror of *her* kidnapping. Hundreds of people had died. For the families of the dead, it had been worse than a war, because men in war expect death to come to friends and companions. The people accompanying Kit and Arl had been entirely unaware there was any danger and had been massacred without a chance to defend themselves. But even that nightmare could not keep Karne awake long. He felt so tired, so drained . . .

After three days in bed, Karne could walk around if he did not walk around too much. After a week he could manage a whole day in the library catching up on necessary business, the most important of which was the search for Charlotte. He knew Wynter, Nik, the Halarek and von Schuss's allies, and the citizens of Lews—everyone had searched for Charlotte and no one had found even a clue as to where she might have gone.

The other important matters were Paul IV Druma's fealty ceremony and Benjmin Roul's punishment. Roul *had* sent the two centuries as quickly as possible. The fines could wait a few days more. Paul IV Druma's fealty ceremony would have to wait until Charlotte was found. That meant Garren Odonnel would have to wait, too, to take Paul's oath. Karne felt a little smug satisfaction in that; Paul must swear first to Karne, because House Halarek had won the short war.

Priorities set, Karne commed Wynter to come to the library. Wynter greeted his lord with a small bow and a sharp click of his polished heels.

"Weisman told me earlier you wanted to know exactly what's been done to find the Larga, milord, so I assembled what we have. Much of this you've heard, milord, in the summaries we've given you every day." The general's tone was curt and impatient.

Karne looked at Wynter sharply. This was not the general's usual style. "I want to hear all at one time what's been done. The first two days I was home, I wasn't too clear in the head, General."

Karne thought a little stiffness went out of the general's stance. Wynter nodded his head slightly in acknowledgment and began. "None of the farmers in their fields heard any screaming or loud noises, milord, though that may be explained by the fact that the Larga's escort was stunned from a distance. We assumed all of them were—stunned, I mean. Including the Larga. I wouldn't have stunned her myself, unless I had to, because an able rider is far easier to transport than an unconscious lump. Be that as it may, no one screamed or shouted.

"No one in Lews or the fields saw either armed horsemen or fliers in the vicinity. There was no sign of struggle at the site where the other members of Charlotte's party were found. That means she was either unconscious when taken or she was willing.

"Two days ago, the aldermen of Lews tri-ded to you their regrets that the Larga Halarek had gotten lost on their *landkreis*. As soon as they learned of the attack, they ordered the entire city searched. They found no evidence that anyone had expected her to arrive."

Karne's head came up straighter.

"That's right, milord. The ladies she said she was going to meet, the shops where she said she had orders—all said they hadn't heard from her in weeks. Since the day you confined her strictly to her quarters, as a matter of fact, milord."

"And who cleared her to leave Ontar?"

Wynter stared at Karne a moment in silence. "Why, you did, milord. I'm sure the note giving permission was mentioned to you."

Karne stared back, a dreadful idea running through his head. "I gave no permission to leave the manor house. I sent no permission."

Wynter's jaw thrust out, making his lower lip almost disappear. "When Orkonan told me about it, I said that couldn't be your note, no matter that it looked like your writing. You wouldn't allow that lady out, especially not with only twenty men as guard." Wynter smiled a thin, cold smile. "Or maybe you wouldn't've let her out with *men* at all."

"A note? In my handwriting?"

"You don't remember being told about it, milord?"

Karne thought hard, but too many things had happened as Odonnel's army pulled out. "Nothing. And you say Orkonan okayed it? Where were you at the time?"

"It came while I was at Druma, advising your vassals, milord. Weisman and Orkonan were in charge here. Weisman showed it to Orkonan, said one of the wounded had given it to Charlotte while she was visiting the clinic."

"Wounded? Guardians! No man who came back from McNeece was really wounded and Tane knew it."

"I'm sure it was just security, milord. After all, Larga Charlotte didn't know no one was wounded. We did put some men in clinic beds precisely to prevent her from finding that out."

"Did you question Charlotte about the note? Someone told me she refused to visit the wounded at all."

"Weisman said Larga Charlotte asked him to bring the note to Tane first because she was afraid of me. Anyway, as I said, I didn't return to the manor until later and then no one thought to mention the matter to me."

"So you didn't ask her who the man was or even what he looked like?"

"No, milord. Orkonan did, or rather, he tried. She gibbered like an idiot when he came to her door, she would not come out to talk (if any sense could've been made of what she was saying), and the deaconesses wouldn't let him in. Of course."

"Do you think that was a performance?"

"I have no idea, milord. She had gone by the time anyone thought to mention the matter to me. I sent a troop out after her immediately, but it was too late."

Karne sighed. At least Wynter had suspected the note and had done the best he could in the situation. "What else have you found out?"

"Gild pix of the area around Lews that day show only the Larga's party on its way to Lews, milord. No other people. The orbital was elsewhere at the time the abduction probably took place and this suggests that the kidnapping, if that was what it was and not an escape, was timed with the orbital's position in mind."

Karne looked up at the dour face of his commanding general. "And?"

"I don't think she *was* kidnapped, milord. Much as you might wish to think otherwise, I and my investigators (and the aldermen, though they're unlikely to say it to your face) believe the lack of either clues or notice shows the Larga left willingly with whoever took her."

With sinking heart, Karne acknowledged to himself that that had become his belief, too. "And what did the aldermen tell you, Wynter?"

"She was traveling with two female companions and a guard. Two decades. The group was attacked, but no one was seriously hurt."

"Maybe her escort collaborated."

"Doubtful, milord. Its squadman was the same person who escaped the massacre of Lady Kathryn's wedding procession. Though seriously wounded and pursued closely by Odonnel men, he rode here to tell what had happened. Surely you remember that?"

Karne nodded.

"That man is bone-deep loyal to Halarek, my lord, and brave as well."

Karne grasped at his last straw, unwilling that a woman of the Nine, even Charlotte, would entirely abandon her marriage House. "Do you think one of her companions was a spy or collaborator, then?"

Wynter came around the table to stand face-to-face with his lord and look him straight in the eye. He did not deign to respond to the accusation against career members of a Retreat House. "Lord Karne, there were no signs of struggle after the kidnapping party left the site of the attack. There were no bits of clothing or jewelry dropped to give a clue in which direction to begin searching. Larga Charlotte didn't scream for help, though many workers from Lews were weeding and watering their vegetable patches well outside the city and sound carries well on open plains."

"Then someone probably saw what happened."

Wynter gripped Karne's right arm above the elbow. "Stop ducking the truth! She's not worth the effort. You've been told the attack happened behind a slight rise and was hidden from any gardeners from Lews. You can guess as well as I can what happened. By posting the deaconesses and Lady Agnes as guards here, you've already publicly admitted Larga Charlotte would be unfaithful if she could. Take the next step and see this 'kidnapping' as proof of how much she wants outside pleasures. Look at me, lord, and think! We've looked everywhere, your allies have, our townspeople have. Much as you may want to deny it, your lady very likely collaborated in her own 'kidnapping.' "

CHAPTER 12

The air carried a damp scent, as well as the piney smell that had dogged them most of the way from Lews. Across the open plains, Brander had stayed in the hollows between the rolling hills whenever possible, among the pines there and their everlasting stench. He had hated being in the open for that half day near Lews, but there had been no way to avoid it. Horses were small. Horses could hide in dips and hollows. Horses were much harder to track than flitters, too. Flitters would be noticed by all the holdings and smallholdings they passed over, though only the holdings would hail for identification.

Brander inhaled deeply. Lake St. Paul put that dampness into the air. Breven could not be far if he could smell the dampness from the lake. He would be very glad to get inside the walls and out of that everlasting stink. And away from the Larga. The woman had been complaining for hours about riding so long. Again she was complaining. Well, it had been a hard two days, but hard riding had kept them ahead of any pursuit and they were close to the end of the journey now.

So accommodating of Halarek to go directly to Druma from Holding McNeece. Made my work so much easier.

The Larga Halarek brought her horse beside his, muttering about how sore she was, how tired, how thirsty. There had been no need to guard her, though. She had come willingly, so willingly he had needed no helpers at all to take her from her escort. That could be very useful later, the fact that there were just two witnesses to her kidnapping, the Larga Halarek and himself. It had been no problem to spray-stun her companions into unconsciousness, which was good, because it would not have been wise to kill them. People had not forgotten Lady Kathryn's abduction and might make connections between two similar attacks. Brander smiled secretly. It was interesting, though, how often the same trick worked two, even three times, sometimes even on the same people. Like smuggling a woman into Breven in a deacon's habit.

When the thick gray wall of Breven loomed against the light of its clearing, Brander drew up his horse. It stamped on fallen needles and blew disgust at the pause. Brander turned in his saddle to face the Larga.

"Lord Richard waits for you with great eagerness, my lady," he said. *Like any randy tup.* "You must put on the habit now, and turn up the hood." *This might be worth the risk, if it puts a bastard in you. Unlikely though that is. Refusing to bring you might have started Richard asking awkward questions of his faithful cousin, though.*

Larga Charlotte turned at once to her saddlebag, her complaining forgotten.

Eager, isn't she? Believing Richard's reputation as a lover, no doubt. I'd bet this disguise will work again, too. "My lady, you may as well dismount. It'll be easier to change and we have to walk from here, anyway." *A horse at the garden gate would be terribly obvious.*

Brander swung from his own saddle and gallantly handed the Larga down. The moment her feet hit the ground, she turned to face him and looked at him speculatively.

Habit. Several months' acquaintance has to have taught her that nothing she could offer interests me.

Charlotte walked a few steps away, slipped the habit down over her head, and took off everything else under its enveloping folds. She looked at him coyly.

No, not me, Charlotte. Other men would probably be stimulated, thinking about what's under that habit, or, rather, what's not under it, but not me. I can almost pity Halarek, having to live with that constant demand for action.

Charlotte shrugged, stuck her hands through the sleeves, checked them for length, and threw her arms over her head with a shout of triumph.

"I've made it! I'm out of that place! No more restrictions on this woman!"

"Quiet!" Brander snarled.

Charlotte cowered away from him and covered her mouth with her hand.

Brander looked at her, trying to hide his contempt. *You can believe that? After already spending a year in a Retreat House like this one?* Brander took a deep breath to erase his irritation. "It's time to go, my lady. If we walk at a reasonable pace, we should be at the gate by dusk. Put up your hood."

She made a face at him, but she quickly braided her long dark hair, wound it up, tucked it down the back of the habit, and pulled the hood up to conceal her face.

"No one will speak to you as long as the hood's up," Brander reminded her. *A year in a Retreat House and she has to be reminded. Stupid bitch!* "You can escape detection no other way, my lady." *I can escape detection no other way.*

"I know, I know, I know."

But will you obey, obey, obey?

Fallen needles slithered under their feet and silenced their footsteps, though Breven had no guards outside to notice. No matter. Brander firmly believed it did not hurt to be cautious.

The pines created their own dusk, long before the sun approached the horizon. A squirrel scolded as they passed. Birds twittered and rustled among the pine needles. A wik-wik cried, "Who's there? Who's there?" making the Larga jump. Soon Brander heard the lapping of water against gravel and then saw glints of water among the trees. They had arrived more quickly than he had estimated. It was a time of day to be extra careful. He motioned toward a flattish boulder.

"We have a little while to wait, Larga, until the chimes call everyone in for nightmeal. If you'll sit on this rock, you can be comfortable and out of sight until the sun goes down."

The woman sat obediently and they waited while the ball of sun got redder and redder and finally touched the horizon. When Brander beckoned, the Larga rose obediently, silently. Brander nodded. Good. Now for the assault of the fortress.

They walked, heads down and hoods up, just inside the line of trees that bounded Breven's outer wall. The shadows there were deep and purple. They reached the low wooden door that led into Breven's garden and recreation area. The Larga started toward the door, but Brander clutched her arm.

"The chimes. Remember the nightmeal chimes. There may be men in the garden still."

The Larga nodded and ceased her resistance to his hold. Soon the chimes rang loudly, calling the community to eat. Brander waited another ten minutes, to allow all stragglers time to reach the refectory, then opened the gate and entered the dim garden. He wound through the shrubbery with the ease of memorization and opened a narrow door that led up a narrower set of stairs.

"Servants' stair," he murmured. "At least that's what the archaeologists think. Did the Old Ones *have* servants? Now the only servants here are the deacons themselves."

"The Old Ones—?"

"Shut up!"

Brander could feel her eyes staring balefully at his back, but she shut up and followed.

He stuck his head around the corner at the top of the first flight of stairs before he risked stepping out into the corridor. He beckoned the Larga to follow him.

There were no Council guards at Richard's door. Richard had taken one of his rare whims, prearranged, of course, and joined the community for nightmeal. Brander tried the door. Locked, as it should be. The guards would have checked the door before they left. He crouched on the floor and looked under the door's edge. The key lay there, as planned. Brander scraped it out into the corridor with the blade of his belt knife.

Council fools. It's a wonder they've been able to keep Richard in as long as they have. If my cousins weren't so intent on fighting each other, they would've spirited Richard out of here or killed him years ago. The soldiers aren't thinking about someone breaking into Richard's room. Fools!

Brander shoved open the door and motioned the Larga in ahead of him. He shut the door and locked it, just in case a Council patrol thought to check it, then showed the Larga the tiny sleeping room and the Sanitary. This room was a remnant of the luxurious suites that used to belong to the Nine on retreats here. The new abbot had converted all but this one back to the small, stark rooms they were supposed to be.

And this one was stark, too, comparatively. No thick rugs anymore, no tapestries on the walls, no polished wood desk or thick-mattressed bed, no pantry full of rich food and expensive wines. The pantry closet that had held them was still behind the door, though, to be used for Richard's clothes.

Little does the Larga guess that's where she'll have to hide if there's a surprise inspection.

Brander chuckled, thinking of the beautiful young Larga stretched thin and flat in the pantry, holding her breath to avoid discovery. The Larga gave him an odd look and he wiped the amusement from his face. He swung open one of the pantry doors to reveal rows of hooks in the top half, a stack of drawers in the bottom half.

"For your clothes, Larga," and he laughed, because the habit was all she had. He made a mental note to pick up the wardrobe she had left in the forest.

The Larga prowled the small living room and the smaller sleeping room. When she opened the room's only other door, her face fell.

Surprise! Just the Sanitary. No more space, lady. Just what you see. You should have thought with more than your loins.

"Is this all?" Charlotte finally managed to ask.

"This is a Retreat House, Larga. You're familiar with Retreat Houses. This is luxurious, compared to everywhere else, as you know. The duke has *two* rooms and his own Sanitary." *The Sanitary is another possible hiding place, Larga. How about the shower?*

"But I thought . . ."

Uh-huh. You listened to your sire's tales of what it was like here. Well, that was under the previous abbot. He lost all rank for five years because of his taste for luxuries and his pandering to the tastes of the Nine. Men like your sire.

"But you said—"

"I told you nothing that wasn't true, my lady." *Though I did leave out some details, like the surprise inspections.* "I didn't describe Lord Richard's rooms, because you were so recently come from a Retreat House yourself. I didn't think it necessary. I talked to you of the advantages of an *alliance* with Lord Richard." *Like the hours he'd have to dally with you, because he has nothing else to do (unlike your husband). Like the benefits of being the mistress of the man who'll be the*

*most powerful man on Starker IV when he gets out. I showed
you what you'd turned down by accepting Halarek. I didn't
mention that I don't intend for Richard to leave here alive.
The shame to you, the gain to me.*

Charlotte took another turn around the room and stopped by
the window. The view was of the lake and the forest and, on
a clear day, of the com dishes of the freecity of Loch. *You're
alone here, lady. You can look at the freecity, but you can't
visit it, not from here. Your stay will be with Richard, and
Richard only. May you have joy of each other!*

Brander glanced ostentatiously at his chrono. "It's almost
time for everyone to return from nightmeal, Larga. It wouldn't
do for *me* to be found here, let alone you. Council's soldiers
often come in with Lord Richard, just to check on what he may
have been doing. Making a ladder from sheets, for example."
Brander laughed. "As if anyone in his right mind would try that
over those rocks below. I suggest you hide in the shower. They
won't likely look there. It isn't a good place to hide anything
perishable."

Without another look at her, Brander left the room.

To avoid drawing the Council guards' attention, Brander
kept to his strict once-a-week schedule of visits to Breven.
He wanted no one wondering why, after four years of faithful
attention to his head-of-House, he did not come or came early,
so he came next on the tenth. Charlotte was wearing a sated
look, like a lounging cat after a delicious and illegal meal.
Richard glowed, as much because he had had Halarek's wife,
Brander was sure, as from the satisfaction she gave him after
so long without any. The next week, their appearances were
much the same.

By the third visit, matters changed. Brander sensed it as soon
as the guard opened the door. He assumed the change had been
caused by the news he had sent ahead with Isan Grent about
Odonnel's retreat from Druma, not even two days after Halarek
and its allies arrived. Richard looked preoccupied. Charlotte
hovered at the edges of the room, pouting. Richard seated
himself at the small desk as soon as Brander came fully
into the room. He still looked preoccupied. Brander hoped
he was thinking of ways to do away with the Lord of the
Mark. Leader of vassals. Thorn in the side. Brander planned

to deliver the good news first, because there was not much of it. The good news was that the seeds Richard had sown in Benjmin III Roul while the young man was at Breven were finally bearing fruit.

"Roul refused service at Druma. And there was an assassination attempt against Halarek at McNeece. Did I mention that? There was some thought he might be Roul's." *It will be amusing to see what Halarek does about Roul. Or the assassin.*

Richard's eyes lit up for a moment, then he frowned. " 'Attempt'? That means the assassin failed?"

"Unfortunately, yes." *And if I ever get a chance at him, he won't live to fail again.* "Halarek has him."

"Has he revealed who hired him?"

I certainly hope not. "Not that our spy in Ontar has heard, he hasn't. He may not, either. Halarek is rather squeamish about torture."

"What else is there?" Richard's tone suggested he knew the rest would be bad.

Brander stalled and hemmed and hawed, wooing Richard's anger, teasing it. He had been saving the bad news for several weeks, cautioning Isan Grent and Dannel of Jura not to mention it, should they happen to visit Richard. The effect of a pile of trouble was always more interesting to watch.

Richard spun, eyes blazing. "Damn you to hell! TELL ME WHAT'S GOING ON."

Brander let his eyes go wide and innocent. "Nothing much, milord. I told you the motion to change the line of succession was defeated."

"Narrowly."

"Narrowly, but defeated. Rooder and Gannet haven't been punished yet." *That* you *would have to order, Richard my boy, and you haven't.* "And the measures you ordered against Kath were never carried out. Without your hand on the sword, so to speak, our House is tottering." *And will fall if someone doesn't take it in hand soon.* "It's not in the Mark's interest, or any other vassal's, for Harlan to return to the strength it had before Halarek had you sentenced here, Richard."

"Yes?"

Brander let himself go wide-eyed. Richard lunged for him.

"Tell me or I'll wring your neck right here in this 'holy' place!"

"McNeece drove Kath back across the river, then they settled and there seem to have been very few casualties. Halarek defeated Odonnel at Druma, or rather, Garren retreated into the fingers of the Frozen Zone and took his men away. Worse, perhaps, for us was that most of Halarek's captured vassals fought with him, including Roul at the end.

"Lews is making an extraordinary effort to help Halarek find the Larga. Other Freemen are acting out of pattern, too. The aldermen of Loch, Lews, and Neeran met with Halarek and his allies at the Freemen's Ball. That can't mean anything good for us. For you."

Richard slammed his fist down onto the desk. "By my Mother's Blood and the Four Guardians, too! What I wouldn't give to be out of here! I can't take spy reports myself. I can't hire good help . . ." He stood so quickly that his chair tumbled backward with a crash. He turned his back to Brander. "Everyone else is grabbing for land and position and using their hard money to buy alliances or mercenaries."

Brander nodded. He had heard the envy and frustration in Richard's voice. "That's true."

Brander waited a few minutes until Richard had gained control of himself, turned around, and sat down again. Brander sat then, too, and the two of them discussed the possible political effects of Halarek's cowardly punishment—mere fines—for Roul and of the freecities moving closer to Halarek. Then Brander said goodbye, leaving Richard with many unpleasant thoughts to occupy him for the next week.

On the fourth visit, Brander could see a big change in Richard and Charlotte. Richard's face looked taut and much thinner. Charlotte had dark circles under her eyes, and her mouth drew tight whenever she looked at Richard. Richard wanted to know which cousin was on top in the battle for control at the moment, if the Lord of the Mark could still control the vassals, if any more had defected, if Karne Halarek had paid any political price for attacking Roul with fuel shutoffs and fines instead of with fliers and men.

Charlotte wasn't interested in news about Harlan, or about Halarek, either, for that matter. When Richard sat at the room's small desk, Charlotte pulled a stool up beside him. While Richard questioned Brander intently and listened just as intently to news from the outside world, Charlotte stroked Richard's arm. He ignored her. She stood, leaned against his back with her arms loosely around his neck, and moved suggestively side to side. Richard snarled at her and pushed her away.

Too demanding even for him, eh? Or is it that she wants control? This will bear watching carefully. And she's asked nothing at all about her husband.

When Richard ran out of questions, Brander delivered the rest of the news, and not much of it was good.

Richard began to pace around the perimeter of the room, swearing viciously. Charlotte sidled cautiously nearer to Brander, slipped a folded slip of paper into his hand, then scuttled into the sleeping room. Brander felt a surge of triumph.

If this says what I think it will, Richard and the Lharr Halarek are about to take almost-mortal political wounds.

Brander walked nonchalantly past the fuming Richard and into the Sanitary and shut the door. He unfolded the note and spread it flat on his knee. The printed letters wavered diagonally down the paper.

I wanta go home. Its no fun here anymor. Richard dos not like me.

Brander smiled in satisfaction. *She had to be desperate to get out if she tried writing.* He dropped the note down the Sanitary's chute, arranged his face into concerned lines with help from the mirror, and returned to Charlotte and Richard.

I can get her back to her husband by the end of next week. His birthday. Richard's sort of timing. What a nice birthday present, the return of a wildly unfaithful wife.

Brander settled into the room's only chair to make plans for the Larga's return and to wait out Richard's rage.

CHAPTER 13

Karne and his three chief officers sat around the big work-table in the library, silent. Warm rolls and mugs of hot klag sat at each place because it was First Day and everyone had fasted until after the service. It was also the morning of Karne's birthday, but no one felt like celebrating. Weisman picked at a fray on the edge of his cuff. Orkonan stared into the steam from his mug. Wynter's face looked more stern than usual. The Larga had been gone a month, vanished, and no amount of searching had produced any clues to where she had gone or even if she were still alive.

Orkonan broke the silence. "About the assassin, my lord. It's time to do something about the assassin. A month of questioning and he still claims to be Odonnel's man and Odonnel still denies it. It would seem best to me to give up the questioning and execute the man. He's never going to change his story."

Karne looked toward his administrator. "Do you still think he's Odonnel's?"

"No, milord, not anymore. Wynter and Anse-the-smith have convinced me that that answer came too easily. It now seems odd to me, too, that Odonnel would send an assassin *after* he'd given up and withdrawn."

Karne nodded. "That's what I thought." He looked at Weisman. "Write an order of execution and take it to the officer of the watch. No." Karne raised his hand to stop whatever Weisman had been about to say. "I won't have him tortured. People make up stories under torture. They'll say anything to stop the pain. Such 'confessions' are utterly useless."

Weisman's face fell, but he bent his head in acknowledgment, scribbled an order, extended it across the table for Karne to sign, then called a page to carry the message to the officer of the watch.

"Who do *you* think sent him?" Wynter asked. "Roul?"

Karne shook his head. "I wouldn't rule him out, but I think it's unlikely." Karne said aloud what he had often thought since Roul's refusal of service. "He's too new in office and he was too long in Breven to be able to arrange something like that. It will take a while for him to win the trust of his sire's contacts." Karne paused, frowning. "Unless either Richard or Brander helped him with the hiring."

"I'll check on that," Weisman said.

Orkonan considered the Harlan possibilities. "You did say he was one of the Breven deacons guarding Richard's door the night you went to a party there, didn't you?"

Karne nodded. "I'm sure he didn't recognize me in the Freeman he let by. No one else did. If he had, he would have said something then or since."

"No, he's never been reticent." Orkonan picked up some of the documents spread on the table. "These fines should keep him cash-short, at least till spring, and that will make hiring spies or assassins harder. He'll continue to be a problem, though, milord. There's no way he'll ever forgive you for his father's death, or the deaths of his siblings, even though none were your fault. He's even convinced himself the Gild autopsy was designed by you and a lie."

There was another long silence around the table. Suspicion was a way of life for all the Houses, but it fed on itself and often resulted in contorted thinking and peculiar conclusions.

"I suspect someone's interfering in Roul," Wynter said finally. "The young man isn't the quickest-witted in the world, but he's not stupid, and declaring so soon, by refusing service, his intent to rebel was stupid. Someone's playing on his emotions, encouraging him to let his feelings instead of his brain make his decisions."

"Dangerous," Orkonan said.

"Letting feelings control you is always dangerous," Karne said, his own example only too fresh in his mind. "His sire wasn't stupid, either, but he was touchy about honor and as stubborn a man as you can imagine. Benjmin III will hold to his beliefs with equal stubbornness."

"The first payment on his fines arrived this afternoon, my lord," Weisman put in.

"That gets him off the hook for now, but Tane's right. This won't end our troubles with him. The new lord was raised with rebellion." Karne looked down at the battered and paper-strewn surface of the table. "I agree that the fines will probably hold him through the winter, though."

That evening, with Family nightmeal going on around him, Karne sat in the Lharr's place on the dais, looking out over the crowd of cousins. He was pushing the food around on his platter and thinking about Charlotte. There had been no sign of her. Anywhere. No one had claimed to have her. No one claimed to have killed her. That made Karne very sure she was still alive. He only wished he knew where. He pushed the remains of his meal into a pile with his fork and stared at the platter's gilded edge.

He was somewhat aware of the click of bootheels coming across the floor, but it was not until Rad, captain of Blues, cleared his throat that Karne noticed the man was standing right beside him. Rad ran a finger around inside his collar and then tugged at the hem of his uniform tunic. When he saw Karne noticing, he flushed. His nervousness interested Karne. Captain Rad was rarely nervous about anything. That was one of the factors that made him such a good leader.

"My—lord." Rad seemed to choke on the words. He cleared his throat and began again. "My lord, there's someone ringing at the northeast entrance shelter most insistently. When commed for ID, she says she's the Larga Halarek and to let her in at once."

At the Larga's name, Karne stiffened. Could it be true? On the other hand, this would be an easy trap to lay, hoping for an easy kill if the Lharr himself came to see if it were truly the Larga at the door. Trap. Traps. So many things on this world were traps, including love and desire. "What's the matter? *Was* it the Larga?"

"I—I didn't order the door unlocked, milord. Considering the assassination attempt—the viewer—don't ask me more here, milord."

Karne let his fingers, out of sight under the table, touch the light bandage that now covered the assassin's slash. He nodded. "Good judgment. I haven't been careful enough, I guess." He grinned ruefully. "Better see who it is. I could do with a wife."

Rad shook his head. "You must come, lord."

Karne read the urgency and worry in Rad's voice, nodded, and stood. They had been battle companions long enough that he trusted Rad's judgment completely. They left the Hall decorously, but the moment they were out of sight of the Family, Rad broke into a run.

"Stairs are faster than the lifts, milord," he said over his shoulder as he ran past the lift and started up the stairs, "and no one must see her now but you, lord."

Karne felt an icy shiver of apprehension. "Is she injured? Dying?"

"No, milord. Or at least she didn't look to be."

Clearly, he was going to get no more information from Rad. Karne saved his breath for the three flights of stairs.

They passed a guard posted at the entrance to the emergency-exit plaza and then entered the plaza itself. Karne gave Rad points for setting the guard, if what awaited on the plaza were as bad as he seemed to think.

Survival suits and masks hung in tidy rows along one wall of the plaza. Coils of rope hung beside the exit stair. Rad motioned Karne to precede him up toward the exit. At the top, the bar still lay across the heavy outer door. Karne palmed the viewer control. The screen beside the door lit up and revealed Charlotte hovering outside the door, dressed in a deacon's habit. A *deacon's* habit. Rad had been right to leave her outside.

"This is what you thought should be kept secret?"

Rad nodded.

"Good man!"

Karne turned his head toward the grille on his side so the sound of his voice would be transmitted better. "Charlotte?"

He heard a gasp, then "My lord?"

Karne swallowed. It was definitely Charlotte's voice. Part of him stood aside and analyzed the mildness of his reaction to that voice: She had been gone a month, yet the sound of her voice did not set him on fire. Karne felt a tingle of relief. Her betrayal had broken the spell her beauty and sensuality had set on him. If he was not now free of it, he could be. Rad elbowed him.

"My lord, she's speaking to you. Has been for a bit."

Karne tuned in to her words, which had turned whining.

"I'm wet and cold, Karne. I've been out here a long time. Let me in. I'm sorry. I'll make this up to you."

Karne took the key that hung from the bar and turned it in the lock. At the sound, Charlotte began pounding vigorously. The sound came through the reinforcing and insulation into the stair as muted thuds, with a peculiar echo from the viewer/intercom beside the door. Karne motioned Rad to lift the bar. Rad put a hand to his stunner and looked at Karne. Karne nodded. It could do no harm. Only the Guardians knew if Charlotte were a decoy for Harlan, a tool to open a door to Ontar for soldiers of its enemy.

Rad dialed the weapon to "stun," then opened the door. Charlotte stood outside, apparently alone. As clearly as if she had told him, Karne knew Charlotte was wearing nothing underneath the robe. He felt just as sure that other men would know it, too. Rad's judgment in keeping her out of sight had been doubly good; the Larga Halarek, returning naked except for a *deacon's* robe . . .

She had been in a Retreat House. There was no other explanation. How many men had she had and in what Retreat House? That question would come to the mind of everyone who learned about her "disguise" and her method of arrival. Karne knew if he did not handle this scandal exactly right, he was looking at his political death.

Karne considered the possible witnesses to Charlotte's arrival. The household Blues knew nothing yet, but at least one border guard did, or should. If that border guard talked to anyone, anyone at all, the tale would spread and change. Men and women would talk about Charlotte at parties. They would laugh at Karne's weakness and her daring. They would point fingers at the cuckold and jeer at him, as if this kind of betrayal had never happened to any of them.

Keeping his eyes on Charlotte, Karne asked, "How many men saw her this way, Captain?"

"Just border guards. I checked on my way down to get you, milord. The border captain reported she and her traveling companion were stopped at our border. Unfortunately for possibilities of secrecy, she and her escort ran into a *squad* of guards going on shift, before they had all separated to go to their posts in the hills. They didn't recognize the man, though they recognized the Harlan nose, but his identity isn't necessary for this to become a terrible scandal, milord. Even if she had *no* escort, milord."

"The Four Guardians have mercy!" A squad! Karne's mind raced. Eleven men, including their officer. Could that "accidental" meeting have been arranged by the Harlans? Was that too bizarre to be possible? Was he himself beginning to see plots where none existed? Karne turned to Charlotte for the first time.

"Who was your escort, Charlotte?" He tried to keep the acid from his voice and failed.

"B—Brander Harlan, my lord."

"By my Mother's Blood!" Karne took a deep, calming breath. The border patrol had seen her, then, not only dressed up in a deacon's habit, but with Brander as escort. Even a child could put escort and deacon's habit and absence together and figure out where Charlotte had been and what she had been doing.

From the corner of his eye, Karne saw Rad lick his lips with a quick flick of his tongue.

"I'll leave you alone, milord," Rad said. He spun and went down the stairs two at a time. At the bottom, he ordered the guard away, then crossed the plaza himself and disappeared from sight.

Karne turned on the woman who seemed bent on his destruction. "Where are your brains, madam? If you bring this House down with your lust, you bring it down on your own head, too."

Charlotte threw herself into his arms, crying, sniffling, trying to get as close to him as she could. The heavy wool robe was soggy and smelled of wet goat. "Oh, Karne, it was awful, awful. He's not as good a lover as you so I decided to come home and that meant I had to escape his quarters somehow and then that awful Brander made me ride all the way even though it rained for hours right after we left the forest and we spent the night without a tent and he made me get off my horse more than a kilometer from our garden and walk the rest of the way and—"

Karne gripped her shoulders and pried her away from him. He forced her head up until she had to meet his eyes. "Brander, escape, forest, *walking*. What are you talking about? Where *were* you?"

She blinked at him, her lashes dark and sparkling with tears. "Breven, of course. Richard—they promised me so much—"

"*Richard!*" Karne had never felt such rage before. He wanted to strangle her right there and he knew the law would consider it justified. He felt his hands sliding across her shoulders toward her throat and shoved her away lest he actually kill her. "You've spent the last month with *Richard*? The worst enemy Halarek has? You—"

"Richard sent you a message saying I had run to him. Or at least he said he did."

"I'll bet he did." Karne gripped her shoulders and shook her. "I'll bet the two of you—" He recognized the terror in her eyes and stopped the shaking.

"Maybe the abbot stopped the letter," she whimpered. "I didn't want you to worry about where I was. I wanted—"

"Don't take me for a fool, Charlotte. You wanted to get back at me with your conquest. That's what you wanted. This was *much* better than taking Shjell to bed, wasn't it? When you get back at someone, you really get back, don't you? Well, this is the last time you leave this manor. At all. Ever. You understand me?" He punctuated his question with a savage shake.

Charlotte nodded, tears streaming down her face. "You're hurting me."

"I mean to hurt you. Guardians! You may have destroyed this House and House Rhiz with your wantonness. Did you ever think about the consequences before you fell for Brander's line?"

Charlotte threw back her head and glared at him. "You know you couldn't keep going as long as I needed. What did you expect me to do, lie here and suffer?"

"Suffer? You call that *suffering*?" Karne's grip tightened until she whimpered. "Could Richard keep going? Tell me the truth? Could Richard?"

The fire and fight went out of her. "No," she whispered. "He couldn't. And you're a better lover, too. Gentler, more careful to please me . . ."

Karne dropped his hands and stepped backward. "I hope you didn't say that to Richard."

Charlotte gave a pathetic little hiccup. "Of course. Why not? It was true."

For a second, Karne could not think at all. She had given Richard Harlan the most powerful insult she could have thought of. She had given him an insult worth razing several Houses to redeem. And she had not given her words a second thought, either before speaking them or afterward. The enormity of that kept Karne silent for some moments after his brain started to function again.

The insult to Halarek seemed to escape her, too. Richard had succeeded with Charlotte where he had failed with Kit. This would not stay secret. Even if the border patrol stayed absolutely silent about what they had seen, this matter would not stay secret. House Harlan would flaunt what Charlotte and Richard had done, and in a way calculated to do House Halarek the most harm. As if going to Halarek's chief rival because Karne was not lover enough for her were not harm enough. As if a noble lady willingly living in sin in a *male* Retreat House were not harm enough. Charlotte could not have done more harm if she had planned it carefully instead of acting on a whim.

Karne took Charlotte's arm ungently and pulled her down the stair after him. Humiliation after humiliation, that was what Charlotte had become. He became angrier and angrier with each jarring step down toward the emergency plaza. Charlotte whimpered and that made him feel angrier yet. She had put his potency publicly into question with her secret preventatives. Now she had done the same to his sexual performance. Richard's, too, was now also in question, but that was Richard's problem and irrelevant to Halarek's danger. A man must perform as a man, or lose his political and military support.

When they stood in the plaza, Karne shouted for the guard. Rad and the plaza guard came back on the double. Karne looked at the guard.

"Squadman, take this woman to the old guest quarters out-

side the wall and lock her in. Post a guard, then tell Lady
Agnes she's needed there. Captain Rad, see that these orders
are carried out exactly and report immediately back to me in
my quarters when they are done."

Charlotte looked frozen for a moment, then she lunged
toward Karne. The squadman caught her and pinned her arms
behind her back. He looked questioningly at Karne, his look
saying, "Is this all right?" Karne nodded.

With that nod, Charlotte's face instantly changed from spit-
ting rage to tremulous pleading. A big tear crept slowly down
one cheek. "Sweetheart, lover," she whispered, her voice trembling. "I came back. *You're* the man I really want. I'll have the
babies you want so much. Don't treat me like this."

"Shut your mouth, Charlotte, and keep it shut." His tone
must have been vicious, because her eyes got big and dark
and her face went white. *Good! You're frightened. It's about
time. I've been frightened since I saw your deacon's habit.*

"Blindfold her," he ordered Rad. "I don't want her seeing
the path to her new quarters. And take her through the servants'
passages as much as you can. I don't want any more people
than necessary seeing her, indecently dressed as she is." Karne
spun and walked swiftly away.

He spent the next several hours alone in his quarters, sitting on his bed tailor fashion. For most of that time, his mind
would not believe what Charlotte, with Brander's help, had
done. Brander's help. Brander's idea, probably. And the story
that would soon be whispered in the Halls and living quarters of the Houses would be Brander's invention and more fiction than fact, sordid as the facts were. There was no way to
avoid the public humiliation. Keeping silent would allow Brander and Richard kilometers of leeway for invention. He would
have to tell what happened before they did. He would have
to get to the Houses first, with as bare a version as he could
get away with, but something to stop Brander from reaching
whatever goal this procuring for Richard represented. Brander Harlan. Brander had not done this just to satisfy Richard.
There was more to this than that. And he had thought Brander
was just Richard's closest confidant and most valued spy.
Brander was playing a game of his own here. He had to be or
he would have avoided damaging Richard. Karne resolved
to set men to finding out what that game was as soon as he

had Charlotte's imprisonment taken care of.

He called Lady Agnes to him. She entered with only the most perfunctory knock and came to stand in front of the rok-hide chest at the foot of the bed.

"My lord?" She stood with exaggerated patience, one wrinkled hand clasping the back of the other and both suspended across her flat belly. "I had understood you wanted me to go to your lady somewhere outside the manor."

Long years of acquaintance had accustomed Karne to Lady Agnes's acid tongue, so he ignored it. "I must make a very painful tri-d announcement tomorrow and I need your help to do it. I want you to see that the Larga arrives at seven hours in the tri-d room, dressed just as you will find her when you reach her new quarters. She has betrayed this House in unforgivable ways and we all must pay for it. I hope this will lessen the price."

Her rigid face softened somewhat. "Seven hours, dressed as she is now. Do I have that correct, Lord Karne?"

Karne nodded.

"She will be there, if I have to drag her by that hair she's so proud of."

"Thank you. You may see to her now."

Lady Agnes bowed, as elegantly as stiff joints and a stiffer attitude permitted, and left.

Karne next told Captain Rad to order the squadman of Blues from the emergency plaza and his squad to accompany Charlotte to the tri-d room in the morning. Then he made a secured-channel call to Rhiz to prepare Lord Cherek for what he was going to do.

At six hours the next morning, Karne was in the tri-d room. He had not slept all night. At half-seven, he had the tri-d techs send out the audio signal that was an invitation to a worldwide broadcast, then he shielded himself inside from the emotions that would come with what had to be the most humiliating performance of his life. At exactly seven hours, Lady Agnes appeared in the doorway, her lean, wrinkled hand fastened like a bracelet of iron around one of Charlotte's wrists. A Blues escort filled the corridor behind them.

"I commanded more help, my lord," Lady Agnes said, dragging Charlotte farther into the room. "The Larga refused to come. In fact, she refused to dress. It took three deaconesses almost half an hour to get that one piece of clothing on her."

If circumstances had been different, Lady Agnes's refusal to name the garment the Larga was wearing would have been amusing. Ladies did not wear men's garments, *especially* the garments of holy men.

Karne took Charlotte from Lady Agnes's grip and stepped with Charlotte into the line-of-sight of the cameras. He bent his head and studied his boottips until the master cameraman said, "Ready, lord."

Karne raised his head and looked straight at the spot where his audience would be had they been in Halarek. He had learned, over the years, the impact on an audience of that sudden flash of his unique golden eyes. He refused the temptation to clear his throat.

"Lords and Freemen of Starker IV, I ask you to listen to a true story about recent events in Halarek. This truth is very unpleasant and damaging to my House, but it must be told before my enemies tell you a fiction far worse than the truth."

Charlotte tugged at her arm and Karne tightened his grip. He hoped strongly that his hard-won reputation for honesty would incline his listeners to stick with him. He glanced at Charlotte. He hoped his story and his reputation for honesty would outweigh Charlotte's seductive beauty and her present pose of beleaguered innocence.

"As I think everyone knows, I married a woman from Rhiz, a House aligned with Harlan until recently. Though our contract was for children, Charlotte secretly used preventatives."

That would get to a number of men in the audience, Karne knew. Some Houses did not even know preventatives existed. Others prohibited them outright, believing their lords could only prove their maleness by the number of children they produced. Everyone knew Karne Halarek had no living children.

Karne took a deep, steadying breath. The very hardest part of the story was yet to come. "She began looking elsewhere for her bed-play, lords and Freemen. Men who would not want children of her." Karne licked his lips and took a steadying breath. "She looked at parties and Council meetings and, when winter made that impossible, among Family here in Ontar."

Everyone in the tri-d room heard the gasp from the connected Houses and freecities. To lie with Family from the same manor, even if not personal family, was to commit incest. Karne heard Charlotte take a breath and saw her lips part.

"Don't say a *word*," he warned her, his voice too quiet for the tri-d equipment to transmit it.

"My sire—" she began.

Karne kept his voice under transmission levels only by a strong act of will. "Your sire knows. And he agrees with my plan for you. You've shamed your own House, too."

Karne looked out again at his invisible audience. "I don't know if she succeeded in her searching, but her very looking embarrassed this House. When I learned she was using preventatives, I took them away."

A buzz of approval came into the tri-d room. Charlotte squirmed, but said nothing.

Karne swallowed. There was support out there. He opened his mouth to continue and for a moment could not force the words out. "She wanted revenge, lords and Freemen, for the loss of her preventatives, so she plotted with Brander Harlan to betray me." Karne looked squarely at the center of the tri-d screen. "A Harlan, lords and Freemen. She worked with a Harlan. Brander helped her into the bed of another Harlan, in *Breven*, which is where she's been for the past month while everyone was looking for her. In Breven, lords and Freemen, with Richard Harlan, chief enemy of her House-by-marriage, and without preventatives of any kind."

The murmuring that came into the Halarek tri-d room rose to a roar and sometimes separated into understandable words against background sounds of anger and disgust.

"Breven again!"

" . . . in the line of succession."

"Perhaps a bastard—"

" . . . the humiliation . . ."

"Lord Richard again."

Karne looked down at the floor, unable to continue even if he could have been heard over the noise. The Houses, whatever their opinions of him, would stand behind a lord trying to protect the purity of his bloodline. The Houses already knew of Richard's licentiousness within the Retreat House from revelations made when Kit had been recaptured, and they disapproved. The Freemen would be outraged that Richard had managed to violate Breven's sanctity again.

When the sounds of anger and sympathy for him faded, Karne looked up. He was trembling and he put his free hand behind his back so no one could see that weakness. "I declare before you now that Larga Charlotte is no longer my companion in life or in bed. I will get from her two heirs as efficiently as possible and then I will set her aside. She'll *stay* locked away from the moment of setting-aside until the moment of her death."

Charlotte moaned. Karne turned to her.

"I'll make sure that only the complete destruction of this House will release you sooner. You'll stay in special quarters, alone, until I can be quite sure, on Lady Agnes's and Dr. Othneil's evaluation, that you carry no bastard by Richard, then I'll visit you in your fertile periods and in those periods only. If it's within my power, you'll never again see a man other than your father, your brothers, Ontar's pastor, and me as long as you live!"

She stared at him, her eyes widened in horror, and then she fell to the floor, unconscious. Karne let go of her as she fell.

Karne indicated the end of transmission to the tri-d techs with a sharp sideways cut of his hand, then he left the room.

CHAPTER 14

Brander let his small flitter glide to rest just outside Breven's courtyard wall. He sat quietly, waiting for the serf attendant to come out to shed his flitter, and thought with both glee and trepidation of his impending visit to Richard. Thank the Guardians both Isan Grent and the abbot were abiding by their orders. Isan told Richard no bad news. Brander had known persuading him to do that would be easy: No one wanted to bring bad news to Richard of Harlan. Even better, this abbot was sticking with Council orders, so Richard saw no tri-d and ate in his quarters. Therefore he saw no one at mealtimes who would tell him about Halarek's tri-d cast.

Brander remembered with pleasure the impact of the news that McNeece had driven Kath back across the river. Richard had been livid. How much more powerful would be the effect of today's bad news. Brander bent and touched the hilt of the small knife he had slipped into his boot. Protection might be necessary, and Brander was a prudent man. The immediate question, though, was, would the courtyard deacon who searched all visitors find it?

He did and Brander climbed the stairs to the third level with a heavy heart. Now he would have to ask the Council guards to come into the room with him, and that might alert Richard to the possibilities of a plot against him. It was too soon for him to figure that out. There were a few matters to clean up first. As it had been necessary to clear up the matter of Dannel of Jura. Jura had had to die. Brander could not afford to have anyone giving Richard another set of facts at this late date. And Jura had come to share nightmeal with Richard on the very same day Charlotte had disappeared. He had been turned away, thanks to Brander's own quick thinking, but he had come off his schedule.

It had looked like a flitter accident, Jura's death, an unfortunate pilot error that had landed Jura in the Great Swamp instead of on his own flitter pad. It had looked so natural, no one had even considered other possibilities. That meant Jura Holding was, for the time being, in the hands of Charlotte Halarek, but right now, from what Brander was hearing, that meant the hands of Karne Halarek. Charlotte was imprisoned outside Ontar somewhere, waiting the coming of her monthly cycle. Richard would be most disappointed when it came, as it surely would.

Brander stopped at the top of the stairs and looked down the hall. Two Council guards stood at Richard's door, as always. Brander shook his head.

What I wouldn't give to find the way into those minds! What I couldn't do with a few Council guards in my pay! My final step would be so much easier if I could just bribe both of them to go to the Sanitary for a few minutes. Or one go and the other fall asleep outside the door.

But over all these months he had found the soldiers wanted nothing he offered enough to desert their post or to aid him in any way.

Damned Freemen. They don't just think they're better than us, they believe *they are.*

At Brander's approach, one guard positioned himself across the door and the other came forward to search Brander. Brander stood still with his arms out at shoulder height. He very carefully kept his face blank. Inside, he seethed. The constant and careful searching made bringing in a weapon to use against Richard almost impossible.

I'm Harlan and these are the sons of tradesmen! I'm fourth in line for the dukedom, not counting Richard, and these peasants are touching me! I'll get back at them and all their kind when I'm duke. All of them!

He indulged himself for a moment in thoughts of what he could do once he was head of House Harlan, then the guard searching him stepped back and motioned him through Richard's door.

Brander whispered in the first guard's ear as he passed him, "Stay in the room this time. I have bad news and I fear for my life."

The guard nodded, gave his companion a meaningful glance, followed Brander into the room, and stopped just inside the door. Richard spun from the window as the door swung open. He looked at the guard for a long moment and, when the man did not leave, glared at Brander.

"What's the matter? Afraid I'll attack you for the way you've messed up my life? Whatever possessed you to think Charlotte would be good for me? And what kept you? I expected you yesterday."

And why was that, cousin mine? Something to do with Charlotte's disappearance, perhaps. "I had business that couldn't wait, Richard." *Like making arrangements for Cousin Hemmil to have what will look like a fatal heart attack before I get back. Like resting a day after that interminable ride with Charlotte. Wouldn't you like to know what kept me, cousin?* "I'm sorry. I'll try not to come late again."

"Charlotte's gone. Vanished. Disappeared four days ago."

Brander struggled to keep his face solemn and concerned. "I'd heard something about that." *Like the Halarek on tri-d, announcing what the two of you did together. You could've beaten him to the punch, Richard. You could've convinced the abbot you had some emergency news to send out. He'd probably let you make an* emergency *tri-d cast. Instead, you've brought worldwide humiliation to our House, you and your lusts. Halarek lost his alliances with Justin, Koort, and Frieden because of Charlotte, but if you'd told a tale first, many more would've left him.* "She showed up in Halarek two days ago, blithering some tale of spending a month in Breven, with you."

"It was your idea, bringing her here."

"Was it? I seem to remember you wanted to disgrace the Halarek publicly by getting his wife to choose you over him in the end. And then there was a personal competition with Halarek, wasn't there? The matter of proving you were the better lover? We see now how that went, don't we, Richard?"

Richard spun toward the window with an oath. "May the Guardians destroy her for her fickleness! May she be brought to bed of *my* get!" He stared out over the graying evening landscape.

Brander choked so he would not laugh. *Her fickleness suited you fine when it was* you *she chose*. "You tried the baby claim with Lady Kathryn, remember? Don't make a fool of yourself twice, Richard."

Richard seemed to swell with anger. His shoulders hunched. Brander sucked in air quickly. Maybe he had pushed Richard too far. Richard whirled and stalked menacingly toward Brander. Brander quickly beckoned the guard standing inside the door to come closer.

"Don't threaten me, cousin." His voice was not as steady as he would have liked. Richard had killed with his bare hands before. One of the Halarek brothers, in fact.

Richard lunged. The nearer guard sprang between Brander and Richard. They grappled. The second guard plunged through the door and together the two soldiers wrestled Richard up against a wall, where they held him until he stopped struggling. Brander could see by the rage in his cousin's eyes that he had been baited enough. It was time for soothing words.

Brander quit reluctantly. This was the first time in their almost thirty years of competition that Brander had really had the upper hand, but continuing might set Richard to wondering, despite the obvious courage-increaser of two guards, where Brander was suddenly getting confidence, and there were still ways Richard could find out. The Lord of the Mark, for example. Grent could not be killed or even slowed down significantly without making matters worse for Brander: The vassals might vote in an even more objectionable leader in his place. No, Isan Grent must be misled, deluded, perhaps temporarily disabled, but not killed, and Richard must be allowed to cool off. The best way to do that was probably to distract him. There might come another opportunity to twist a knife later.

Brander pushed his anger and resentment deep inside and began soothingly. "It's possible a child of yours will come of this. I'm sorry for dismissing the idea out of hand like that."

"Bitch!" Richard snarled. He struggled to get free. The guards only pushed him harder against the wall. Richard stopped fighting and let out a stream of curses on Charlotte, Council, House Halarek, Karne Halarek, Lady Kathryn, and

Dannel of Jura. When he finally stopped, panting, Brander continued.

"It may ease you somewhat to know that Halarek has confined Charlotte very strictly to quarters outside the manor." Brander paused to check Richard's comprehension. Was he still too angry to hear? "She may not even attend First Day services anymore: Pastor Jarvis must come to her and I understand the once he tried that, Charlotte threw two plates and a two-pot full of klag at him."

At that image, Richard's mouth twitched a little and his body relaxed visibly. After a moment he spat. "Bitch couldn't get around him anymore, eh?"

The guards relaxed their holds a little.

"Put that report on tri-d," Richard went on. "Let's put that on tri-d. With all the details we can think of, of what Charlotte and I did here."

Brander could imagine what kind of tales Richard could have invented. It was too bad he was not going to get the chance. Brander made his face look regretful. Now came one of the good parts.

"I'm really sorry, Richard. That would've worked if you'd done it the day she disappeared. As it is, Halarek was on the tri-d yesterday, describing every usable detail. He's beat you to it, Richard. He's squashed all the lovely possibilities for disgrace and humiliation that incident had. Even the tale he told may be disgrace enough to make him completely ineffective in Council this next meeting. He lost powerful, longtime allies over it. No one will believe any story from you, though. You're days too late."

Richard went livid. "Why didn't you tell me?"

Brander shrugged. "What good would it have done? Halarek has already lost whatever allies he's going to. Besides, for some time in the future, Halarek's attention will be on controlling his wife and providing heirs for his House. We could take advantage of that. Try to force House Rhiz back into line, for example." *Take some action for your* House, *you fool! Stop making so much of the injuries to your reputation!* "Our spies report Halarek is going to ask Dr. Alterinn in for a fertility consultation. It's ironic, don't you think, that Halarek has to ask advice of Odonnel's Family physician, who is, coincidentally, the chief adviser to Harlan's genetic council?"

"Alterinn's a Freeman. He can talk to whom he pleases. Besides, it's most unlikely the Lharr knows about the genetic council. How would he find out?"

"Think, Richard! Alterinn's special interests are fertility and genetics. How would Halarek know that, unless Ennis told Lady Kathryn about the genetic council?"

Richard stood straighter and shook the guards off. "You see plots behind every pillar. Physicians talk to each other. That's how new ideas get passed around."

"I think you're taking this too lightly, Richard. It worries me." *By all the gods, it worries me! Alterinn might discover how infertile you are in the process of discovering why Charlotte doesn't conceive, and then where would I be?*

Richard discounted Brander's worry with a slice of his hand. "Forget that. If Halarek's worried about fertility, we may yet have a chance to take that House. Now's the time to get rid of Kerel's boys. Make it an accident, the kind little boys are likely to have."

"Of course, my lord." *May you never find out I sent an assassin into Durlin two days ago.*

Brander did not especially care if Richard caught the sarcasm in being addressed by title. Jura was dead. Hemmil would be. That left only three cousins to go, two in the Jennen line, one in Richard's. Soon House Halarek's heirs would die, too, taking Halarek's attention almost entirely away from Harlan and whatever might be going on there. Three cousins were not a problem. The Council would eventually see things his way, too. Especially after that tri-d cast of Halarek's and what it told about Richard. Summer Council was only three days away. The righteous anger, especially among the Freemen, at Richard's arrogance and blatant violation of the sanctity of a Retreat House for the second time, would not have had time to burn itself out. In three days, the Jennen line within Harlan would become the hereditary rulers by Council vote, and that would mean only two more cousins would have to die before Richard did. Three days. Only three days.

"Brander? Brander! You're miles away. I asked you what's happened to Jura. He missed his scheduled visit altogether this week."

As he will miss all the others, forever. "Haven't you heard? I would've thought the abbot would've told you, Dannel coming here every two weeks or so as he did. Of course, he did come extra last week." *And I wonder what news he had that couldn't wait until his scheduled visit. I'm glad I convinced Grent to tell your guards to tell Jura you weren't receiving guests. Damnably roundabout way of doing things, but necessary.*

"Dannel died in a flitter crash three days ago, apparently right after dropping Charlotte off at Ontar. At least, our spy in Ontar reports she arrived that same day. His holding is her dower property, after all. Perhaps he felt he owed her the help. *You* know how unhappy Charlotte was that last week. Obviously she got word to her vassal somehow." *And there goes another source of outside information, right, Richard? Too bad.* "He did come, but he waited until you went to nightmeal, then he lifted Charlotte off the roof. He dropped a rope down for her so she could climb up the wall."

"Jura, eh? Somehow I'd figured you had a hand in Charlotte's disappearance, Brander. Your disinterest in women is notorious, but this woman could interest a stone. And you seemed to have some feeling for her. Lucky for you it was Jura."

Lucky for me Jura can't tell you differently.

Richard brightened considerably. He looked at the nearer of the Council soldiers. "Get the abbot for me. I have urgent business with him."

The soldier looked at Brander for directions. Brander considered the matter. Richard was calmer now. Letting the soldier leave would not be much of a risk. Brander nodded to the soldier.

Richard watched until the soldier left the room, then turned to the other. "You wait outside."

This soldier, too, looked toward Brander.

"*Inside* the door," Brander said.

Richard's hand flashed for the weapon that was not on his hip. Even five years a prisoner could not quench that reflex. Brander could hear Richard's teeth grate when he realized he had no weapon.

Richard seemed to swell. His face reddened. "Obey me! I'm the Duke of Harlan."

"Duke-designate, milord," the soldier said quite calmly, "and a prisoner here. You can no more give me orders than the deacon in the scullery can."

Richard growled deep in his throat and grabbed for the soldier. The man's stunner was in his hand in an instant. Richard's left leg buckled under him. Richard hit the floor hard and lay very still for a moment. Brander could see the shock on his face. He assumed it was the first time in Richard's life anyone had ever refused one of his orders, let alone enforced the refusal. This would be a good time to lay on the capping blows.

"The Lharr Halarek not only announced to the world Charlotte had been here, lying with you, he plans to set her aside as soon as she's given him heirs. And not yours, Richard. He's making sure she's carrying nothing of yours."

Richard struggled to sit up. Brander resisted a mighty urge to kick him.

So close. So close now to the top. It would be insane to show him how I really feel when I'm so close to the top.

Brander stepped back to make temptation easier to resist. After there was no possibility of stopping the changeover, *then* he could say what he had been saving up for almost thirty years, do what he had been wanting to do for almost thirty years. Just a few moves more and Richard could cease to exist. Brander looked forward to that moment. He could begin planning how it was to happen. He wanted to kill Richard with his own hands and he wanted Richard to know how thoroughly he had been betrayed first.

CHAPTER 15

Karne strode along the hall at such a pace that some of his personal bodyguard had to trot to keep up. He did not even look back to see that his orders regarding Charlotte were obeyed. He trusted Lady Agnes as he trusted few other people, male or female, and knew Charlotte would be returned expeditiously to her quarters. Karne had to take care of too many problems caused by Charlotte's behavior to bother about Charlotte herself, and he was only too aware he must have at least ideas about the solutions to those problems within four days, in time for the Summer Council.

Karne shoved through the library door so quickly that it banged into the wall behind it, and that set up a nasty vibration of the door's metal fittings. The library was empty. It was too early yet for either Tane or Weisman to be at work. Karne dismissed his guard. They left, shutting the door behind them, but he knew they would patrol the hall both outside the door and outside his quarters so no unknowns could get in. There was both reassurance and despair in that knowledge. It was at such times, when the pressure of constant vigilance became oppressive, that Karne regretted ever having lived on Balder, because if he had not lived there, he would not miss freedom of movement. People did not kill each other in feuds on Balder. They settled feuds with saga-singing contests or weregeld or, at worst case, with Drinn wrestling. In the Drinn ring, occasionally, a man died. Here, there was death on every hand.

Karne shook off the longing for peace and safety. He had chosen to return. It had been his duty, but he could have refused it and he had not.

He went around the worktable and pressed Weisman's "call" button. Weisman took a long time answering, or rather, it took a long time for a page to bring Karne Weisman's message. Frem Kurt Weisman regretted to inform his lordship that he would be unable to attend him this day or the next, at the least. He had a very bad cough and a runny nose and a fever and Dr. Othneil had ordered him to stay in bed at least two days and probably three.

Karne stared at the message in his hand for a long moment. He needed information *now* from Halarek's spies. There were only four days to Council. If Weisman were in bed for three days . . . On the other hand, Weisman had always been extremely faithful; he had come to work even when miserably sick, so he must be sick indeed to stay in bed.

Karne dropped the message onto the table and looked at it for a moment, then he crossed the room, passed under the stair, and stopped before a small sliding door in the wall. He looked at the array of buttons beside it, punched in a combination, and waited. In a few minutes, a discreet beeping, quiet enough not to disturb work in the library, told him to open the door. Inside were a steaming cup of klag and a platter of rolls and sausage. He took a napkin and utensils from a drawer under the machine and carried his fast-breaking meal over to the table.

He sat down, leaned back in the chair, and shut his eyes for a moment. One more thing to go wrong before Council; he had to work without Halarek's spies. With a sigh, he sat forward and reached for the stylus and pad Orkonan always left on the table and wrote himself a reminder to assign someone to work with Weisman from now on so two people would know and be known by Halarek's contacts in other Houses.

He picked up the steaming cup. The hot, thick smell of klag drifted away in tails of steam. Karne sniffed appreciatively and took a sip. Klag. Necessary for thinking early in the morning. He leaned back in the chair again, immediately more comfortable. He cradled the warmth between his hands and thought.

Why had Brander himself brought Charlotte back? Why he would have brought her to Richard needed no explanation, but why had he not sent her home with a servant or a cousin

or even by herself? Because there was value to Brander in
Halarek knowing he had been the escort. That had to be the
answer. No one would expect Charlotte to keep such a thing
secret, especially when she had so clearly felt abused by the
manner and speed of travel. So why would Brander want to
be known?

He could be presenting himself as a possible ally, so when
Richard found out he had helped Charlotte escape, Halarek
would defend him out of gratitude.

It was possible, though not likely, that either Charlotte or
House Rhiz had some sort of hold on Brander, so he had been
forced to help Charlotte escape.

Or it could be that he had just wanted to stay off the screens
of the holdings between Breven and Halarek and so had come
with Charlotte on horseback. That way, only a few people
would know where he had gone or even, if he had planned
carefully, that he had been out of Harlan's manor house at all.
No, that could not be the answer, because he could just as well
have ridden directly home alone.

Then what? It was important for Karne to know Brander
was with Charlotte. That would tie Charlotte's disappearance
to Richard, yet, if Charlotte accused Brander of aiding her
escape, it would be her word against his, and Charlotte's
reputation as well as her femaleness would weigh listeners
toward Brander's story. Plus Brander would probably have
a backup candidate for the role of rescuer, to keep himself
safe from Richard. The most likely answer, then, seemed
to be that Charlotte's stay in Breven served Brander's purposes as well as Richard's and Brander wanted as few people as possible to know he was even involved in Charlotte's
escapade.

And what would Brander's purposes be? He had supported
the move at Thawtime Council to change the Harlan line of
succession. Was that his plan, to move into the line of succession? If so, Charlotte's visit to Breven was possibly designed
to discredit Richard, too, and if that were the case, Charlotte's whereabouts would have to be publicized by Brander
somehow. Interesting thought. Karne had always seen Brander
as Richard's errand boy, trusted messenger, and confidant
(because he was out of the line of succession). He would be
willing to bet most lords of the Nine thought the same. He

had even interpreted Brander's help to Charlotte—the preventatives, the introductions and bits of information—that way, as something that was useful to Richard.

Thinking of Charlotte and preventatives reminded Karne that Charlotte had had none when she fled to Breven. He leaned across the table and touched the com panel. When Othneil came on, Karne told him to check Charlotte for pregnancy. Karne released the "talk" button with a bitter thought: Whatever Othneil found—pregnant or not pregnant—would have to be announced to the world. There could be no question at all about the bloodlines of a Halarek heir. Brander was a clever man. He had seen how Charlotte's return must go. His presence as an escort was a threat—you expose your wife's transgressions, and Richard's, or I'll expose hers. Would Brander link her to Richard? All lines of thought led to Brander with an agenda of his own.

Karne finished his fast-breaking while thinking about Brander in new ways. When he had finished, he called a page to take the dishes away and walked back to the tri-d room. He called Baron von Schuss and, after a few minutes spent explaining his train of thought, persuaded the baron to set von Schuss's spies to learning what they could about Brander Harlan. Karne then tri-ded the abbot at Breven to get a list of Richard's visitors over the last four months. Abbot Godwin promised to com the list as soon as it was assembled. Karne turned to leave the tri-d room, then changed his mind.

"Raise House Durlin," he said to the nearest tech.

He waited while the necessary technical matters were attended to, then Sindt of Durlin appeared on the wall, his long face set into that look of cool contempt he usually presented to Karne.

"What is it now, Halarek?"

Karne clenched his teeth on a sharp reply. Emotion would only feed Sindt's prejudice against the "woman" of Halarek. "I am 'Lharr' or 'Lord Karne' or 'my lord' to you, Sindt." He held up his hand the moment Sindt's mouth opened. "No argument. I am the head-of-House, no matter how much you dislike the idea. You will treat me with at least surface respect. I've subsidized the continuing existence of your House since I took my place as Lharr, but the Guardians desert me if I send you even one more credit if you *ever* show public disrespect for me again."

Sindt flushed and bit his lip, but he bent his head in acknowledgment.

"Now, for the news I called to give you. Something's up. We don't know what yet, but I'm going to assume it puts the boys in danger. My contacts report you still take no precautions to guard them."

"Your 'contacts'?" Sindt spat out the words. "Your spies, you mean."

Karne ignored the rush of anger inside and went on. "My contacts report you still take no precautions to guard them."

"They're only children, but they're *male* children. You're the only male in House Halarek with a bodyguard." Sindt made that into an insult and a sneer.

Karne had heard this before, and from more than this cousin. He had hardened himself not to feel the insult anymore. "I'm still alive. I want the boys to stay alive. Because you're reluctant to risk your public image of manliness, Sindt, I'll dispatch two squads of Blues to bring the boys here where they can be fully protected."

"You can't. I won't permit—"

"You have nothing to say in the matter. You are their uncle, but so am I, and I'm lord in this House and I say they'll be adequately protected. Have them and their mother ready to leave by nightmeal on the thirteenth. I've left them to your whim too long already. Refuse, or attempt to block this, and I'll absorb House Durlin into House Halarek and you'll be no more than a minor cousin among minor cousins."

Sindt gasped and turned red and then he and his tri-d room vanished. Karne looked at the empty screen. He hoped this move was not too late. The idea of Brander with an agenda of his own, different from or even opposed to Richard's, made Karne distinctly uneasy.

He returned to the library.

The visitors list arrived from Breven in late afternoon. There were deacons, by name, deacons (2) not by name, family members of deacons, the Lord of the Mark, Dannel of Jura, Brander Harlan, and Dr. J. J. Gebbits of Harlan.

Not very promising, Karne thought, but I'll forward it to the baron, anyway, so his spies can get at it. The physician's visits indicate Richard might be sick. That's not something we'd ordinarily hear about. I wonder what could be wrong that requires a physician visit every month.

Karne considered sending the list to Weisman, so it could proceed to von Schuss through the usual channels, but Weisman had sounded very sick and so, in the end, Karne returned to the tri-d room to pass the information to the baron himself.

"In the process of setting up a call to you myself, boy," the baron said the moment he appeared on the wall. "Secured channel."

Karne motioned to the techs to secure the channel.

"Urgent messages from Harlan, Karne. Hemmil Harlan died of a heart attack two hours ago. My spies have also been hearing things that suggest there's a plot to kill Kerel and Netta's boys soon in an 'accident.' "

Karne's heart sank. There was no pleasure in learning his suspicion about an attempt against the boys had been correct. This news only made Brander's involvement in a plot against Richard more probable.

"I'm giving the techs a list of guests at Breven, Emil. My spy master's too sick to work. Have your people find out what you can, will you? I have to get protection to the boys."

Baron von Schuss nodded and waved and disappeared.

Karne ordered Captain Phillipson to assemble a fighter escort to bring the boys to Ontar immediately. The boys' flitter and its escort took off shortly after dark. Karne watched, hoping all his concern was for nothing. It was only later, when Karne had resumed his work in the library, that he had time to think how convenient for Brander the death of Hemmil was.

Three hours after the flitter and its escort had left, Phillipson commed from Durlin. He refused to speak to anyone but Karne or Tane Orkonan, so both men ended up in the com center. The voice that came out of the speakers was heavy and sad.

"My lord, we've just arrived and we were too late. Both boys had their throats slashed by a kitchen worker gone berserk not more than an hour ago. Lord Sindt was afraid to tell you and Lady Netta is in hysterics and cannot speak coherently at all. I'm sorry to have to give you such news, milord."

Karne wanted to sit down, but dared not in front of the techs. He shut his eyes, bit his lip, and held his breath for a moment until the fiercest grief and anger had passed. He opened his eyes and looked at Orkonan.

"It's almost as if someone told Harlan we were taking the boys away," Orkonan said, his voice revealing his stunned disbelief. "What else could explain it?"

Karne shook his head, not yet trusting his voice.

"Lord Karne, what shall I do?" Phillipson let the question hang in the air.

"Bring them here for burial," Karne finally said. "Bring their mother, too, and I'll send her back, adequately escorted, after the funeral. Without delay, Captain."

"What about the spy, my lord?"

"Let Sindt deal with him as he will. If he will. I'll announce at Council what's happened." Karne turned to one of the comtechs. "Notify House von Schuss, emergency channel, of what has happened. Kit and Jemmy may be in danger, too." Karne spun and left the room.

He would do as he had threatened, Karne decided as he strode through the hallways and charged up six sets of stairs to the conservatory, his bewildered bodyguard trailing behind. This was too much, too much, too much. Those little boys, dead, because they had a Halarek for a father. The brutality of the attack was not Richard's style, either. These deaths were by someone else's orders. Brander's? And Sindt had helped the killer. Through his own arrogance, he had helped the killer.

Karne heard the vicious snap of his leather soles on the stone floor and did not care. Betrayed, by an in-law's contempt and arrogance. Well, he would dissolve Durlin, as he had promised. He would make Sindt the minor cousin he had been before Netta married Kerel and Trev Halarek had given his Family House status in return. Dissolution and the announcement of Sindt's criminal negligence to Council would finish forever any political ambitions Sindt might have had. But that would not be enough. Nothing would ever be enough.

Karne burst through the door to the conservatory. He did not come here often, but often enough that his guard knew to stay outside. Karne stood for a moment just inside the door, transfixed for the moment by the warm, damp, fragrant, welcoming air. The gardener, who lived in an apartment at the back of the conservatory, stuck his head out the small window that looked out onto his kingdom. He nodded to Karne and withdrew. Karne shut the door, dropped the bar across to lock it, and sat down on a bench under the skylight. This was his refuge of last resort and today he really needed it.

Karne's clasped hands sagged down between his knees. He stared at the graystone floor. Dead. Both boys were dead. And at Harlan orders. It had to be at Harlan orders. No one else would profit, really, from the deaths of Halarek heirs. All the young Halarek heirs but Jemmy.

The boys' deaths meant the Harlan spy inside Ontar had struck again. There was no other explanation of how the message about Halarek's military escort could have gotten to Durlin so fast. Everyone knew there was a Harlan spy in Ontar, had been for years, but no one had found a way to smoke him out. There was some question of whether the spy had been the same person all the time, since actions identifiable as internal treachery were infrequent, but there was no way to answer that. Trev had at one time considered replacing Ontar's entire staff to get rid of the spy, but that would only have provided opportunity for countless spies to be hired in the places of loyal servants and household officers.

Karne shook his head, then straightened. There was so much grief, so much death. He must get rid of the weight or he would cease to function effectively. Karne tipped his head back and let himself feel the sun falling on his face. The heat and light loosened muscles in his face and shoulders that had tightened almost to snapping with his effort at public control. He let himself feel grief for the little boys who had been killed only because their sire had been Trev's second son. He let himself cry for them there in the sunshine and silence. Once the grief had been let out, he would have better control of his other emotions.

When the worst of the grief was over, Karne stood. He sniffed deeply. The air smelled of damp earth, green leaves, wet stone, and tam-tam flowers. He walked slowly over to the tiny grove of tam-tam trees. These exotics, imported indirectly from Terra, bloomed pink and orange and red almost continuously and their flowers smelled of spice and warm honey. Karne touched several of the huge flowers and stroked the blades of the ferns growing at the bases of the trees. The fronds, filmed with water, left his fingertips damp. Karne ran a fingertip along the fern leaf's edge, feeling the delicate springiness of the leaflets with pleasure. He brushed the water from his fingers onto his trouser leg and wandered deeper into the conservatory. Each step lifted some of the weight of grief and responsibility from him.

Karne stayed among the plants until the light coming through the skylight faded to pink and lavender. He went down to his quarters, then instructed the squadman in charge of the night patrol that he was not to be disturbed for anything except the arrival from Durlin, commed Orkonan from his quarters to set funeral arrangements into motion, and went to bed.

Karne awoke most reluctantly to shaking by Gareth, newly apprenticed to the seneschal in Ontar and no longer sent on administrative errands much. "My lord, Lord Karne, you must get up. Lady Netta wails and moans and won't be comforted and Lord Sindt wounded two of our Blues while they were preparing the boys' bodies for transport."

Karne groaned and rolled over so his face was in his pillow. How could he face another day like the last one? How could he face a day only half as bad as the last one?

Gareth pushed on his shoulder. "Tane says you must take care of the Lady Netta. You're the only one here of appropriate rank."

Karne rolled onto his back and stared up at Orkonan's younger cousin. "I will *not* take care of Netta. Call Lady Agnes. Charlotte can do without company until the funeral's over if necessary. Request Lady Kathryn to come. She'll have to come eventually, anyway. I will *not* take care of Netta."

Gareth turned to leave.

"Don't tell anyone what I just said, in case you didn't know that. Request Lady Agnes's presence most graciously on my behalf. Make a similar request from me to Kit." Karne sat up and rubbed the sleep out of his eyes. He sighed. "No, on the other hand, I must tri-d von Schuss myself. No one else should break the news of what's happened. But take care of getting Netta into Lady A's hands, Gareth."

Gareth made a quick bow and left.

The tri-d to House von Schuss was not the only one Karne had to make. He had to notify Council chairman Gashen that he would be late to Council due to the funerals. He had to ask Childreth Konnor to sit at Halarek's prep table and speak for Halarek, with the advice of Halarek's vassals, until Karne arrived. He had to call Ronnif Halarek and tell him to prepare himself to be Heir; Jemmy was too young to be accepted by the vassals and retaining him as Heir also put him at unacceptable risk. To be Heir in von Schuss was enough and it was safer.

The next two days passed in a blur and by the time of the funerals on the morning of 15 Aden, Karne felt numb. There were too many mourners and guests to hold the boys' funeral in the chapel, so it was held in the Great Hall. Karne performed his duties as uncle and lord, then retreated to the quiet of the conservatory for an hour to recover before flying to Council. Council required a different role and a different set of mind. He could not let himself think about the murdered boys again until after Council, except as an example of the lengths to which Harlan would go to destroy Halarek.

Karne slipped silently into an empty space on the bench behind Childreth, whose attention was wholly focused on the debate about Richard's recent defiance, again, of Council sentence and the rules of The Way. This time no one but Gormsby seemed to be speaking for Richard. Garren Odonnel sat silent and Isan Grent's only comment was a statement of utter disbelief that the same disguise could work twice. This comment roused angry shouting from House Rhiz, which defended the abbot's innocence in the entire matter, roaring that Godwin Rhiz was upright and honest and that the problem was with the Council guard. A few urged that Richard be sentenced to the Desert of Zinn now, as common criminals were. The debate surged in one direction and then another, like treetops in a storm, but Karne could see the direction it was heading. Slowly and subtly the argument was being made that Richard had forfeited his right to live as one of the Nine. The telling points, such as Richard demonstrating by his behavior his contempt for The Way and the customs of the Nine, had been rehearsed ahead of time, Karne was sure. They came too glibly to be spontaneous. They could not possibly be of Richard's design, either, because they pointed to the logical next step, installing a new line of succession in Harlan.

A new line in Harlan. A new line in Halarek. Much as he hated the idea, Karne knew he could not be a responsible lord and do otherwise. Ronnif would make a good lharr. That he was a second cousin would bother some on Council, but that was too bad. Richard had killed all the men of Karne's generation but Karne himself, and Trev and battles had killed off Trev's brothers and most of the first cousins.

I have no near cousins, Karne reminded himself. It has to be Ronnif.

So absorbed had Karne been in his own thoughts that he had missed Chairman Gashen's signal to the techs to acknowledge an incoming broadcast. He was not so absorbed that he missed the screen brightening and the figure of Richard Harlan appearing. There were a few gasps from the Council and some brief protests that the subject of debate, who was supposedly restricted from using tri-d, should so suddenly appear.

"The abbot," Gashen said, his voice fierce.

The graying, benign face of Godwin Rhiz appeared at Richard's side.

"What does this mean, my lord abbot?"

The abbot's hand rested quietly on his paunch. "Lord Richard has convinced me that without access to tri-d for information or to defend himself, as in this case, he would soon be dead. Lord Richard convinced me there is a conspiracy against him inside his own House, Frem Chairman. I cannot passively stand by and allow a man to be killed."

"You passively stood by and allowed him to bring a woman into Breven again!" The voice came from the Freemen's benches and the man did not stand to be identified.

The abbot bristled. His right hand dropped to his side where his weapon had once rested, before he entered the religious life. He looked at the hand as if it were a traitor to him, then looked back at the men in the Council chamber.

"Lord Richard did not bring the woman in. She was brought in most cleverly in a deacon's robe, *while all members of the community were in the refectory,* and she was concealed in his room before he and his Council guards returned from nightmeal. The guards searched the room, as they often do, lords and Freemen, and they found no one and nothing. The guards are not at fault, nor am I. We were outsmarted."

"How many times more will you be 'outsmarted' while Lord Richard's with you, Lord Abbot?" someone from McNeece jeered.

The abbot drew himself up taller. "Council and I have already made arrangements that such a thing can never happen again. I'm not responsible for what happened under the previous abbot. This, at least, was not as extensive and I do take responsibility for this incident. It will *not* happen again." He glanced toward Richard. "However, Lord Richard has, as I said, convinced me that use of the tri-d is necessary to the preserving of his life. He has discovered his present sources of information are either limited or contaminated. That part of Council sentence will have to be modified. I repeat, I'll not be responsible for a man's death. Lord Richard?"

Richard's face was stern. He stepped closer to his audience. "I admit I had the woman, Charlotte Rhiz, here with me. She offered. I accepted. My cousin Brander got her in."

Karne gripped his knees and stared at the floor in front of his feet. The shame again, in front of all these people again, as part of Richard's excuse for his behavior: Charlotte had offered herself. Though it was possible, it was more likely Brander had tempted her repeatedly with such an important conquest as Richard. Richard had been no innocent bystander, irresistibly tempted. The intensity of the anger that flooded Karne surprised him. Apparently, some matters having to do with that woman still had the power to move him.

He glanced toward Brander, the fourth party to the Breven arrangement. Brander's face looked swollen and red and a vein beat heavily in his near temple.

So Richard betrays you, too. Karne longed to shout the words. *You've served him so well for so long and he betrays you to lessen the damage Council will inflict on him. Well, I'll find some way to betray you, too, Brander, for what you've done to my House in serving yours.*

CHAPTER 16

Brander stared at the figure of his cousin. *How did you manage that, you bastard! I thought I'd made the abbot excuse-proof.*

Richard with access to the tri-d room. Richard with access to vassals other than Isan Grent. Richard free to talk to other Houses. There was too much he could learn, yet it was too early to kill him. Richard's appearance made the day's business near impossible, too. How could cousins, let alone allies, vote to change the line of succession with Richard, vengeful, still-powerful Richard, watching?

Brander chewed thoughtfully at a hangnail. Could he stop the process? Could he get word to the second set of speakers he had arranged for—the ones who were to support changing the succession away from a man unfit to live as one of the Nine—in time to keep them from bringing up the subject? Or maybe Richard knew about that proposal. Maybe that was why he had appeared so inopportunely. Brander began looking around the chamber, locating the men with speeches on the issue. All were back-bench men, with no assigned places, and had to be found without making the looking obvious.

Suddenly, Brander realized he was missing what Richard was saying. He listened more carefully.

"—Charlotte Rhiz, here with me. She offered. I accepted. My cousin Brander got her in."

Red rage flooded Brander. He controlled it with great difficulty. He wanted to pound on the prep table. He wanted to stamp and scream how unjust this was. He had served Richard faithfully and secretly for years and years and here was Richard making the bringing of Charlotte to Breven Brander's idea.

How like you, you craven son of a whore. You haven't faced up to your responsibilities your whole life. You take on the fun things, like feuds and duels and beautiful women, and let me and your allies do the work of keeping Harlan together. Well, no more. You're in Breven and can't get out. I'm here. I don't have to go to Breven ever again. I'm safe from you, Richard, and I'm going to take Harlan from you.

He shed his childhood fear of Richard in that moment and it was like dropping an M-ton of stone from his back. Brander felt taller, though he was sure he had not moved.

"Point of order." The Duke deVree was standing to be recognized.

Gashen inclined his head toward him. "Your point, milord?"

"There is business already on the floor, Frem Chairman. Richard Harlan, with his plea for modification of sentence and his abbot, is out of order."

Brander watched the abbot bristle at being called Richard's abbot.

Gashen thought for a moment. "You're right, mostly, milord, but I'm going to allow Lord Richard to continue, since his points may have bearing on the matter of both his sentence and the next item, the line of inheritance in Harlan." Gashen turned to Richard.

Richard bowed. "Thank you, Frem Chairman. I present these bits to you, lords and Freemen, as evidence that someone is moving against me in Harlan and that to move against me is, in the end, to threaten my life.

"My cousin Ennis was assassinated while attempting to rescue his wife from that trap in Breven. Breven is not the sort of place *I* would chose for an assassination, lords and Freemen. Assignation, yes, assassination, no.

"Dannel of Jura died, I'm told, after being turned away from visiting me. I was told Jura had taken Larga Charlotte with him. The Lharr Halarek says her abductor was my cousin Brander. In this case, I believe the Lharr. Coincidentally, my cousin Hemmil, my Heir, died a few days after Charlotte left. I was told it was a heart attack."

Richard's eyes found Brander's.

What are you going to do, now you know, cousin? Kill me? How, when I've been your contact for such arrangements for years?

Richard looked back at the chairman. "I think, Frem Chairman, that's too many deaths of people close to me in too short a time. If Council retrieved Jura's flitter, it might find the crash was not a mistake, but sabotage or outright murder. Finally, I come to the most recent deaths—the sons of Kerel Halarek were brutally murdered three days ago in such a way that blame would seem to be House Harlan's. Halarek has no enemies within his own House, so what other House had any reason to kill Halarek heirs? Harlan, because that weakens our ancient enemy, or so the reasoning goes. Richard Harlan, because I'm head-of-House. But I swear to you, lords and Freemen, that I had nothing to do with those murders. I swear, by my Mother's Blood, such killing is *not* my style. I prefer to do my own killing, for one thing, and I've never killed a child. There's no challenge in it." Richard gave the members of Council a challenging look, then turned his hand so he could examine his fingernails.

As though this were a small matter. This is no small matter. I don't like the way you lined up the deaths for these dolts to see.

Brander glanced at the Halarek to see how he was taking this interruption, then looked back at Richard in disgust. Trying to read Karne Halarek was like trying to read a stone wall most of the time; he had been too well trained to let his emotions show except under the most extreme circumstances. He had showed something in his tri-d announcement about the Larga's unfaithfulness, for instance, but not as much as Brander was certain he had been feeling. That was a definite handicap in dealing with the Halarek, his deliberately blank face.

The men of Council were whispering to each other, walking from one House's benches to another's, gathering in small clusters here and there. Brander glared at the chairman in disapproval, but Gashen did nothing to stop this out-of-order moving around. Several more minutes passed. Brander nudged the Lord of the Mark.

"The business of Richard's sentence."

Grent gave Brander a look of distaste and returned his attention to the circulating Council members.

Finally, deVree stood again. "Frem Chairman, Charl deVree, House deVree. There is still the matter of Lord Richard's extensive and blatant violation both of his sentence and of the rules of The Way."

Gashen nodded. "True enough. The matter of sentence needs to be decided before the matter of inheritance."

Richard, suspended in lifelike detail on the wall behind the chairman, returned his attention to the chamber, folding his arms across his chest as he did so. Brander thought he detected traces of a frown.

Worried, are you? Anything you get, you deserve.

The debate swirled here and there in the chamber, but finished more quickly than such things usually did. The final agreement said that Richard Harlan might keep tri-d privileges, since they truly seemed necessary to the preserving of his life, and death had not been his sentence; but, because the interlude with Larga Charlotte had been the second such in a short time, Richard would be more strictly confined and more guards would be added at Breven. For the remainder of his stay there, guards would check every person entering and every person leaving the Retreat House and a guard would be posted in his rooms at all times. These guards would be in addition to those already assigned to guard Lord Richard's quarters. The Council voted funds for the additional soldiers and moved on to the next business.

Brander watched the debate sourly. Richard's appearance had spoiled a magnificent opportunity to change the line of succession. Not only that, but he did not go away once the sentence problem had been solved, but hung around, watching, making it impossible to bring up the subject of the change of inheritance. Though Gormsby would speak about the reasons such a change would benefit Starker IV, Richard would see through Gormsby to the originator of the idea and Brander was not yet ready to be recognized.

Oh, no, my handsome cousin, I won't reveal myself yet. But you will know, before you die, who will take your place.

Then Gormsby rose, the plasti slate with his speech notes on it in his hand. The old man did not think bringing up the subject was impossible. Or maybe the old man did not think. Brander controlled panic with difficulty. For a fraction of a second, he hesitated between standing up and interrupting or going to the old man and pushing him back into his seat. In the end, he decided to stay where he was and hope for the best. The risk in trying to stop the marquis was more than the risk of Richard figuring out who was behind his speech. The speech had been written from the Old Party point of view and Gormsby's strict adherence to the Old Party's theories and beliefs was well known. Maybe Richard would not suspect Brander's involvement, after all. Brander told his taut muscles to relax, but did not succeed.

Brander had to admit the old man delivered the speech well. There was even a spattering of applause from the benches of Harlan's allies after the old man sat down. The debate afterward was very restrained, perhaps because Richard was watching it and he still held enough power to intimidate a great number of the Houses or at least to keep them from open opposition. Yet, slowly, more and more arguments in favor of changing to the Jennen line came forward. Jennen, the founder of the line, still had a reputation for tolerance and reasonableness generations after his death. Richard was not known for either tolerance or reasonableness, and tolerance and reasonableness seemed to be coming into fashion. Brander had carefully cultivated his own public image to match his ancestor's. Brander signaled his advocates, many of whom had been injured financially or even physically by Richard's ambitions, to do their parts. They spoke in turn, many of them about the danger to other Houses if House Harlan collapsed, as it seemed on the verge of doing for lack of leadership. Most of them, though they did not say so directly for fear of being named cowards, spoke for the change in order to lessen House Harlan's power in Council and outside it.

"Call the question," someone over toward Druma cried.

"Karne Halarek, Lharr in Halarek," the Halarek said at the same time.

Brander, assuming the chairman would call the question, twisted in his seat to see who had stood in Druma. If it had been in Druma. Druma was a gutless House. On the other hand, Odonnel had very recently attacked Druma in a bald-faced power bid and Odonnel had always been tightly connected to

Harlan, especially Richard Harlan, so perhaps Druma thought to get back at Odonnel by emasculating Richard.

Brander smiled at the word that had come to mind. By this time, Richard should be very close to that. He reminded himself to check with Gebbits when he got home and have the doctor examine Richard again on some pretext or other. If the count were low enough, or gone, Brander would consider telling Richard about it.

To be forever free of your interminable bragging, Richard. To know that you will never produce get to challenge me—

"Thank you, Frem Chairman." Karne bowed slightly in the chairman's direction, a courtesy almost never extended to Freemen.

Halarek! He's letting the Halarek speak first!

"I've listened carefully to this debate, lords and Freemen, and I see danger. Lord Richard thinks his life is at risk. He may be right. That's not for me to judge. Harlan is disintegrating, true, but my experience with similar events on other worlds leads me to think Harlan will survive intact until Lord Richard's sentence ends and he can better attend to his House's business. To change the line of inheritance while the ruling lord is still living sets a dangerous precedent. Never, in all of Starker IV's history, has the line of a living ruler been removed from the succession. When the line of inheritance has changed, it has been on the death of an entire line, as has so nearly happened in my House."

Karne Halarek looked with set face at Richard. "You know the history of my House's feud with Harlan, lords and Freemen. You know the lengths to which Lord Richard and his supporters have gone to destroy my Family. You know I buried my two young nephews just this morning."

Halarek looked down at the battered surface of his Family's prep table and his forefinger followed a groove for a short distance. "So when I speak against changing the line of inheritance, you know how serious this matter seems to me." He swept the chamber with his peculiar golden eyes. "Don't change the succession in Harlan, lords and Freemen, or we'll have feuds and wars such as this world has never seen in all its violent history."

Halarek sat down. The room was silent.

"Question!"

This time the call came from Emil von Schuss, baron in von Schuss. Gashen motioned to the bailiffs who always hovered at the doors to the back of the room, awaiting orders. The bailiffs came rapidly down all the aisles, distributing paper ballots and counting voters at the same time. When they had finished distributing, they counted again.

Double counting! That's Halarek's doing! I know that's Halarek's doing!

Brander shook his head at the allies who looked toward him for advice. The plan to load the ballots with votes for Jennen would not work after a double count; it would only mean everyone had to sit for the count, be notified of the overage, and vote again and wait again and . . .

Bastard, Halarek. You bastard! You'll pay for interfering. By all the gods, you'll pay!

Brander watched helplessly as his plan crumbled and the vote to change the succession in Harlan failed. He would have to change the succession by killing Richard. Richard had no legitimate heirs of his body. His death would change the succession. And he would get back at Halarek. He would kill someone in Halarek whose loss would really hurt the Lharr and his House. He wanted the Lharr to *feel* the loss. He wanted the Halarek to see his dreams destroyed as Brander's own had just been destroyed. Who should it be? Charlotte? Lady Kathryn? The baby boy? He must do it soon, though, so the Lharr could not miss the connection between the speech in Richard's favor and the death.

CHAPTER 17

To make Halarek pay, Brander needed to find the Gypsy caravan that had helped Odonnel, sort of, carry Lady Kathryn to Breven. He began searching the evening after Council. He listened to his spies and read the portions of their reports that had to do with Gypsy activities. He visited many freecities, because the Freemen often traded for Gypsy crafts. He examined Gild pix of the caravan routes with great care. Without the Gypsies, Brander's revenge on Halarek could not take place, because the Gypsies had a unique way of killing secretly.

Over several years, Brander had observed that people who injured or killed Gypsies almost always died. Odonnel's executioner had been the most notable death, just a little more than a year ago. He had cut the tongue out of a Gypsy girl, who had seen Garren strangling one of his paramours, because Garren wanted no witness talking to the freecity's court. The executioner had gotten sick within days and had died for two weeks, slowly, in agony, his flesh falling from his bones in stinking pieces.

Other offenders had died in other ways, some faster, some slower, but always in agony, and the deaths came too quickly to be disease. They had to have been caused by poison, though how poison had been gotten to Odonnel's executioner, safe in Odonnel's house in Erinn, Brander could not understand. No Gypsies worked in Erinn, no Gypsies worked on Odonnel Holding, but poison it had to have been and poison he would have. No one would even think of poison in connection with a death in Halarek. The Gharr did not use poison. It was cowardly. It was unmanly. But it would work. If the Gypsies could get poison into Odonnel, Brander Harlan could get poison into Halarek.

Brander did little traveling in his search. If a Gild photo seemed to include a likely caravan, Brander would fly over the caravan personally to check it out; otherwise, he let his spies do the work. *His* spies, loyal only to him. Richard had withdrawn his access to the Family Harlan spy network the day after Council, but Brander had financed his own spy network for some time against just such a possibility. Withdrawing his privilege, though, that was a warning. Richard suspected him. If he did not already know Brander's plan, he suspected it. Richard was tightly confined, though, and Brander was free. Brander did not worry about what Richard would do to him, because he did not intend to go near Richard again until it was time to deliver the death-blow.

Brander wanted no one in the House to think he had changed for fear of Richard, now Richard was showing his distrust, so, during the three-week search, Brander kept mostly to his usual routine. He made one small change: He posted a soldier guard at his door at night. On the inside, so it would not be obvious, but a guard just the same. It was here, guarded and alone, that Brander read his personal spies' reports.

The reports from his spy in Halarek troubled him. He looked them over again and again. The Larga was not pregnant by Richard and her non-pregnancy had been verified by the specialist Alterinn. That he had expected. If she *had* been pregnant, he would have to have had a serious and painful (for the physician) talk with Dr. Gebbits. He had not expected the Lharr to make a public announcement of Alterinn's findings, though. He knew something of the Halarek's pride and had assumed one tri-d humiliation would be enough. That the Halarek made such an announcement probably indicated how heavy his losses in allies and freecity support were after the first tri-d announcement. Apparently, the Lharr believed he had little left to lose and much to gain by proving as well as could be proved that any child Charlotte bore would be his. The Lharr Halarek clearly did not shrink from doing the difficult, if it had to be done.

The more Brander thought about it, the more Brander believed that second humiliating announcement had actually been aimed at Richard, now he had tri-d privileges. It might have been a subtle dig suggesting Richard *couldn't* sire a child.

Brander crumpled the reports into a ball. Richard would have had no reason to watch that cast. The abbot would not have let him. Humiliation in Halarek had nothing to do with danger to Richard, and therefore, the abbot would not have let him see the cast.

But the abbot would probably not prohibit Richard calls from friends. That had been an important point in Richard's argument to Council, that his life depended on having many sources of information (*other than me was the implication*). Richard's friends, perhaps a vassal, perhaps a still-loyal cousin, might call to tell him about that tri-d cast and about the subtle insult—

You're letting your imagination run away with you! There's no reason for Halarek to suspect Richard's infertility, let alone my arrogant cousin. Get a grip on yourself! You're too near your goal to panic.

Brander flattened the ball of papers and smoothed the sheets so he could read them again. There was an old report from Richard's deep spy inside Halarek and a new one from Brander's own, but neither could tell him anything about conditions inside the Larga's quarters. The deaconesses were incorruptible, the soldiers liked their lord more than they liked Harlan money, and there was, of course, absolutely no point in trying to get anything out of the dragon who lived with the Larga. Brander had now lost the use of the deep spy in Halarek, of course, thanks to Richard, but that man had not been able to get close to the Larga anyway, so that did not matter.

Brander's spy did report that the Lharr entered the Larga's quarters only during the Larga's most fertile week. That was interesting, considering the Larga's proven seductiveness. That was very interesting. It looked as if the Lharr had lost his obsession with his wife. Evidence of her wanton behavior had destroyed her power over him, probably.

The Halarek's a prude, but he has more iron in him than I'd thought. Doing without may be punishment for him, but it's a worse punishment for her by far. And his method of heir-making is efficient. I have to give him that. It's efficient. He should have an heir by spring.

The Lharr's heirs were *his* problem. They would not be Brander's problem until Richard was dead. The Lharr's interference in Harlan, though, *was* Brander's problem and he intended to take care of it as quickly as possible, but it was necessary to find the Gypsies first.

Near the end of the third week after Council, Gild satellite pix showed a caravan on the plains of Gormsby Holding, near the southern Frozen Zone. Brander moved quickly, because Gypsies were notoriously elusive, especially if they learned someone wanted to get hold of them, as these must have by now. He slipped out of the manor house, unnoticed, he hoped, and flew to the spot where the caravan had been last seen. It was no longer there, but wagon tracks still showed in the drying autumn grasses and Brander sent his flitter skimming close to the ground along that trail.

The Gypsies had set up camp in a hollow and were washing clothes, mending wagons, and doing the other maintenance work that people who live on the road must attend to now and then. Brander circled the camp once, so the Gypsies would expect him, then set the flitter down out of sight, to avoid frightening the cart animals.

Brander walked up the rise, trying to look both confident and not aggressive. After all, what could one man do against a caravan? Just the same, it did not hurt to be careful. Three men waited just over the top, blocking the path into the hollow. The center man, a stocky person with thick, black, curly hair and a curly, graying beard, took a step forward from the rest.

"What's your business here, stranger?" His voice was rough but not discourteous.

"I'm Brander, out of House Harlan, and I have business to discuss with the headman."

"I'm the headman. What do you want?"

"It's customary among my people to exchange names before conducting business."

The stocky man set himself more solidly in the path. "Among mine, it's not."

And either the word "Harlan" doesn't mean anything to you or you're very good at hiding it. Maybe I should have said I was Odonnel.

But Brander remembered the surprising carnage this Gypsy band had made of trained Odonnel soldiers outside Breven and decided Odonnel would not have been a good name to try.

"Your business, sir?" one of the other two prompted.

"Private. As I've already said. With the headman."

Brander felt more than saw the men bristle, but the headman waved the other two back. Brander waited until the men were well out of earshot. Even then, he spoke in a low voice.

"I have a personal matter I want to take care of very quietly. I have observed, as I've said, that over the years people who kill or injure Gypsies die slowly and in great pain. In every instance of Gypsy injury or death that Council has record of, the perpetrator died."

The headman had clasped his hands behind his back. He stared at Brander and said nothing.

"I have been injured and I want such a solution to my problem."

The headman pursed his mouth and looked up at the sky.

"I'll pay very well." *Why doesn't he say anything?*

"We are not murderers," the headman said at last, angrily. "We do not kill for money, sir, only for honor."

Honor? In this day and age? "I'm not asking you to murder anyone, only to supply me enough poison to kill one man quickly, if quickly's an option."

"*Poison,* sir?"

Don't play the idiot with me! "Every perpetrator has died. What else kills silently and without visible wounds? That you use poison for vengeance might be information Council—and the Gild, since you seem to deal much with the Gild—would be interested in."

The headman was frowning. "Are you threatening us, sir?"

Brander swallowed his impatience. "Threatening? Of course not. Why would I want to threaten you? I only want to pay you extremely well for a small amount of a deadly substance you obviously own several varieties of."

The headman turned away. "Get such from your own people. We don't soil our hand in gorgio quarrels."

"Wait! Can you really walk away from a hundred decacredits, Gild currency?"

The headman turned back. "*Gild* currency, sir?"

"That's what I said." Brander could not keep the impatience from his voice.

"Something might be arranged for *Gild* currency, sir. Our last 'employer' used blackmail and force as payment. We returned his payment in full, sir."

Brander knew the headman meant the killing of so many Odonnel soldiers outside Breven. It would be hard money or nothing, then. Brander hoped he could unearth that much Gild currency.

"I'll have to return to my holding to gather so much—"

"Two hundred decacredits, sir."

"Preposterous!"

"Two-fifty sir. On this matter I do not haggle. I inform you of the price."

"But—"

"Three hundred, sir."

Brander shut his mouth. *Three hundred! I'll have to raid the vaults to get that. If Richard hasn't already thought to lock them against me.* He looked off across the hollow, as if considering the price. "I'll bring it to you here, tomorrow."

The headman shook his head. "You may have been seen coming here, at least by the Gild. That's how you found us, wasn't it? Through Gild pix?" He did not wait for an answer. "Meet me at the foot of the tower of the Old Ones that lies at the edge of the Great Waste, where the mountains of the Frozen Zone jut into the grasses. Two days. Noon."

The headman spun and walked away without giving Brander a moment to question or reply.

Two days was longer than he wanted to wait. That would mean it would be almost a week before he could figure a way to use the stuff and get away. Almost a month since Halarek spoke up so surprisingly for Richard. But it would have to be so. He had no choice. Karne Halarek must pay, and before he could miss the connection between his Council speech and the death.

The Gypsies and I are alike in this. We take our revenge quickly and secretly. Only the offender knows who's responsible.

CHAPTER 18

Karne left the Larga's quarters as rapidly as he could without looking like he was running away. The process of engendering a child on the woman who had betrayed him in so many ways was ugly and humiliating, something to be gotten through as quickly as possible. Karne felt grateful toward Lady Agnes every time he went to Charlotte, a feeling he had never thought to have toward the acerbic old lady. It was she who had convinced Charlotte that physical resistance to these necessary visits would be foolish and perhaps dangerous, considering her sins and Karne's temper, tightly restrained too long. Lady Agnes and Karne knew he could never hurt a woman badly, but Charlotte did not, and her own imagination kept her in line.

Still, the process was nothing like it had been. Karne could no longer summon up the wild desire he had once felt. He could no longer even think of her as beautiful. Her beauty was a trap into which he had fallen. As Shjell and Richard and the unknown Harlan who had helped her with the preventatives had fallen. Perhaps even Brander.

Maybe one child would be enough. Then he would not have to go through this unpleasantness fertile week after fertile week in another year. But Karne knew one child was never enough in the Houses of Starker IV.

Karne made a circuit by the chapel before returning to his quarters for the day, but time spent in prayer did not help. There was no way to ease the burden of Charlotte and of providing Halarek with heirs. Karne rose from the altar rail and went to his quarters.

He commed the kitchen for an All Night and then flopped into the old leather chair that had been such a comfort to him throughout his boyhood. Some of that comfort lingered in it still, though he had been a man five years now. He shut his eyes and let his thoughts go where they would. That was a mistake. The thoughts spun round and round the announcement he had made of Charlotte's non-pregnancy, though that was nearly a month past. In front of everyone on Starker IV, he had, for the second time, declared himself a cuckold and Charlotte a whore. What had he to lose? Her adventure with Richard had cost him so many alliances it would be years before he would again be in a place to influence Council. So he had made the announcement to at least be sure children from this cursed union would not be called bastards. The word of Dr. Alterinn of House Odonnel about Charlotte's condition added the final surety of that. House employee or not, no Freeman would lie to help an enemy of his employer, just as no House would dare punish a Freeman for telling the truth, even if the truth helped an enemy. Everyone who had tuned in would believe Alterinn.

Even in memory, the humiliation of revealing details of Charlotte's sex life and history to anyone who wanted to listen burned, but this time the humiliation was worse for Charlotte and her House than for him. This announcement would cost House Rhiz a heavy price in prestige and allies. There was satisfaction in that, at least. Cherek Rhiz had defrauded House Halarek. Now he would pay politically for as long as anyone remembered Charlotte.

Karne shut off the circling thoughts. He would do what had to be done and no more. He stood abruptly and took a quick turn around the room. Thinking about Charlotte did that to him more and more these days, making him want to run or hit someone or break something. He hoped the All Night would help him regain control, the precious control of which he had once been so proud. Before Charlotte.

There was a knock on the door, then the door opened and a page about eight years old stuck his head cautiously around the edge. "My—my lord?"

Do I really look as fierce as that? Karne asked himself. He forced his taut face muscles to relax a little. "My All Night?"

The boy looked relieved, nodded, and came more confident-ly into the room. He set a steaming mug on the rok-hide chest and started to leave.

One of the new ones, Karne thought. They never have courage enough to say anything to me that's not required. "Have you been in Halarek long, son?" he asked. "I don't recognize you."

The boy stopped and turned to look at his lord in surprise. He nodded slowly. Karne beckoned the child toward him and gradually, over almost half an hour, coaxed out of the boy who his Family was, where his personal family lived, and why he had come as a page into Halarek. By the time the boy skipped out of the room with a small, new pocket knife in his hand, Karne felt cleaner and less depressed.

By morning, life looked better, largely because Karne had no need to see Charlotte for another twenty-one days. He sat up, swung his legs over the edge of his bed, and stretched. Kit and Nik and Jemmy were coming for a visit. Dr. Alterinn was due to give a report on Karne and Charlotte's fertility tests. Both of those should be cheering events.

"They can't hurt, some fertility tests," Othneil had said when Alterinn had come to examine and test Charlotte, "and Alterinn's here, anyway. Let him do tests on the two of you to be sure there's nothing slowing the process down." Othneil had looked at Karne with genuine concern. "You two have been married for almost a year, with nothing to show for it."

Karne stood and stretched and headed toward the ward-robe. The results of Dr. Othneil's tests should be in by late afternoon and the rest of the House's business was winding down in preparation for winter. Come Uhl, only seven or eight weeks, winter would shut everything down and House Halarek could enjoy four months or so of peace and qui-et. Peace and quiet, rare things on this world. Come Uhl— Karne had never looked forward to Uhl before. Always before, winter had been a time of tense waiting for spring. Enemies plotted sieges over winter and announced the laying of siege forty days before the first thaws were due, so siege could be laid the first moment men could be moved. Kidnappings and assassinations could be prepared for very thoroughly in four months. Political conspiracies were planned using closed-channel tri-d.

This winter Karne was not going to worry about political problems. House Harlan was too disorganized and Richard too closely confined to cause serious trouble. Odonnel rarely moved without Harlan. Charlotte should soon be pregnant, and if not, she at least could get into no more trouble. Roul was paying his fine while laying in enough supplies to withstand a spring siege, though he did not know his lord knew what he was doing. Rhiz had resisted financial pressure to re-ally itself with Harlan, at least so far, and there was nothing much Richard could do to increase pressure on Cherek after the middle of Uhl. As for the former Harlan vassals, fighting for Halarek against Odonnel had seemed to settle some of the more restless of them: They seemed to fit into the Halarek way of governing more afterward. Karne decided he did not need to worry about any of them rebelling in the spring. The settlement between McNeece and Kath seemed to be working out, too, to their satisfaction as well as Karne's.

Karne took a slow, deep breath and let it out with luxurious slowness. Of the important matters that had needed taking care of at the time of Odonnel's attack on Druma, only Druma's swearing of fealty was yet undone. And the engendering of an heir. Druma's swearing-in could be scheduled for the last week of the month. That would force Odonnel to stew more than two weeks extra and would make scheduling *his* taking of Druma's oath before the winter much more difficult. Karne looked thoughtfully at the ceiling. Perhaps he could reschedule Druma's swearing so it would not *be* possible for Odonnel to schedule Druma's oath before spring. Karne was whistling by the time he was dressed and ready to go down to the library for fast-breaking and paperwork.

When Karne stepped out onto the little platform at the top of the iron stair, he saw Weisman nervously arranging and rearranging the papers on the worktable and the books standing down the middle of it. Weisman looked up and his rearranging stopped.

"My lord, news from Odonnel."

Karne hurried down the stairs. "From Dr. Alterinn? It's early."

Weisman looked at Karne with a strange, almost savage, expression in his eyes. "One of the men in my network found a document, milord, in a place in House Odonnel where it should never have been, Dr. Othneil's files. It's a top-security House Harlan document concerning Lord Richard and some *very* personal matters. Perhaps someone had stored it in Dr. Alterinn's files for transfer at some safer time. Perhaps Dr. Alterinn did. Perhaps he intended blackmail. Ordinarily, I would've held it until I could get a medical expert to look at it, but, whatever its background, I thought this document was important enough that you should read it yourself immediately." Weisman handed Karne a thick envelope and watched intently as he opened it and unfolded the paper inside.

Karne skimmed the paper. "These are medical terms, right enough, Weisman, but just being about Richard doesn't make them important."

Weisman bristled. "I've run Halarek's spy network since before your time, Lord Karne. I don't disturb my lord with frivolous matters. Read the sheet carefully. The information on it means death to whoever took it, if I've deciphered it correctly. Because of this, I took the liberty of awakening Dr. Othneil and Frem Orkonan, my lord. Dr. Othneil can surely translate the more technical terms and double-check my estimation of the meaning." Weisman picked up two books from the center of the table and walked to the back of the room to shelve them.

Karne watched him. Weisman slid the books into place, then busied himself at the far end of the room. He moved stiffly, as if angry or offended. Or, perhaps, afraid.

Karne hefted the envelope. It was thick, quality paper, not plasti, and bore the frank of House Odonnel. Karne walked over to the fireplace, waved a hand at it to start the flames going, and sat down in one of the chairs to read. He slid the envelope's contents out. They could not rightly be called a letter. Inside were several sheets of brief, handwritten summaries of some of Richard Harlan's medical records. The dates at the heads of the summaries were five years apart, but within the past year, the gap had narrowed rapidly to one month apart. The summaries seemed to show the results of a series of fertility tests, beginning with the test given by the genetic council to all Harlan boys when they turn fifteen.

Karne turned the sheet of paper over, then checked inside the envelope. There were no notations, no message identifying the author or the thief or the purpose of the theft, not even explanatory notes about the medical terms. Karne read the document again, slowly. Many of the terms were not in his vocabulary, but the gist seemed clear enough: Richard's fertility was declining rapidly. The last test, given in late Verdain, showed fertility so low as to be almost non-existent.

Karne let his hands and the papers in them rest in his lap. His eyes looked at the wall ahead of him, but he did not see it. Clearly, the summaries had not been meant to be seen by anyone outside Harlan's medical facilities, probably not by anyone but Family Harlan's physician, Dr. Gebbits. Harlan's genetic council could not know about them, or more Harlan cousins would have voted in Council to install the Jennen line. Karne also felt sure Richard did not know, because knowing what the summaries contained *had* to take the swagger out of such a man. Someone had taken a great risk, going into Harlan and copying out the important details of files as damaging as these. How had this report come into Odonnel and from Odonnel here? Alterinn? Was he also the copier? His specialty would probably give him access to Harlan files . . .

Dr. Othneil came through the main door, not bothering to shut it behind himself. The sharp, determined click of his bootheels identified him before he came into Karne's range of vision. "Weisman said the matter was urgent. What's the problem, my lord?"

Karne glanced at Weisman's back in irritation. "The matter may be urgent, but it's not my problem. It seems to be Richard Harlan's." Karne handed Othneil the test summaries.

Othneil went through them quickly. "Umm," was all he said at first. He read them again, more slowly, then sat in the chair opposite Karne.

"The handwriting is Alterinn's, for all the lack of a signature. We've been corresponding on medical matters for more than twenty years. I suggest copying these and then burning the originals so no one can learn from the writing who stole them." Othneil glanced at the unread sheets in his other hand. "These are in medical-student code. It's a special way of abbreviating we used to take notes quickly. I'll look at them in a minute." He laid the coded sheets in his lap.

"The tests here seem to show that Richard Harlan will soon be unable to sire children. Gebbits has been testing him for disease and getting fertility measures at the same time. That suggests Lord Richard doesn't know these tests were done. Alterinn commed me *your* test results just a short while ago, by the way. Those show there's no reason why you and the Larga can't produce children quickly and on a regular basis." Othneil's face took on a severe cast. "But the Larga probably now has an unpleasant disease. Curable, my lord, but unpleasant."

Anger stirred in Karne. *On top of everything else!* "Why didn't you tell me this before, Othneil? You checked her when she returned."

"She had no signs of it, milord. May not have any still. This has a long latency period, but infection is almost certain. I wouldn't know about it yet if I didn't have these reports. I'll start both of you on a treatment program today. Stay away from her until your supply of pills is gone."

Othneil's eyes strayed back to the coded sheets. He glanced at Karne and, with no objection forthcoming, read slowly through them. Afterward, he looked unseeingly at the wall for a long time, his mouth pursed.

He cleared his throat and sat straighter. "Alterinn added these to the summaries, but in code, to explain what was going on in case he did not survive." Othneil looked down at the papers. "His tests on the two of you led him to wonder why, with Lord Richard's vaunted sex life, there were so few of his bastards around. The larga, for instance, had had enough time with him in Breven to conceive. If Richard has been infected for a while, though, long enough to produce symptoms for Gebbits to find, that could have lessened his fertility and that would have explained the infrequency of bastards, because House Harlan is not a believer in preventatives.

"Alterinn says here he asked Gebbits about tests—Richard *must* have taken such tests, regularly, considering his appetites—and Gebbits was evasive. More than evasive. He refused to give any information at all on security grounds, though revealing who carries an infectious disease is, of necessity, commonly shared medical information. Even after Alterinn explained that he needed the information to treat the larga for anything she might have been exposed to, Gebbits refused to share test results, said there had never been a problem. You *know* that couldn't be true. All Alterinn got were the standard tests given at puberty and every five years after that."

Othneil rattled the stiff paper. "It's obvious why Gebbits lied: He had put the tests for disease and for fertility on the same record each time; therefore, to see the disease record is to see the fertility record. That Gebbits *kept* the fertility results suggests he had to show them to someone. They'd be too dangerous to keep otherwise. That measurement has fallen precipitously over the last six months. I think Alterinn knew Gebbits was lying and checked for himself. Disease *might* have had some bearing on the Larga Charlotte's not conceiving." Othneil shook his head. "It probably wasn't even very difficult for Alterinn to find the information: He consults in Harlan frequently and has complete access to the files and, as I said, Gebbits probably had to show the results to someone. What amazes me is that he would leave documents like these *in* the regular files."

"Who would look? Who but Richard would care?"

Othneil looked grim. "If that's what he thought, he made a fatal error. Richard isn't likely to let anyone live who knows he can't get heirs." Othneil looked over his shoulder at the tense, unmoving Weisman and lowered his voice. "I don't think this decline is natural, milord, or disease caused. There are drugs that have this effect. They're usually used for diseases that depend on male hormones to survive, but the effect on a healthy man is the same: used long enough, a man becomes sterile."

"Will Alterinn confirm your opinion?"

Othneil snorted. "He's done enough, milord, providing these summaries."

"Alterinn's an Odonnel man. Why did he take this risk for an enemy House?"

Othneil looked at Karne as he might at the town idiot. "A physician swears to do no harm, milord. Gebbits has definitely done harm. I don't believe there's any other way the results can have fallen off so sharply. That you got these summaries shows Alterinn doesn't believe there is, either. Gebbits has betrayed his patient, probably for money. We're physicians first, my lord, Alterinn and I, and employees of the Houses second. This is deadly information. Alterinn took great risks to get this and even greater to send it to you. You're the only man who can use this information without being immediately killed."

Karne looked at Othneil quizzically.

"Richard is confined, milord, and he has only one or two spies in this House. Spies he can't reach quickly without your knowledge, since he must use the tri-d to do it. Men in Odonnel and Harlan are at far, far greater risk. Plus, for them, these"—he rattled the papers at Karne—"represent the most basic sort of betrayal. Betrayal means death and in Odonnel and Harlan, every fourth person is either a spy or an assassin." Othneil looked at the paper, his face darkening. "Of course, the moment you use these, my lord, Gebbits is dead, but he deserves to be."

Karne leaned back in the chair and looked at the physician with interest. He had not known Othneil had any interest in Family politics and he had never even imagined that Othneil, who fought death so hard, could accept death for anyone easily. "How would you suggest I use these?" he asked with interest.

"You can tell Lord Richard outright, by tri-d, though that risks Alterinn's life. You could send him the summaries, transcribed, of course, so the handwriting won't betray Alterinn. That's what I'd do. It's Gebbits's death sentence, as I said, but he's conspired to end an entire Family line. How ever you do it, if you tell Lord Richard, you may earn yourself a respite from Harlan attacks for a time, because the physical changes in Lord Richard stop when the drug stops, so the sooner you tell him, the sooner he can stop eating or drinking whatever had the medication in it. If these summaries are accurate, Lord Richard can still have children, though the getting of them will take a lot longer than any House will like, but even that possibility won't last more than two or three months longer."

Karne nodded. The advantages of telling Richard what was being done to him were overwhelming. Richard still had enough power to take care of the perpetrator. Dr. Gebbits, physician in Harlan, and his unknown employer, were as good as dead.

"If you wish, milord, I'll set the network in Harlan to work finding Gebbits's employer at once." Weisman's voice came from close behind Karne's chair.

Karne started, then turned in anger. "You were eavesdropping, Weisman! I won't have it!"

Weisman smiled deprecatingly. "Eavesdropping, at least elsewhere, is the definition of my job, my lord. It's become a habit. Please excuse me for forgetting that this isn't a proper place."

Karne collected his thoughts. Weisman was right, in a way. Karne sighed. "Excuse my impatience. I've learned it's better to be overcautious than not cautious enough."

Weisman bowed his acceptance. "I'll get right to this matter, my lord." He bowed again and left the room.

Karne watched him leave. That was a trouble with spies: They could not help spying all the time. Karne sighed again. Spies and assassins and armies were how life was for the survivors on this world.

A connected item he had not thought of for a long time came to mind, the visitors list from Breven. Had either von Schuss or Weisman checked it out? Karne checked if he had any other business he had to attend to immediately and could remember none. He stood to go to the tri-d room and saw Orkonan standing beside the worktable.

"I came as called, milord," Orkonan said, "but you seemed so intent I didn't interrupt. I caught some of what you and Dr. Othneil talked about, the rest was too quiet."

Karne summarized what had happened, then told him to com Richard the medical summaries.

Von Schuss's report on Richard's visitors arrived the next day. Orkonan summarized the information at the daily officers' meeting. "All the visitors have been identified, milord, and checked with," Orkonan said. "One doesn't *question* a lord of the Houses, of course, but none of Richard's visitors minded saying they'd been there and a few even said what they'd talked about. Dr. Gebbits's visits would fit with the delivery of the necessary medication, Dr. Othneil says. The only unknowns remaining are the two nameless deacons, who were seen in the halls on 8 Aden. None of the male Retreat Houses had had anyone out that day, Lord Karne, let alone as far afield as Breven." ·

Karne looked across the worktable at Orkonan. "Send the correlations between Gebbits's visits and the probable dosing schedule of the drug to Lord Richard." He looked at Weisman. "Check Brander's whereabouts on that day. I'd bet this holding that those two deacons were Brander and Charlotte on their way back here. Charlotte whined a lot about how long Brander kept her riding. It would be possible to get here from Breven in two days if one rode very hard. I'd guessed three or four days, knowing how Charlotte whines at the slightest refusal of her whims, but two would be possible. Maybe you or Weisman can find out if Brander was seen in either Harlan or Odonnel that day."

Orkonan nodded and left.

A few hours after that, Nik and Kit arrived. Nik's first words were, "Did you hear Jurnig Harlan fell down a flight of stairs yesterday and broke his neck? That leaves only two men between Brander and the head of the Jennen line. Makes his support of the change in succession more interesting, doesn't it?"

Kit gave Karne a quick hug. "Isn't that an interesting bit of news, when he could've told you how big and handsome Jemmy's getting?" Kit laughed and motioned the child's nurse forward.

Karne dutifully admired the baby's thick dark hair, his fine eyes, his sweet smile, then his mother went off to the old nursery to feed her son and put him down for a nap. "It's been a long trip for a five-month-old," Kit called over her shoulder as she hurried down the corridor toward the nearest lift.

Karne and Nik went to the private dining room of the Lharr's personal family, seldom used since Charlotte's arrival. Karne commed for a warm snack and summarized the new medical information while they waited for the food.

Karne sat down and motioned Nik into a nearby chair. "Jurnig Harlan's dead, eh? And Hemmil not so long ago. One an 'accident' and the other a 'heart attack.' "

"That's what House Harlan says."

"I smell a rat." Karne shoved his straying forelock out of his eyes, sat forward, and looked keenly at his best friend. "I'd wager it's the same rat that's been giving me trouble. And you trouble, come to think of it. Kidnapping, Nik. Assassination. Murder. Inciting vassals to rebellion. Sterility pills. Who benefits from Richard dying childless? Who benefits from focusing Richard's attention on women from his worst enemy's House instead of what's happening in his own?"

Nik smiled a small, wintery smile. "A rat with the Harlan nose, no doubt. I'm sure Richard's medical scores will be 'leaked' as soon as they hit zero. The Jennens probably hope to take the dukedom when the cousins rise up in uproar over a duke without possibility of heirs."

"And who benefits from murders in the Jennen line?"

Nik's face grew stern. Karne could almost see memories of what Brander and Richard's plotting had done to Kit pass through his mind. Brander Harlan had not clearly been the center of the plan until now. Until now, Brander had been very skillful in presenting himself as Richard's loyal cousin and aide.

"Brander Harlan," Nik finally answered. "He's third in line now, he was fifth. I'd be willing to bet that the remaining two men between Brander and the top of the Jennen list disappear or die before winter. That will make Brander's plot fairly obvious, but he's probably counting on that making no difference by the time it happens: He'll be so close to being duke that no one will dare oppose him. He wouldn't've had Hemmil and Jurnig killed if he weren't pretty sure he'd get away with that." Nik's face drew into even sterner lines. "My woman he takes, then yours," he said.

"Because they were connected to me," Karne added bitterly. "I think I'd kill myself if I had to live as a woman in most Houses on this world." He shut his eyes and willed that darkness away. "I sent those summaries to Richard."

"Goodbye, Brander Harlan," Nik said, with satisfaction in his voice.

CHAPTER 19

Brander Harlan heard the buzz of an approaching flier.

Just when I get to the Great Swamp, where the footing is always bad and running is almost as risky as waiting for the flier.

Brander jabbed his spurs into his horse, which sprang forward and raced into the trees as fast as it could. Brander slumped forward over the horse's neck to make his outline harder to identify. It did not help that the trees were losing their leaves for winter. He pulled the horse to a stop as soon as they were completely under the trees.

There were fliers out yesterday, too, looking. There may be riders out as well, and just when I was so close to taking Richard's place. Damn Halarek for an interfering bastard!

Behind him he heard the whisper of the Ednov River as it ran to its end in the morasses, quicksand, and lagoons of the swamp. Overhead, the flier buzzed closer. It flew over, followed by two others perhaps five hundred meters on either side of it. All were Harlan green.

Richard really wants me, to send men over Halarek in marked machines!

Then Brander remembered it had been Halarek who had given Richard the test results. *That whoreson swine! It wasn't any of his business.*

Richard had told Brander by tri-d what he had just learned. He had apparently lured Dr. Gebbits to Breven on the pretext of a consultation with Dr. Alterinn. Clever Richard. Gebbits had obviously swallowed whatever the story was, because he had been visible in the abbot's office, hovering in the background of the tri-d cast. Richard had given Halarek every credit for the discovery. Then he had jerked Gebbits into camera range and slit his throat before the abbot could blink an eye.

Richard had looked directly at Brander then, and said, "Watch every step, you treacherous . . ." and Richard had run on for some time in words too terrible to remember. "You're a dead man," Richard said finally, "at my hands or Halarek's. You'd better start running now."

Brander clenched his teeth and looked toward Ontar. He had started, but not into Zinn yet. He had a better chance in the Desert of Zinn among the convict Runners and their gods than he did among the holdings. But he had one debt to pay first.

Many kilometers to the northeast of Brander's hiding place rose the foothills of the mountains of Zinn. On the plains side of those foothills, a kilometer or two out onto the grass, the com dishes and entrance shelters of Ontar manor threw small noon shadows on the ground. Closer still were the com dishes and entrance shelters of the freecity of Ontar. Brander touched the tiny vial of Gypsy poison that hung like an amulet from his neck, then repeated the litany. The Gharr did not think in terms of poison. No one used poison. This would be a killing without clues.

He dropped the vial and looked at his hand. It was still dark brown, like suntan.

The stain lasts. Good. No one will suspect a farm serf come to work in the kitchens for the winter.

Brander pulled gloves from a tab on his belt and slipped them over his hands. They were black horsehide, with silver embroidery and the silver insignia of House Justin. He held his hands out to admire the effect.

A minor cousin of House Justin comes to shop in Ontar because it's closer to his smallholding than any of Justin's freecities or manor towns. What could be more natural?

He pulled a soft black hat with the same silver insignia from an inside pocket of his jacket and set it on his head. It drooped low over his forehead and ears, shadowing his face.

The latest fashion. How convenient for me that it draws attention to itself and away from my unfortunate nose. Harlan hasn't married into Justin enough to produce Harlan noses there. A disguise within a disguise within a disguise.

He felt some satisfaction in that. No one would connect the serf to the Justin or to the prefet of Blues, nor the prefet of Blues to the Justin. Brander patted his horse's neck, then spurred it forward toward the freecity.

Once there, Brander led the horse into the animal-entrance shelter, tied the horse in the lift, stepped back out, and pressed the button that would send the lift down to Ontar's stabling area. The horse's saddle tag would identify it as a Justin horse and its care would be billed to that House. Months from now, perhaps, the stable's business manager might com Justin to ask when it planned to reclaim its animal.

I'll go in and leave as a serf, and no one will ever know how an assassin managed to kill the Larga. I'll get back at both of them at once.

The thought steadied him. This was a very dangerous project. But he would carry it off, as he had so many others. Life was meaningless without danger.

Brander stepped into the passenger lift and, moments later, out into the noisy craft-center plaza, where serfs sold the goods they made in their spare time. There were brightly embroidered tunics and skirts, scarves woven in curious patterns and textures, carved wooden toys and furniture, leather goods, and plants that grew indoors.

Brander stood at the edge of the plaza, inhaling the special smell of that place, a combination of hot cooking oil, onions, tam-tam flowers, sweat, and fresh-cut wood. He looked around. Only serfs moved about the plaza at the moment. A real waste, all this potential serf work time, spent for the serfs' benefit and not for Halarek's.

Ah, well, I've always said he was a fool.

Brander sauntered toward the center of the city. Somewhere beyond that were the alleyways that led to the door into the lowest level of Ontar manor. Somewhere between here and there, he would find a prefet of Blues about his size. Or perhaps he would have to find one on the lower levels of Ontar manor itself. He played for a moment with the idea of appearing in his Justin gear in Ontar.

Maybe Halarek would blame the death on Justin, then. Serve them right, not stopping my cousins from fighting and breaking away while Justin was trustee of Harlan.

It might be a thrill, but it would be stupid. A prefect of Blues can just disappear among the rest of them. Someone from Justin is distinctive. Justin would be commed. Halarek would learn no one from Justin was here today.

Brander strolled through the city, stopping in this shop and that, eating a snack in an inn near city center, buying a belt in the square from which the alley to Ontar manor went. Every moment, he watched for spies, followers, assassins. Richard had said Halarek was after him, too. It would have been surprising if he were not.

I did lead the raid against the deVree wedding procession. I did arrange Charlotte's disappearance. I did arrange Ennis's killing (though perhaps that did not matter to Lady Kathryn, since she had loved Lord Nicholas all the time). No, Halarek holds no fondness for me, either.

After one last look over his shoulder (an alley was a very quiet place to kill someone, as he had plenty of reason to know), Brander entered the alley. He waited at its entrance a moment, his back to the square, to let his eyes adjust to the much dimmer light. The serfs who lived here did not need the day/night lights the Freemen lined the streets with. It would have been a waste of money. One of the few signs of prudence on the Freemen's part.

Brander walked to the first of the alcoves that were used to store street-cleaning supplies. He slipped inside, removed the Justin clothes, and dropped the hat and gloves with their Justin insignia into a can of caustic. He resealed the can's lid carefully and stepped out into the alley again in the clothing of a kitchen serf.

By the time anyone learns there's something in the caustic, it will be too late to tell what. If anyone opens the caustic soon enough to find anything, that is.

Brander let his eyelids droop and took up the springy walk of a clodhopper.

Over the furrows. Eyes squinted against the sun until he can't open them completely anymore. Strong arms. Weak brain. No one expects much of a farm serf. That's why they work in the kitchen and scullery.

The path to Ontar's lower levels did not proceed straight there, as Brander had hoped, but zigzagged from one alleyway to another. Dark blue arrows with green-tipped tails, painted at women's eye level, marked the way. Farther in, the walls dripped, making the floor slippery and dank. Brander heard the clank of military equipment. He ducked into an alcove and waited, as a serf would have done. A patrol of four soldiers in Ontar city colors marched past. Brander let out a quiet sigh. A good thing he had heard them in time. His documents were good only for a Halarek Holding serf *inside* Ontar manor.

One more corner and he was in front of a plain black door. He tried it. It was open.

Why wouldn't it be, fool? The manor gets deliveries all day. No one would invade Ontar from here. No respectable assassin would choose a stinking alley for access, either. Relax.

Telling himself to relax was easier than doing it. Hope of deposing Richard was gone. Even hope of living comfortably in Harlan was gone. He was going to have to live on the run, but he was going to pay Halarek back first.

He's destroyed my life. With one flip of a com-tech's switch, Karne Halarek destroyed my life.

Brander pulled open the door and sprinted up the steps behind it. *I was going to be rich, I was going to marry well, I was going to control what was once and would have been again the most powerful House on Starker IV, and Karne Halarek finds Richard's test results and tells him about them.*

The door at the top was closed. Brander laid his ear against it. He heard no sounds from the other side. That could be because there were no sounds or it could be because the door was soundproofed. He had no choice. He had to open it or give up his plan. He opened it a crack. No one was in sight. He ran down the steps, closed the lower door, and ran back up again. Still there was no one in sight. Brander opened the door wider and stepped into the corridor.

Safe, for the moment. Now to find the Blues. Brander moved down the corridor in the direction of the nearest lift. He had had no good map of the serf areas of the freecity, but he had not only had floor maps of Ontar manor, he had memorized them.

He's going to pay, Brander chanted in his head as he walked. He's going to pay, pay, pay.

The nearest lift was really quite close, near one of the arena exits. The smell of horses stung Brander's nose and made his eyes water.

Good old softhearted Halarek. Obviously he doesn't have his serfs beaten often enough to keep his stables as clean as they should be. Brander had a momentary vision of the stable of his smallholding, the smallholding he would have had for relaxation and private pleasures if he had been duke. The stables there would never have stunk like these.

Gone, that dream. Like all the others. Well, I'm going to take Karne Halarek's dreams.

The lift doors opened and Brander stepped inside. He dared go no higher than the kitchen level in these clothes, but there was a small barracks on this side of the kitchen. If he were in luck, there would be a Blues prefet there he could lure out into the corridor, someone about his size.

Luck was with him. At the kitchen level, a squad of Blues crowded into the lift before he could get out. They were laughing, joking, shoving, obviously going off shift and not noticing, or perhaps not caring, that there was a serf huddled in one corner of the lift. Eight prefets and their squadleader. All he had to do was make one of them miss the lift. Brander, head humbly down, said timidly he had to get off on this floor. Two of the more rambunctious prefets shoved and tickled him as he wormed his way toward the door. The door was beginning to close.

"Please, lords," Brander whined, "I have to get out. I'm not allowed above this level."

"Clodhopper," sneered one man, blocking his way. "What happens if we don't let you off?"

Brander whimpered. "I get beaten, lord, till I bleed. An' I don't get nothing to eat tomorrow."

"That won't bother me," his tormentor said.

The door was halfway closed, moving slowly because of the tunic hems and weapons ends telling its safety the opening was not yet clear.

Brander ducked to one side. He really did have to get off on this level. One of the other men stepped to block his way.

"Let be," the squadleader snapped.

At that moment, Brander threw himself through the narrowing opening, taking his first tormentor outside with him by the force of surprise and weight. The door thudded shut and the lift started upward before anyone inside had time to stop it. Brander clubbed the thrashing, cursing man under him with relish until he went limp, then dragged him into the stairwell just around the corner and stripped him.

His uniform fit passably well. It would do for the necessary time. Brander bound and gagged the man with the rope and cloth strips he had brought along and dragged him out of sight under the stair. No one would be likely to look for him there until they had looked everywhere else. And they would look. Eventually. When he did not show up for roll call sometime, or for nightmeal. Brander stuck his head out of the stairwell. The lift was already on level 4. Apparently, the squad figured what had happened was an accident and their comrade would take the next lift up. Clearly, they did not consider the incident important enough to come back after him.

Brander checked the man's bonds again, to make sure they were tight. He stashed the serf clothing under the bottom step, then stood, went over in his mind the path to the Larga's quarters outside the manor house, and reentered the corridor. No one would suspect a prefet of Blues with a message from the Lharr and a small gift. If he were not allowed into her quarters, and from what he had gathered, he would not be, he had worded the message to play on Charlotte's vanity, especially her vanity about her attractiveness to men. One sip of the "aphrodisiac" and she would never tempt a man again. The message could not stand up to careful scrutiny, but it was good enough to pass for the Lharr's handwriting when presented to soldiers who rotated at that post and to an old woman.

It's too bad my usual forger died. Richard's work, too, probably. He could have done Karne Halarek's hand to perfection.

Brander touched the vial around his neck and then the paper tied to his chest so it would stay flat. *No heirs for Karne Halarek now, or ever. When this wife dies, no one will waste another daughter on him, not with women as scarce as they are. And he doesn't have the cash to space out for one. His line is doomed, as he doomed mine.*

CHAPTER 20

A red light flashing, visible from the corner of his eye, made Karne look up from the book he was reading. The emergency blinker on the wall near the iron stair was on. In all his years in Ontar manor, Karne had never seen that light come on. He sprinted to the worktable and slapped the com square on it.

"Lharr here. What is it?"

"Intruder, Lord Karne." The com-tech's voice was crisp and rapid. "A man in serf's clothes knocked a prefect of Blues out of a lift on level one. The soldier just showed up here, milord, naked as the day he was born. He'd been knocked out and stripped, milord."

"How long ago?"

"Fifteen minutes, my lord. He and his squad were due on shift fifteen minutes ago."

"Assume the intruder's an assassin. Notify Wynter. I'm going to the Larga's quarters immediately. We're the only targets here. Tell Weisman to meet me there as soon as possible. I want an observer to keep track of everything that happens."

Karne reached for his stunner, temporarily draped over the back of his chair. He cursed himself for stupidity in sending his bodyguards to nightmeal all at once. No time to locate them now. Wynter would do that.

Orkonan, who had been working on the other side of the table, unsnapped the retainer on his belt knife and had the door on the library supply room side open by the time Karne reached it. "I'm coming, too, Karne," was all Orkonan said.

"Watch my back, then," Karne ordered.

Stunner drawn, Karne sprinted down the hall past the personal-family dining room and the tri-d room, whipped around the corner, and ran past the House officer's quarters to the stair, Orkonan right on his heels. Karne flew down to the next level and along the corridor past Orkonan's office and personal quarters. There was a minor corridor there that led to the guest quarters outside the manor and to the Larga. He almost collided with a very young prefet coming around the corner from the outside.

"My lord!" The young man skidded to a stop and made a quick salute. "Tomas Karel Oroark, milord. Wynter sent me to guard you."

Karne gave him a skeptical glance, but this was no time to argue. Wynter had always been an excellent judge of character. However, the order might be a lie and this the intruder. Karne looked over his shoulder. Orkonan gave a curt nod and continued on his heels.

Several squads of Blues milled in the corridor outside the Larga's door. The highest-ranking officers present seemed to be squadleaders. The soldiers, then, were the manor's patrols, summoned by the emergency flasher but no information beyond where to go. Karne thought he saw Weisman's slightly hunched figure working its way toward him through the crowd. If the Larga had been attacked, or was going to be attacked, there were too many soldiers here and too few elsewhere. The manor could not be left unprotected like this, with tens of hiding holes left unguarded or unsearched.

"All squads but the ones for level three return to your posts," Karne shouted. "You'll be commed if needed." Karne grabbed the first squadleader to pass him. "Send your men ahead," he told the man, who obeyed. "Block all possible exits on your level at once," Karne shouted to everyone. To the squadman in his hands he said, "Go to the com center. Tell Wynter to double or triple the manor patrols at once. Then—"

A piercing keening silenced everyone in the corridor. Lady Agnes. Karne felt turned to ice. He knew, without knowing how, that the intruder/assassin had succeeded. Somehow, the Larga was dead. Nothing else would make Lady Agnes violate her dignity in such a noisy, painful way. Charlotte was dead. Karne pushed through the soldiers toward the door.

Someone behind him shouted, "Look out! A Harlan!"

Karne saw a flash of Blues uniform charging through the crowd around the door. It was so unexpected, everyone stood frozen for a fatal moment. The man drew a beamer. A lean Blues body leaped between Karne and the man. The beamer swung upward.

Brander Harlan! Karne's astonished mind said.

The world narrowed to the tiny segment of corridor with Brander and Karne and the young Blues prefet in it. Karne began leveling his stunner, feeling as if he were moving in slow motion, knowing he would be too late. A man flashed by Karne, knocked Brander's arm down, then jammed a knife into Brander's throat. Brander's beamer bolt sprayed across the stone, setting many soldiers dancing and filling the corridor with the smell of singed leather. The man was Weisman. Brander looked at Weisman with what appeared to be astonishment. His mouth moved, but no sound could come out. He crumpled to the floor.

Everyone stood very still for what seemed to be a long time. An assassin in Blues uniform. A *Harlan* in Blues uniform. A lord so nearly killed. The details took time to soak in.

Karne wet his lips and swallowed very carefully. So close to burning, and this time nothing Othneil could have done would have saved him. A terrible death, burning. His scarred shoulders twitched, remembering the pain without end. The keening from the Larga's quarters went on and on, several women's voices now. Karne wet his lips and swallowed again. That seemed to help him find his voice.

"Frem Weisman." He stopped, choking still on the memory of burning and pain. "Frem Weisman, I owe you and this young man my life."

Weisman bowed ceremonially. "I did only my duty, my lord. If my information had been better, or faster, this man"—he prodded the body with one toe—"would never have entered the manor."

"And you, prefet?" Karne said the words carefully, so his men would not hear his trembling. "I owe you, too, my life."

The young man turned. He could not have been more than sixteen. "Oroark, my lord. I was assigned to protect you. I did no more than that. I regret my equipment malfunction." The young man's freckled face was very pale.

He *knew* what he was risking, Karne told himself. He *knew* and he stood between me and that beamer, anyway.

Karne did not know if he would have had that kind of courage in a similar situation. He bowed to both men, an honor a lharr almost never extended to men not of noble blood. "I'm deeply honored to have such brave men on my staff," he said. "It takes great courage to stand fast when faced with a beamer." He swallowed, trying to make the remaining lump of fear in his throat disappear. "More about this later. We must see what happened inside."

Karne, Oroark, Weisman, Orkonan, and the squadleader for level 3 entered the room. The Larga Charlotte Rhiz-Halarek lay on top of her coverlet, dressed in the barest of night garments. Karne heard Orkonan cough nervously and saw Oroark turn deep red.

"She's dead," he snapped at them all. To the soldiers hovering in the doorway he said, "Send for Othneil to be sure."

He turned back to the Larga and her companions. Lady Agnes sat on the Larga's bed, holding her hand and wailing in ritual grief. The deaconesses who were the Larga's guards stood on either side of the bed, keening, too. When they saw Karne, all three of them turned gray and one of them fainted.

"We didn't know, milord," one of the two remaining deaconesses whispered.

"A prefet of Blues brought a small bottle and your note to her saying this was an aphrodisiac that she was to take, that you had taken some, too, and in an hour you would come to her bed to enjoy its effects."

"The note was in your hand," the first deaconess cried.

"She showed it to us," the other said, almost at the same time.

"Give it to me," Orkonan snapped, holding out his hand.

Karne felt despair. He had protected her in every way he could think of, in every way General Wynter and the best military minds in Halarek could think of, but none of them had considered the possibility that an assassin would dress as one of Halarek's own soldiers. None of them considered poison, or an approach through her greatest weakness, her need to be fiercely desired.

We should have. We should have. We should have, Karne told himself.

But it was too late for blaming. Karne walked to the edge of the bed and laid his fingertips against the Larga's neck vein. It was still. Lady Agnes stopped her keening to hand him a mirror and he held the mirror before the Larga's mouth. There was no mist of breath.

"The Guardians have mercy." Karne said the ritual words with feeling. Charlotte's soul would need mercy.

He knelt beside the bed and said a prayer for her soul and her safe passage to the other side. He rose, stood for a moment looking down at the beautiful woman who had once driven him mad with desire, then squeezed Lady Agnes's shoulder in comfort and appreciation and left the room, his ritual duties completed. Lady Agnes and the deaconesses would prepare the Larga's body for burial. Pastor Jarvis would say more prayers for her soul and complete The Way's burial rituals. Karne returned to the corridor and the body still lying in it.

Brander's corpse lay on a litter now. Karne looked down at this other dead person, amazed that he felt so little. It would have been nice if Brander had lived long enough to tell if the Larga's murder had been his idea or Richard's. Well, Weisman and Wynter would find out why Brander had gotten in. How seemed pretty clear. He would contact Richard himself and see what he could learn about who was responsible for this.

The apparent brilliance of that idea lasted only a second or two. It was all too late. It no longer mattered who had been killed and why. Halarek was without direct heirs and Charlotte's murder would make marrying again close to impossible. No one would send an only daughter, or, in lucky Houses with more than one daughter, any daughter, into a House that could not protect its women. Lizanne had died through no fault of House Halarek's, really, but she had died at her own hand and many blamed Karne. Kit had been kidnapped, from a wedding procession that had had no outriders or guards by command of the Duke deVree, who designed and financed the procession. It had been deVree's responsibility, but Kit was Halarek and had been kidnapped because she was Halarek. Now Charlotte, dead also, probably because she was Halarek. All in less than four years. No, Karne Halarek would not be able to find a wife again for a long, long time, if ever.

The reality of that finally hit Karne. Likely never again would he marry. No children. No heirs of his body. Fights among the cousins over the inheritance, as there was in Harlan. Rage burned through him then, rage that the Guardians would leave him so unprotected, rage that the Allfather had allowed Charlotte to be murdered, bitch-in-heat though she was; rage that he had been left alone and without hope. Karne fought to keep that rage from his face and his movements. This was not the feeling his soldiers expected to see after such a sudden crime. Grief, perhaps. Cold anger, perhaps. Not rage that burned like fire. He must act in public as a Gharr lord was expected to, and smash and pound things later in private. That would be necessary, later, the smashing and pounding, if he were not to lose his mind. When he was newly Lharr—it seemed decades ago, though it had been only six years—he had thought he could keep all his feelings under complete control. He had been a fool. Charlotte had taught him that.

Karne looked across the litter to see Wynter watching him.

"No apologies can be sufficient, my lord," Wynter said. "I've been told the Larga also is dead. I resign the generalship of this House as of this moment. I've failed in my most basic duty, keeping my lord's family from harm."

Karne stared at Wynter, his mind refusing to function for a moment. His adviser from the first, his friend, wanted to quit? Now, when he had lost his future, Wynter wanted to leave? Weariness conquered Karne's rage. He felt his face and shoulders sag too late to stop them. He caught the flash of compassion in Wynter's eyes before the general could conceal it.

"Assassins manage to do their work in spite of the best precautions, General," Karne said at last. "Resignation denied."

Wynter bowed with a sharp click of heels and, turning, ordered the soldiers of the watch to return to their posts. A few minutes later, he headed down the corridor toward the nearest com panel.

Karne felt a hand fall comfortingly on his shoulder.

"My lord?"

"Tane?"

"What do you want done with the bodies?"

"Has Othneil seen them?"

Weisman stepped forward. "My lord, he had an emergency delivery in the serf quarters. He said to tell you that a dead woman will wait. An arriving baby won't."

Karne could tell from Weisman's tone that he disapproved of the physician's impudence. "Tell him to come up as soon as he can. It's the official death declaration for the Larga I'm most interested in. I'm sending this"—Karne pointed to the litter—"back to Harlan." Karne glanced over his shoulder at Orkonan. "Litters move slowly, as you know. Go get Richard on the tri-d. I want to see how he looks when he sees his cousin. Perhaps it will tell me whose idea this murder was."

"As you say, milord." Orkonan made his perfunctory bow and was gone.

"You and you," Karne ordered, pointing to two men of the watch. "Pick up the ends of this litter and hurry it along."

The men dialed the litter's propulsion to "hover only" and picked it up by the handles. The machine carried the weight and the men provided considerably more speed than the machine alone was capable of.

The litter arrived at the tri-d room almost an hour before Richard was permitted to appear. Karne was feeling angry again, this time at the abbot, who had haggled for most of that hour about whether this call, which Karne refused to explain in detail for security reasons, was sufficient reason to allow Lord Richard the use of his infrequent tri-d privilege.

At last Richard Harlan stood in the abbot's office. He looked the Halarek tri-d room over with obvious contempt. "Well, Halarek," he said almost immediately, his voice sharp and hostile, "what can you possibly have to say to me that's important enough that the abbot calls me from nightmeal for it? Nightmeal is one of the high points of my day anymore, thanks mostly to you."

Karne looked at his handsome enemy, and his weariness increased. "My wife was murdered less than two hours ago," Karne said. "By one of your men."

Two tri-d techs, coached ahead of time, boosted the litter upright at that moment, so Richard got a sudden view of his dead cousin.

"This is the murderer," Karne went on.

Shock flashed across Richard's face, and then satisfaction. "Brander," he said softly, "your schemes fell through at last." He looked at the corpse for some time, then he looked at Karne again. "You got him before I did. I'm sorry he got to Charlotte first. When she was good, she was very, very good."

Karne went rigid with shock and then rage. That Richard would speak so to him, after what had happened—

Richard continued. "I owe you one, Halarek. That man was after my head." His face sobered. "No, actually, I owe you two, because if you hadn't sent along those summaries, I would soon have had no hope of heirs at all. Nor would I have known for sure Brander was the cousin plotting against me, though I knew someone was." He met Karne's eyes. "I pay my debts, Halarek, even to my worst enemies. Let me know what you'll consider as payment. No rush. I'll be here some years yet." Richard waved his hand, and his image vanished from Ontar's tri-d screen.

Debt. Harlan in debt to Halarek. On any other day, the idea would have been ludicrous. Karne stared for some time at the empty wall where Richard had been, his mind still trying to digest the idea of Harlan in debt to Halarek. Finally, he left the room for nightmeal, but slowly. This was no trick. Harlan did pay its debts. What could he ask? A truce several years long? Help lifting the Gild embargo on passengers from the Houses? Hard currency? Land?

Karne paused outside the door to the family dining room. He did not feel like eating among all the cousins and vassals in the Great Hall, hearing the condolences, answering their questions. He wanted quiet and friends. Just friends. He sent young Oroark, who was still at his back, to bring Nik, Kit, Jemmy, and the five Blues officers who had been his friends since they all were pilots in the year of Karne's accession. Then he sat down in the dining room to wait.

Karne heard Jemmy coming first while the baby was still in the hall. In minutes Kit burst through the door with the babbling child and then she was hugging Karne tight with her free arm. Nik followed and gave Karne a hug on the other side. They stood in silence for a time. There really were no words for such a tragedy. Finally, Jemmy squirmed, then whimpered, and the little group separated.

"I'm so sorry, Karne," Kit said. She stood on tiptoe and kissed his cheek, then she slipped out of his arm and handed him Jemmy. "I know this isn't as good as a boy of your own, Karne, but hold him. Halarek isn't lost as long as you and I and Jemmy are alive."

Karne rocked the whimpering baby. Jemmy subsided slowly. He nestled his soft fuzzy head under Karne's chin and went
to sleep. Karne felt pain at the death of his hopes, then a flash
of jealousy that Kit had two living children, then a surge of
love for Kit and Nik and Jemmy. He held the baby closer.
What Kit had said was true. There were three of them still.
Halarek wasn't lost yet.